# Convenient Secrets

*A Novel by*

*Ann Wade*

All characters and situations in this novel are fictional and any resemblance to any person, living or dead, is purely coincidental.

Order this book online at www.trafford.com
or email orders@trafford.com

Most Trafford titles are also available at major online book retailers.

Printed in Victoria, BC, Canada.

ISBN: 9781-4269-0068-6 (soft cover)
ISBN: 9781-4269-0538-4 (hard cover)
ISBN: 9781-4269-0938-2 (eBook)

*Our mission is to efficiently provide the world's finest, most comprehensive book publishing service, enabling every author to experience success. To find out how to publish your book, your way, and have it available worldwide, visit us online at www.trafford.com*

*Trafford rev. 12/15/09*

 www.trafford.com

**North America & international**
toll-free: 1 888 232 4444 (USA & Canada)
phone: 250 383 6864 ✦ fax: 812 355 4082

*Dedication*
*To my children,*
*Valerie, Brian, and Kevin*

# Witherston, Minnesota

## Population: 26,500

I N THE SOUTHEASTERN prairie of Minnesota, the immigrants of a German settlement neighboring a natural lake built their huts in 1850. The small colony of farmers struggled through the winter blizzards and the summer windstorms to till land, grow crops, feed cattle, raise families and build a community. These first settlers called the colony Lake Mens. The second generation built stores and a village under the stewardship of Karl Witherston. Karl was the visionary, the force, the glue, and the public servant who brought the settlement of farmers to a full-fledged incorporated town. The citizens voted on renaming the town; Witherston was the only choice on the ballot. Then came the schools, political offices, libraries, a Main Street of businesses, and the resources to sustain an enterprising community.

The town grew around Lake Mens, which was the main source of water for bathing and fishing, both in warm and cold months. Now a twenty-five foot fountain, in the middle of the lake, sprays water fifteen feet high, summer and winter. The main streets of the town stretch south of the Lake meeting the residential neighborhoods that spread north and east. The designers of Witherston wisely sat aside enough lakeside land to build a continuous drive around the lake, and houses are setback, by city ordinance, one hundred yards from the road forming a greenbelt. The city fathers wisely retained enough lakeside land for city parks. The larger of the two is on the south side so that the north end of Main Street is divided east and west at Loren Park where the annual celebrations for Founders' Day and Fourth of July are held by the lakes.

Witherston flourished under the Germanic traits of hardiness of spirit, firmness of mind, strength of purpose, and sense of pride. Hard work, honesty, and principled behavior shaped the heritage and character of the community. Members of ancestral families became the town fathers, respected through second and third generations.

The Brandt family opened the first banking offices and in the late 1930's an insurance business. The town proudly tells the story of how the bank was one of three in the state that remained opened during the depression, providing loans to farmers. Elmer Brandt called upon local businessmen, asking each one for two hundred dollars to build a pool of money. Harold Stassen owned the first general store, which over time expanded into two grocery markets, one on each side of town. Koehler's were the early tailors and opened Koehler department store, now managed by the Toohey family. The Hertzog's family, five boys and three girls with their father and uncle, built the dairy herd to supply the milk, cream and cheese for the townspeople. The farm was ravaged by a tornado in 1944. Sam Rothenkamp perfected meat processing. Kamp's Meats is the largest business in Witherston and posts summer jobs for local students. Members of the Frederick family were the public-minded servants, overseeing the school system and establishing a library (the current Librarian is the great-grandchild of Hans Frederick). They also opened the first health clinic.

The Strutter name is on a construction business, the corner drugstore, and a hardware store on Main Street. All are still owned and managed by one or more of the thirty-three descendents of the Strutter family. Sebastian Strutter was thirty-one years old and a widower when he emigrated from southern Germany to join other settlers by Lake Mens. Sebastian was a carpenter as well as a farmer, and he helped families build their first huts and barns, and then their houses and churches. He was a quiet man, working and living by himself until he married a young woman twenty-two years younger than he. Lottie Rummels bore him two children, John and Gredda. Lottie had skills for healing with natural remedies, learned from her mother and grandmother. What she didn't find in the woods or on the prairie, she grew in her herbal garden. Gredda learned the healing ways of her mother and became a mid-wife for the settlement. Gredda married Ivan Koehler and became an accomplished seamstress, bearing no children for the Koehler family.

Sebastian raised his son, John, to be a carpenter and builder in and of the community and encouraged him to marry young and to rear a large family. John followed his father's advice and married Frances Hertzog when they were both twenty-four. Their first born, Emil raised a family of five; Sarah, the only girl, died of scarlet fever before her sixth year; the next son, Lyle had six children; and Frances, the youngest had one son, named for the grandfather John. Eleven members of the Strutter family reside in Witherston and are involved in one of the family businesses -- construction, the hardware store or drugstore – started either by Sebastian or his son, John.

The oldest church in town is German Lutheran, Our Redeemer, rebuilt on the original plot set aside in 1851 for the settlers' first church; the newest is the Unitarian. The Strutter families attend St. Anne; the oldest Catholic Church built in 1888, enlarged in 1912, and re-modeled in 1948.

The population of Witherston remains fairly stable, fluctuating with births and deaths, but overall holding constant since 1960.

# Grandpa John Strutter

T HE CITIZENS OF Witherston referred to the grandfather as Old John and his grandson as Young John. The young boy, after his mother died on his fifth birthday, was with his grandfather every day. She had baked a yellow cake and placed it with three presents under the Christmas tree, which was always part of John's birthday celebration on the twenty-ninth. John waited all day to blow out the candles and open the presents. He was tucked into bed with a kiss one night by his mother and the next night by his grandfather.

"Where's Mommy? When are we going to open the presents?"

"We'll do that tomorrow, young man. You and I shall be spending the day together."

"Where's Mommy and Daddy? Don't they want to see my birthday?"

"Your father will be here in the morning, John." And after a long pause, "Your mother won't be with him."

"Why Grandpa? Doesn't she wanna come home?"

"John, your mother has died."

The memory of his grandfather's lap and arms etched into John's memory forever. He remembered the smell of Grandma's homemade soap in Grandpa's shirt as Grandpa held him to his chest. He remembered his grandfather's tears wetting the top of his hair.

In a muffled voice, young John asked, "She died? Like Skipper died? Was she hit by a car like Skipper?"

"No, John. She had a sickness that went through her body like lightning. The doctors could not stop it." There was no need to say it was meningitis, for medical terms would have no meaning to the five year old.

John looked up into the old man's face. "I wanna see her. She loved me. She wouldn't go away on my birthday." Grandpa stroked John's body as it shivered with sobs.

"John, she would be here if she could. When a person dies they can't come back . . . just like Skipper."

"I'll never see her again, Grandpa?" asked the wee, soft voice.

"Not to talk to her, John." Grandpa rocked the little boy back and forth. He knew he'd not leave this room tonight; his presence was all he could offer his grandson.

"Where's Daddy? Did he go away with Mommy?"

"No, he's coming later. I'm sure you'll find him in bed with you when you wake up."

"Grandpa, can't you fix it? Can't you ask God?"

"No John, I can't . . . I wish I could. But I can promise you I'll be here with you until you grow up." That meant he'd have to live at least another fifteen years. He silently asked that he'd see his nineties.

"Will I live with you?"

"Sometimes, maybe. Your dad will talk with Grandpa and Grandma about that."

Grandfather John stayed by the boy's bedside, sitting in his favorite rocker brought up from downstairs. He held his grandson's hand and felt the twitch of the fingers as the boy drifted into sleep. He remembered the nights when he'd held another little hand, his daughter Sarah, as her body burned with the dreadful scarlet fever. He and his wife battled death with cool water, wet blankets, liquids, and medicine left by the doctor. None of it saved their only daughter. "How much worse was it for a little boy to lose his mother?" he thought.

Frank, the boy's father, was the youngest of three sons born to John and Frances Strutter, who were in their forties when Frank was born. Lyle, the oldest, took charge of the small hardware store his father had opened, and in ten years, tripled its original size. Emil, four years older than Frank, was the first son into the drugstore business and was glad when Frank joined him after receiving his pharmacy license.

Old John was a carpenter by trade and in their turn his sons each had worked by his side doing construction work. They were proud of the many buildings in the county that were built by the Strutter family. Old John started the hardware business because he liked having his own ready supply of tools and materials. And, in addition, he felt he had fulfilled an ancestral obligation to have successful businesses for his sons.

Young John, Frank's only child, took on more of his grandfather's mannerisms than those of his father. Frank mourned the death of his young wife by shutting himself away from life and into managing the drugstore. The activity, long hours and the stream of people (even though their heartfelt condolences during the first two weeks reminded him of his loss) kept him occupied and tired at the end of the day. He ate breakfast with his son and then walked with him the two blocks to his parents' home, where young John stayed many nights. Frank knew his mother would lull young John to sleep with family stories and mother his son. Sunday was the day for father-son time, but even then it was interwoven with his parents' life; attending Sunday services, family dinner at noon, an afternoon nap, and later a walk uptown for an evening treat -- maybe a sundae or soda. In the early years, Frank played checkers or dominos with his son. When John was eleven, Old John bought a chess set for him. Under the tutelage of his grandfather, the grandson became an astute player.

John's traits became like those of his grandparents. From his grandmother, he took on her gentle nature and loving kindness for all living creatures. Grandma Frances treated her chickens with as much care, concern, and ceremony as she did her family, flowers, and friends. Everything in nature was sacred to Grandma; her neighbors, her strawberry patch, young John's pets. Most sacred was her communion with her church. She never preached her beliefs or broke her devotion to God.

John usually went to evening angelus with Grandma. "Why doesn't Grandpa come with us?"

Her answer, "Maybe he doesn't have someone he wants to talk with. You have your mother, I have my Sarah."

Her words of encouragement to her grandson were unending. "Be a good boy, John. One that Grandpa and your father will be proud of."

"I will, Grandma."

"Your mother would be pleased," when she praised him for a 'good deed'.

"She knows, Grandma?"

"Yes."

"Does God tell her about me?"

"She just knows John, because she still loves you."

And, she always, always told him, "Help the little creatures, John . . . they belong to us also. God would like us to be kind to all things."

"I'll remember, Grandma."

Until he was seven, Grandma gave John his own seat of honor on quilting day. Every Wednesday afternoon, the ladies arrived at Frances's for sewing the pattern pieces or stitching the over-laying design. It was a time for the ladies to share family news, but more engaging were the items of interest heard by the 'grapevine' or by the telephone party line. Often, Grandma would squint and shake her head, "Remember we have little ears listening." John liked the attention of the ladies; they asked him to thread their needles, cut paper patterns, and pass the cookies served with tea

Grandpa would later chide, "John should be with other boys rather than listening to the town gossip."

Grandma had her way this time. "Oh let the little boy be fussed over."

Grandpa John preferred waiting on the customers at the hardware store rather than the drugstore and took the young boy there more often. He had John stack shelves, hand out flyers, sweep the front walk, and deliver small packages if the distance was no more than a few blocks. Young John really felt older than his years because of the responsibility his grandfather granted him, and none no more so than the day Grandpa said, "John, let's see if you can close out the cash register."

"You mean count the money?"

"Yes I do. You can count to one hundred can't you?"

"Yes sir, you know I can." How proud he felt when Grandpa asked him one Saturday afternoon, after his twelfth birthday, to be cashier.

John was a silent witness when watching his grandfather and didn't realize that what he heard and saw was molding his own character. Grandpa's stoic nature magnified when listening to the extravagant pitch of a salesman, "don't get caught in their emotional enthusiasm, you may end up with a backroom of stuff you can't sell." Few shoplifters found their way into the aisles in the Strutter's stores, but when it did happen, Grandpa's direct approach, with a stern voice, left no alternative, "do you want to pay or talk to the police?" His patience let the difficult customers have their say, "give them space to rant and rave, when they cool down they'll talk sense." And old John classified men with a handshake, "that man has chosen an easy life, he has no calluses on his hands." Grandpa was the hundred-year old oak tree, from which, John, the young twig sprouted. John trusted and acted on family principles, although he didn't always trust others. His polite demeanor disguised his distaste when he encountered deception or corruption.

John was not competitive, but this did not mean he wasn't ambitious – an A student in high school and college, and one of the top hitters on Witherston's baseball team. He lived away from

*Ann Wade*

Witherston only once – for college, returning with a degree in pharmacy and a bride, Emily Knowland.

# JOHN AND EMILY

# CHAPTER ONE

# Good News Day

## 1

E MILY GRABBED A kitchen towel, rubbed her hands dry, and rushed to the ringing telephone. The handset was at her ear before the fourth ring. "Hello," she said in a breathless tone.

"Mrs. Strutter? Sally Mason, Catholic Services."

"Yes, Sally. Good to hear your voice." Emily mentally pictured the décor of Mrs. Mason's office from previous Minneapolis visits. An un-cluttered table–top desk neat and organized. Pictures of the Minneapolis Basilica and the cathedral in St. Paul hung on an ivory colored wall and, by her window, a large photograph from an early St. Paul's Winter Carnival of an ice palace bathed in colored lights. Being true to the Minnesotan way in starting a conversation, Emily asked about the weather. "How deep is the snow in Minneapolis? We've got about five inches on the ground."

"Quite a bit more here, we felt the brunt of the storm last week. The sun shines brightly today however and that makes for bitter cold you know."

"Same here. Guess that's our Minnesota winter fare. Are you calling with news?"

"Yes, I am. We have a pregnancy in its fifth month, due in the spring. I wanted to . . ." Mrs. Mason didn't get to finish.

"Oh, how wonderful. Glorious is the word. It's like a Christmas gift . . . the babe arriving." Emily's emotions flowed into tears and muffled breathing. Her left hand pressed on her forehead, and she turned quickly as if to twirl and then caught the telephone as it slid to the edge of the stand. "Oh, we've waited soooo, so long."

"I know this is an exciting moment, but remember this is just a possibility. All we know right now is that the mother has chosen for adoption . . . but still has the option to keep her child. That final decision waits until after she's held the newborn."

"Yes, I remember . . . you've stressed that many times. But . . . but I want to think of this as good news."

"Well, let's keep in mind that whatever the decision is, it is good news."

"Can we be at the hospital?" Emily interjected.

"Possibly, but not usually on the birth day, Mrs. Strutter. We'll work that out and more in the coming months. Meanwhile, you should be prepared for a change of mind. While it doesn't happen often, we do insist that the birth parents see and hold the baby the first twenty-four hours."

Emily spoke quickly, "I know, you're saying it's always chancy, but if she goes for adoption, I could hold my baby the day it is born."

"Or very soon, thereafter," Mrs. Mason assured her.

"Oh, how wonderful! A child in our home. We shall be a complete family." Her voice was like a singing bell.

"Please, Mrs. Strutter, keep in mind there are four months to birth, which in itself is quite a momentous time for the young parents. We should all want the best outcome for the child."

"I know, I know. You do help us keep that in mind. But, we've waited so long . . . had our own disappointments." Emily voice turned into a more sober tone. "What is the probability she'll change her mind?"

"That's hard to really say. Birth is an emotional, life-changing experience, and young mothers are often in a quandary."

"I think I can imagine that. But, what's been your experience? Fifty-fifty? Seventy-thirty?"

"It's a low percentage overall. Though I've seen it happen and sometimes in cases which surprised me. While this young woman I am working with now is quite adamant about adoption, there's always the other possibility. I'm not sure if the young man can persuade her to change her mind."

Emily did not press Mrs. Mason any further. "Well, I'm going to pray the right decision is made. In the end, as you say, it must be what's best for the baby."

"Excellent thoughts to carry with us," Mrs. Mason concurred. "I'm putting a number of things in the mail today. Please read them carefully – both you and Mr. Strutter – and we'll be talking again soon."

"Will we be coming to Minneapolis?"

"Yes, once for sure and maybe again later if necessary."

"Oh, I do feel confident and blessed . . . after so many mishaps." Suddenly, Emily's voice turned up, "What a blessing if it were twins."

"Well, that would be a first for me," Sally chuckled and paused before saying, "Please call me after you've read the packet or if you want to discuss anything."

"Thank you, Sally . . . we'll be in touch. I told John this morning that I felt this was going to be a special day. Can't wait to tell him. Thank you again. What a Christmas present."

Emily danced down the hallway to the kitchen and smiled as she thought back over the breakfast conversation with her husband. She had told John, "Something good is coming our way today."

John lowered his head and looked at Emily over his glasses. "Have you been planning something?"

"No, John, I've not been dreaming up surprises. My intuition tells me this is a special day for us. It's . . . well . . . I just feel it."

"Now, are you sure that it isn't just wishful thinking? You might be full of fancy because Christmas is so near." John spoke in an affectionate tone.

"Oh John, you are such a skeptic." She busied herself filling their coffee cups.

"Emily, what have you been weaving . . . some scheme for the holidays? I notice that you've been a bit more of a sparkle lately, which often means you have a surprise coming our way."

"John, you make me sound like a sorceress."

"Let's say we've seen you make magical things happen before," John smiled lovingly at his wife, "and then pretend it was just a random, *wondrous* happening."

"John . . . John." Emily scrunched her face into a 'here we go again' look.

"Emily, Emily." John mimicked. "Think we all love your magical side, and I'll look forward to hearing about 'the something good' tonight." He laid his napkin next to his plate, now empty of scrambled eggs and toast. "Must be off."

"Don't forget to tell Dad we expect him for dinner Sunday, and we'll all go to the Christmas concert from here."

Emily walked John to the front door and held his winter scarf while he pushed his arms through the sleeves of a black tailored overcoat. She tucked the scarf around his neck and under his coat collar, and then lifted her face for a good-bye kiss. They never started their day or ended their evening without expressions of love. Mr. and Mrs. John Strutter were spoken of as the model married folks in Witherston, Minnesota.

## 2

John Strutter first saw Emily Knowland at Jefferson Junior College, where they both were preparing for a medical professional, she as a nurse, he to be a pharmacist. Professor Jorgensen had just begun his lecture on Anatomy, when a female with a trim body took the empty seat next to John. He nodded with a smile, and she returned the smile with a whispered "Hi." John had noticed this pretty face; once at the doorway entrance at Crawley Hall, several times in this class, and just yesterday in the Malt Shop at the student union. Her deep brown eyes had caught his attention, and he noticed that her lips gave shape to a perpetual smile. Her long-legged figure attracted him. Comparing her height to his six foot-two frame, he gauged her to be five feet six, at least.

The professor began his lecture on the body's circulatory system, including diagrams of the network of vessels that carry blood to and from the heart. Both students busily moved their pens across their notebooks; the terminology describing the construction of the arteries was complex. As the auditorium emptied, the two remained seated comparing their notes, studying the diagram, and helping each other to clarify definitions.

"Guess we should introduce ourselves. I'm John Strutter – my hometown is Witherston."

"Hi. I'm Emily Knowland from Cross Center. Our basketball teams played each year. Were you on the team?"

"Yes, for Central High. I was number six, but I doubt you would have noticed . . . I was not the star player."

"No probably not. My attention was more on pom-poms and leading cheers. Guess I could ask you, don't you remember the four cheerleaders in green and white?" Emily asked coyly.

"Well, at least I can place the school colors," replied John, and she wrinkled her nose in response.

As they walked out and away from the building, they found they were going in the same direction – to the cafeteria for lunch. It seemed easy to share a table and to linger after a sandwich and soda, talking about professors and studies, until class time.

In that first meeting, they found common ground and mutual attraction and seemed a natural fit, suitable in so many ways. Emily had grown up in a Catholic family and community; John was brought up in similar circumstances in a larger town one hundred miles north of Cross Center. They'd been born in the same year, 1930 - Emily in July, John in December. Both were twenty years old, and in four years, they would be married.

## 3

By the end of their first conversation in the school cafeteria, Emily and John said their first good-bye. Her eyes lingered on the tall man as he walked away. *I've just met my love. He's mine. I know it. There's something about his voice . . . like a magnet . . . draws me to him. He's like a caress. I'll marry him . . . I know it.* This type of intuitive knowing was the same as a guarantee to Emily; she accepted the feelings as fact and acted upon them. This trait had been fine-tuned into the art of friendly persuasion, even in one who was barely twenty. She knew how to convince others to follow her dreams and desires, so that the outcome originally sensed came to pass, re-enforcing her belief that her intuition was exempt from error. Others might refer to her as an innocent manipulator, but Emily thought it her right and obligation to follow her instincts. So, from the beginning, Emily treated John as if he were her treasure and her man.

Emily Knowland Strutter was born July 12, 1930, the last in a family of three children. Her siblings were brothers, eight and five years older. They doted on their little sister; giving her the first cookie, the first dish of ice cream for desert, the first choice of toys, and building her first snowman. They read her books, played ball with her, twirled her in make-believe dances, taught her how to brush Toby, the fox terrier and, when she was five, how to play cowboy and Indian. Emily was the maiden princess saved by the cowboy brothers.

Emily came upon the art of persuasion naturally, as she wanted only the best things happening for her. She came to learn that wishes were granted when she asked coyly or playfully. Even her father, Carl, could not deny the pretty face and ever-present dimples that deepened with a smile. Emily learned she needn't whine or cry her way into a win; rather a smile, a laugh, or a kittenish 'maybe I will or maybe I won't' never let her down. The family noticed Emily began to hum at six years of age, and she went on humming into adult life, a sure sign that life was happy and going her way.

She hummed waiting for John outside the classroom – she 'just happened to be there' at the time he was coming down the hallway. Her timing was impeccable; although, John never thought it an accident after it happened more than once, but he was pleased with her ploy. It became a natural for them to have lunch in the student union after class, and they soon began meeting for dinner in the cafeteria, giving them more time to share their personal lives and dreams.

One night they explored their choice of professions. "Where do you think you will nurse?" inquired John. "Will you go to a larger city, like Minneapolis, St. Paul?"

"I'm not sure. I do have to work the hospital floors to finish my training. I'd like Mayo Clinic."

"Good place. I see it always at the top of hospital ratings. I hear people saying Rochester is a nice town to live in, small and friendly."

"I'd really like that. My next two years are primarily working classes, so I have to be near a hospital. My brother is urging me to transfer to the University of Minnesota."

"Why is that? Does he live there?" John asked.

"He and his wife have a home just north of the city. They offered me free room and board. Though, I'd need a car for transportation." Emily spoke hesitantly.

"You sound as if you might have another choice."

"There is a smaller school and hospital in St. Paul . . . St. Mary's which might be more to my liking. And my dad has offered to help with my tuition. Won't you be at Minnesota for your degree in pharmacy?" Emily asked, secretly elated that they'd be in the same city.

"Yes, that's the plan. It's where my father graduated."

"We could explore the big city together." Emily gave a quick smile. "Couldn't we?" He nodded with less than the full enthusiasm she hoped for.

Emily wanted their relationship to move away from being casual into one more serious. *Wonder how strongly he feels about me? Maybe give it a test. I don't want to be taken for granted. Maybe just a nudge. Wonder if he could be jealous.*

Emily was acquainted with the effects of jealousy, both in herself and others. She knew the green-eyed monster could raise doubts, anxiety and fears, particularly when she thought she'd lose out on something she wanted for her own. Thus was her fear about John. She wanted them to be a steady couple, but he seemed satisfied just sitting next to each other in class, sharing a table for a random lunch or cafeteria dinner, or for an occasional movie or student event. She felt sure that he liked her and was interested in hanging out with her, but she wanted the comfortable feeling that he desired only her, although she really hadn't seen him with other girls. She wanted that same intensity he had towards his studies, his assignments and grades coming her way also. *Would jealousy work? Maybe if it was a guy he'd like to protect me from – hum, who?* Emily spent a lot of her hours, which cut into her concentration in class, scheming. *What if this backfires? It won't, I can make it work perfectly. Now, who should it be? C.C.? He's been tagging me for weeks. Maybe it's time to stop playing hard-to-get. Just say 'Yes.'*

John took up Emily's suggestion to stop at the student union for an after-class soda. "Not too many days left of fall and beautiful leaves," Emily opened. "Good weekend to be outside?"

"The best I'll do is walking between dorm and library." John said to her, not picking up on her disappointment. "Tests coming up . . . a paper to finish, and my communications group needs to work on our class presentation. Wish Professor Stone had given us more time. Are you ready for exams?" John asked.

"Sort of, but I'm not going to keep my nose in books all weekend. Don't you get burned out?"

"No. Dad says I inherited the power of concentration from my Grandfather. And, I'd like to make him proud with honor grades." He paused before asking, "Will you be at the library on Saturday?"

"Gosh, no, John. I've got a date to go canoeing," Emily said coyly, rolling her big brown eyes.

20

"Oh, on the little Cedar? With whom?" John raised his eyebrows.

"With C.C. This is the third time he's asked me out but the first time canoeing. Guess he thought it would be more appealing than a movie." Emily waited watchfully.

"With C.C.? That's Chad Conley right? The big man on campus. Didn't know you were next on his list."

"What a small thing to say." Then, in a playful voice, "Do you think I shouldn't go out with him?"

"Emily, you're free to do whatever you want. I have no priority or claims on your time." Certainly not the words Emily wanted to hear. "It's just that he has a reputation for having fun, but not always the best kind." John continued, "But I guess you know that . . . you girls certainly must keep tabs on the guys."

"John it's just a canoe. We'll be on water. He'll be paddling. Would you prefer I cancel out?"

"No, just a heads-up. Canoes can be brought in to shore you know."

"John, do I hear a bit of jealousy?" Emily teased. "We could go canoeing."

"Emily, are you working me? Is there an angle here? I don't play games well," John said with a sharp edge. "Let's leave this topic. I have a date with the library and you have one with C.C. Guess, we'll have to see who gets the most out of their date."

"Well, Kathy and Sheri have both gone out with Chad and had a lot of fun. I didn't see them come back with frowns. In fact, I think they're envious of my date with him." Emily wanted to keep the topic going but got nowhere with the effort. The soda glasses were empty and John was picking up his book pack from the floor ready to head out. At the door he said, "Have fun. Be sure you stay on water."

When next they met, Emily wore a bandage on the right side of her forehead with a bruise peeking beyond the edge and a scowl darkening her eyes. "Hi Emily, what's the scoop? Did you get hit with a paddle?" John said lightly as they entered anatomy class.

"Don't try to be funny John. You're partly to blame for this."

"What?" He stopped and looked at her quizzically. "How did I get in this?

John kept glancing at Emily during the lecture, feeling a little sorry for her, as it was evident that the canoe trip had faults to it. "Do you want to go to lunch?"

In the cafeteria, he listened as Emily told about the struggle in the canoe after Chad guided it to shore and was ready to play a bit with hands and lips. Emily tripped over the seat and fell on the steel rim that edged the canoe, hitting her forehead on a raised piece of steel. As a scalp slash would do, it bled profusely.

"It was awful, blood running down my face, on to our shirts, into my eyes. I was screaming. He was pulling his shirt off to cover my head. By the time we got back to the car and then to the hospital, everything on me was red."

"Gosh, sort of scary. Head wounds can lose a lot of blood. Did they give you a tetanus shot? Being cut with dirty metal is not good." John was looking at the physical aspects of the accident.

"Can't you feel sorry for me? Think of the ugly position I was in. If you'd gone canoeing, this wouldn't have happened. Makes me wonder just how good of a friend you are." Emily's eyes watered.

"Whoa, wait a minute." John held up his left hand, palm out. "You tried to manipulate me last week and now you are doing it again. Yes, I was concerned, not knowing where Chad's ego might take him, but I wasn't going to be pushed into making your decision." John nodded his head, as he told her, "There's a law of physics -- for every action there is a reaction. To put it another way, for every decision there is a payoff. Could it be possible that you got caught in a game?" John reached across the table and touched her arm. "How hurtful for you and maybe to your pride, also."

"Oh, John, why didn't you do something?" Emily scolded.

"Like what?" Both hands came up this time. "Stop you? Get

mad? Demand you not go? Emily if our friendship is going to move into a real thing, I want it to be straightforward, not a game of playing with our emotions."

"God, John you sound like an old man."

"Emily, you like perfect, then let's work for perfect in an open way. Okay?"

"Thanks a lot. I feel like a bad girl," and hesitantly, Emily admitted, "I wish that we were back to before," then added, "did I just learn a lesson without a text book?"

The healing of the stitches on Emily's forehead left a red welt; a painful reminder about scheming too far. Later, it became her habit to rub the spot when John attempted to rein in her persuasive powers.

Their time together during their last months at Jefferson Junior College were carefree. They listened to each other's family stories, shared winter afternoon's cross-country skiing on the trails near the school, strolled those same paths in the spring, attended Sunday services at St. Mathew's, and quietly fell in love, forever – often singing the popular 'I love you a bushel and a peck and a hug around the neck . . . you bet your pretty neck I do'. The only gloom on the horizon was the possibility of John's name being drawn from the draft lottery to serve in the Korean War. Emily secretly prayed constantly and didn't feel unpatriotic in doing so.

They married in Witherston after graduating from the Minneapolis/St. Paul schools. Their home for the first four years was a small two-bedroom bungalow rented from John's uncle Lyle. It was 1930 style, like an over-grown dollhouse, the rooms small and not needing a lot of furniture. Emily worked in a clinic headed by four doctors, and John worked in the pharmacy of the family drug store under his father's guidance, learning the trade of the business and the tendencies of their customers. Emily was blissfully happy and impatient to start their family.

## 4

John was very sensitive, attuned to the needs of others and felt their emotions without falling into them, and he was especially attuned to Emily ways and had the wisdom to carefully guide her highly persuasive powers. He knew her to be capable, committed, independent, and a self-starter with a strong tendency to work things around to what she thought was best. She engaged in work and community with a sole desire to help make things better. Being a top-of-the-list volunteer, Emily was seldom left out of any church or town projects. John was proud of his wife, as was the entire Strutter family.

In their intimate moments, John was a considerate love partner. Emily's arousal came to full satisfaction under John's tender touch. His hands and fingers stroked her face, arms, body – unhurried – like a soft rhythm that played to Emily's humming. He taught her to move with the tempo of the sweet moments and enjoy the intimacy of the act. To Emily, John was gentle, wise, devoted, and totally above reproach.

Within a year of their marriage, Emily believed she was pregnant. "Oh John, we've done it. I'm pregnant!"

"Don't you think it best to have that confirmed by Dr. Burns?" John asked in a teasing tone.

"Oh John, I know . . . I just know it. In fact, remember the night I whispered, 'we've just conceived a baby'? It's true. It's true. It's true," sang Emily as she danced around the room.

"Can you tell me if we're having a boy or girl? Which one did you plan for?" John laughed at her girlish happiness.

Emily twirled into John's arms, "It's a boy, Mr. Strutter." She pulled his head down for enough kisses to cover his face.

## 5

Emily moved their lives into a whirl of planning, converting the extra bedroom into a nursery. She spent her lunch hours at the paint store, fabric counters, furniture show rooms, bringing home blue paint samples, swatches of material for curtains, and pictures of bassinets, small cupboards and chests for baby clothes.

"John do you like this shade of blue or should it be the lighter shade?" Emily asked, holding two colored squares before him.

John reached out for the two samples and put them in his left hand, colored side facing him. "Now pick one, you know either one will do."

She pulled both of them, "No, let's do the Cloudless Sky, the soft blue fits for our little boy." She picked up a pencil, posed to write on the sample, "How much paint should I buy?"

And so Emily hummed, as the second bedroom became a beautiful nest to welcome their baby. Blue walls, one over-painted with fluffy white clouds. White eyelet curtains at the windows. A vintage hand-made crib found at an estate sale, and dresser drawers beginning to fill with tiny clothing. Emily kept a slate propped against the wall on the kitchen counter where names, such as, Thomas, Caleb, Joshua, William, Mathew, Luke, Lyle, Carl were written and erased and then often written again. The name John was a constant.

John came home earlier than usual that particular Thursday. "I'm home," he called out as he hung up his jacket and headed to the kitchen. Emily was at the sink peeling carrots, and John noted that Emily was not humming and only slightly nudged into his greeting kiss.

"Think I'll have a beer tonight," as he opened the refrigerator.

"Supper will be ready in an hour," reported Emily, keeping her head down. "The paper is in the living room."

John poured beer into a mug and stood by the doorway, wondering what was happening with Emily. He saw no trace of the happy wife and soon-to-be mother; instead he heard a tone of voice that was flat and tight-lipped. He knew Emily had something to be told, something she did not want to admit. John's patience and wisdom kept him quiet and waiting.

"Oh John," Emily broke, dropping the paring knife to hold

on to the edge of the sink. "I'm scared . . . so scared."

"Why Emily? What happened?" John asked quietly, holding back his urge to go to her immediately. Emily needed to come slowly to her story; it was always so when the news was distasteful.

"He didn't say."

"Who didn't say and what was it he didn't say?" John waited.

"He wants to see me in seven days – next Thursday morning."

"Who? Dr. Burns?"

"Yes, he just said he wanted to see me more often. That's not normal, John. What do you suppose he's detected?"

"Did you ask?"

"No. Wonder if it is bad news? Oh, John, a whole week to wait." Then she turned and sought John, his arms stretched toward her. She moved into her safe and secure haven.

John never revealed whether he called Dr. Burns or not, and Emily didn't ask. She purposely told John that her appointment was one hour later than nine o'clock. She wanted desperately to hang onto her belief that everything was okay. Emily was trembling when she walked into the waiting room. Dr. Burns saw her immediately. He put his stethoscope to several areas of her rounded stomach; he measured the size of her bulge, and then made his internal exam.

Emily never felt more alone than when she heard Dr. Burns's words.

"Mrs. Strutter, I am not hearing the heartbeat any longer."

"What? Why? What do you mean . . . any longer?"

"Last week, I noted that the measurement of the fetus was the same as the time before. There'd been no growth. The heartbeat was also very faint, and I thought maybe it was the position of the baby. But I am now sure, Mrs. Strutter, the fetus is no longer living and will probably abort."

Emily sat stone-faced, stunned, as the tears slowly rolled down her cheeks. Dr. Burns suggested they call John to come to the office to be with her and hear the rest of his advice.

"Please, don't send me back to the waiting room. I don't want to be with those people right now."

"I understand. Let's go to another room and we'll call John from there." Dr. Burns apologized for the messy desk as they entered his office

Emily had held back the burst of tears until John came through the door. "Oh, John," she wailed, "I'm so sorry." He held her tight, stroking her long brown hair, "Shhhh, shhhh, we'll be okay. I'm sorry too, Em. So much expectation -- so ready to love. Shhhh, we'll be okay."

Dr. Burns gave them the privacy of his office and asked the nurse to bring a glass of water. John sat Emily down on a small sofa and pulled up a chair directly in front of her. He held both her hands and leaned towards her. "Emily?"

She sobbed, head down. "John, I can't bear this . . . our very first . . . what did I do wrong?"

"Emily, you've done nothing wrong. Neither one of us. What happened? I don't know; maybe the doctor doesn't either. Maybe the fetus had a wrong beginning. You did not cause this, Emily. Look at me . . . look at me, Em . . . we'll see this through. Let's hear what more the doctor has to say and then we'll go on home. I'll be with you."

In a caring tone of voice, Dr. Burns told them nature tended to act of its own accord and that they could expect a spontaneous abortion within the next forty-eight hours. His instructions were to call him and go to the hospital immediately with the first cramp or sign of bleeding. "If it doesn't happen tonight, I'll call tomorrow to see how you are doing."

John took Emily to the hospital at 3:36 a.m. the following morning. She kept her face to the wall and never asked the gender of the fetus. Only John knew it was a girl. He stayed the day and night with Emily, their presence for each other had to be enough for now.

Dr. Burns' parting words the next day gave promise. "These

things happen sometimes, with no explanation. An imperfect fertilization often ends itself. There is no reason that you can't have a successful pregnancy. Give yourself some time. Come see me in a couple of weeks and call if you have questions." He reached over to pat Emily's hand. "You're a brave woman. Be active. Plan to go back to work. That helps to heal."

They did wait and their emotions did heal, and the best healing was being pregnant eleven months later. John and Emily were elated. Any apprehensions were left unspoken. They were to face disappointment again within twelve weeks and again sixteen months later when a third pregnancy ended in eight weeks. Tests indicated Emily's body did not provide the right elements to keep the fetus attached to the uterus. Dr. Burns offered no encouragement about future pregnancies and said a full-term pregnancy was unlikely. Over Emily's strong protestations, he attempted to convince them that surgical procedures should be done to halt any further pregnancies and disappointments. "Mrs. Strutter, your health and longevity are the uppermost in my recommendation."

While Emily mourned more openly, John grieved silently. Their intimate moments became awkward. What was sex without the likelihood of creating children? Both John and Emily had talked, planned, expected, and saved for parenthood. It was to be their fulfillment of being partners in building a family in a community where the Strutter name was greatly respected. If they were to follow Dr. Burns' cautions against more pregnancies, what birth control method would they use? It was unlikely to expect the Catholic Church to give dispensation to use anything other than abstinence or the rhythm method. Having sex seemed contrived to Emily and often she cried afterwards knowing their seeds would not produce her dream. John and Emily held off any medical decision.

John made the first visit to Father Mike, the priest who they considered to be their close friend. John's visit paved the way for the discussions later among the three of them. Father gave his blessings in sanctions from the church and his support of the medical procedures recommended by Dr. Burns. And, so it was done.

## 6

The pain of that time could now be erased. Emily stood at the back porch door, looking out on the deep snow covering her flower gardens. She dared to daydream about a baby carriage in the shade of the tree where she planted the spring beds, and she clasped her hands together saying an emotional prayer of thanksgiving. "Thank you, thank you for this gift . . . I'm full of love and excitement . . . my prayers have been answered. Guide me in parenting one of your precious beings . . . and please bestow your love upon the mother to aid her in her courageous decision. As always, thy will be done.'

Emily felt a deep confidence that her time to be a mother had finally arrived. She felt her long-repeated prayers were being answered. Although she'd become anxious at times through all the tragedies of unborn babies, she never doubted that someday she and John would bring a child into their family. She'd trusted and prayed and waited for so many months . . . "Thank you, God, for the blessing of this day."

Emily went to the telephone to call John, stared at it for a few moments, then turned away. She needed to be with him when she told him, to see the joy of his face, to be enclosed in his arms. The telephone wouldn't do, neither would a visit to the drug store. There'd be no privacy amid John's customers and employees. She gave into another inclination instead and bundled up in warm clothing to walk the seven blocks to the church. Emily was particular fond of the picture in the foyer of St. Anne, the mother of the Blessed Virgin. It depicted the saint arrayed in a reddish colored cloak, the cowl resting around her forehead, her right hand reaching for the latch of a door -- the image associated with St. Anne. Emily saw the door as a symbol of expectation and of welcome to an awaited message.

Emily had offered many novenas to St. Anne who also had waited devoutly in prayer for a child to be born to her and her husband. It was in Anne's and Joachim's declining years of life, when an angel appeared to Anne, as she prayed under a laurel tree, with the announcement that she would conceive and bring forth a child who "shall be spoken of in all the world." St. Anne's faithful fervor and belief that she would bear a child inspired Emily to follow the saint's practices. And today, Sally Mason had been her angel, bringing the good news.

She looked around, found the church to be empty, and went to the kneeler in front of Mary and spoke her words: *"Help me to forget the past and accept your blessings. Let the baby arrive safely to my arms. You who have been a mother for all of us, teach me to fulfill the obligations of motherhood."* She prayed her rosary beads, the first of a thirty-day novena for the health and safety of the young mother and the baby she carried. She touched the hem of Mary's robe. *Please don't let me be disappointed again. I'll lose all faith.*

# 7

John heard Rosemary Clooney singing, "Hey there, you with the stars in your eyes . . . " as he walked pass the dining room and into the kitchen. The table was set for a party, candles, wine glasses . . . "Say, what's going on here?"

"Oh, John we have a celebration."

"Well, I suspect 'the something' of this morning is now known and you are waiting to tell me." He moved to her side.

"Yes, dear one," she put her hands up to hold his face, "our child is on the way."

"You heard from Minneapolis?"

"Yes, yes, yes. Mrs. Mason says in four months."

John pulled Emily closer for a wrap-around hug before sharing tender kisses. "How long have you known?"

"Almost all day. I didn't want to tell you over the phone . . .

I wanted to be with you, just like now." She started to tell of her afternoon as she turned her attention to the food on the stove. John walked to the back door, looked out on the snow-covered yard, and lifted a finger to wipe both eyes.

## 8

John was a quiet man, displaying neither elation nor despair. Sadness was little more than a shake of the head and the words 'too bad'. John tended to handle what was in the moment, thoughtfully, efficiently, and thoroughly. When too many tasks were at hand, John became focused and even less talkative – not too say that he ever was over talkative. An astute reader of people, John held an unspoken distaste for glib or unfounded statements and for those who made them.

John was a pleasant-looking man, his deep hazel eyes, behind rimless glasses, were a striking feature under a full brow and a high hairline sculptured by a widow's peak. His sandy colored hair was combed straight back in traditional style, parted on the left. Emily said he was lucky as she predicted any grey hairs would match his natural color so closely that no one would notice he was aging. His cheekbones shaped an oval face; his pointed chin, aquiline nose and flat ears made his face seem long. People spoke of his compassion and sense of humor and referred to him as handsome, but Emily thought they alluded more to his personality than his looks.

He was tall, two inches over six feet, with a lean frame and a strong body. His mind worked crisply, quick to grasp what was happening or what was being said. He did not jump to hasty conclusions or biased thinking; his uncluttered, unemotional perspective led to fair, workable choices for himself and others.

People trusted John Strutter, a trust that trailed back through his father, Frank, and his grandfather for whom he was named. Respect, trust, and love from the community was the basis for the continuing success of the family drugstore and John's longevity in serving on the City Council of Witherston. He'd declined running for mayor two times; mostly under Emily's insistence that he could be more valuable and persuasive in the group if he were without all the administrative duties tied to the mayor's office.

The Strutter name had been on the front of the town's drugstore for two generations and on the hardware store for three. Family stories told of the pharmacy business being even older, having stemmed from John's great-great-grandmother's herbal remedies. John's father, Frank – or Mr. Strutter as the townspeople called him – had been the manager up to five years ago when he gave his portion of ownership of the store to John. Frank was approaching sixty and never missed a day at the drugstore. He came in every morning at nine, went to Elsie's Café at eleven for a two-hour lunch with his long-standing male friends, walked home for an afternoon nap, and returned around four until closing time. John knew the town's people were the important part of his father's daily routine and was careful not to infringe upon his father's patterns or pride.

*Dad will be a proud grandfather. He's been longing and waiting like Emily. I hope there is time to adopt another one or two.*

# 9

John studied Emily across the candle-lit table. The bright eyes and flushed cheeks displayed the elation within her. Her hands were in constant motion and she would scrunch her shoulders and giggle. He loved this side of his wife; her abounding glee when one of her dreams was coming true. Though in her thirties, she still had the charm of the young college girl.

"It's going be hard to hold you down, Em. I haven't seen you so fidgety since the 1960 fourth-of-July baby parade. You're not even eating your dinner, which I must say is very tasty."

"Just think, John, the next baby parade will have our baby in it." She smiled with the thought and sipped her wine slowly. "I'm so glad the Chamber asked me again to do a parade next summer. Do you think it too bold if I walked our carriage at the head of the parade?" She scrunched her shoulders again and squeezed her face into a mask of happiness. "Darling, I know this time is the real thing . . . it's been so long. You are excited, aren't you?"

"Yes, of course, but I think that we should keep this our news for now."

"Tell no one? Not Claire? Father Wentz? Not even Dad?" Emily asked in a sober tone.

"Don't you think it might be prudent to wait closer to the birth time? Once we share with one other person, we have really shared with many. If the girl has a change of heart, it might be harder for us to accept with too many people waiting with us."

"Oh, it would John. But I want others to hear my good news, a lot of the happiness is in sharing." Emily spoke pleadingly.

"Let's just go week by week. For now it can be our happiness, our celebration, our secret." John put his chin down and glanced over his glasses.

"I know, I know. Maybe I should stay apart from people. You know I always have to tell good news." She put her hand to her forehead.

John looked lovingly at her, "When you want to talk about this 'good news' talk with me. It would be the best conversation we could have."

"I love you John Strutter . . . you are a perfect mate. I'll do my best to keep this secret." Emily said with the seriousness of a 'little girl' grin.

"How about this? You tell Father Mike. He'll be delighted to hear it, and you'll have the joy of telling someone."

"Yes, of course. Father Mike would keep the secret with us. It'll be just the three of us until we tell family."

"Now don't run up too many phone bills calling Father Mike." John couldn't resist the tease.

"It's not fair to give and take away at the same time," Emily tossed back. "Phooey on you. Father Mike will welcome all my calls."

Later they looked over the packet from Catholic Charities, which documented their personal information. In their review, details of the home study - background investigation, outside references, psychological testing - all elements of the screening process were in front of John and Emily again. Mrs. Mason wanted them to assure the agency that the information was still true and, if not, to make separate notes of any changes.

In the twenty-two months since gathering the data not much had changed in their financial situation, health, residence, and most importantly their marital compatibility. They would give Mrs. Mason permission to double back to their original references – family members, parish priests, the State Bank, and doctors. Unless something should trigger doubts, Mrs. Mason would not be requiring further psychological tests or written essays. Her packet included the reminder that all administrative, hospital and birthing costs would be borne by Mr. and Mrs. Strutter.

As they put the documents aside, Emily asked, "John do you have any concern about how I'd raise our child? I know I can take a wrong turn at times."

"Em, your deeds mirror your good intentions. Even a wrong turn here or there has never caused harm to another. You're like my grandmother, I doubt you could intentionally hurt a fly."

"That's not true of the Minnesota mosquito." Emily said with a quick grin. "Seriously, dear, I am not perfect or you wouldn't be giving me advice so often. Now really, what would you have me watch out for?"

"Well, maybe your enthusiasm for doing things you've decided should be taken up, all in the effort to make perfect, to make life happy. We've talked about your highly persuasive nature, and it might smother a small child and could cripple their independence." John was straightforward and watched Emily for any sign of offense. "Because you love being with children, I see your emotions play out stronger with them . . showing the best and the also not so good."

"But, John, I will only want the best for our son . . . I only want him to be safe." She thrust out her lips in a semi pout and rubbed the pink welt on her forehead, a sure sign to John that she felt the truth to his statement. "Your sense of responsibility could make him old before they age . . . just as your grandfather did for you." And added a look of pain to the pout.

"Not to worry honey. You and I balance our weaknesses quite well. What can be a better sign than that we can talk reasonably about them?"

"Oh, how I wish our house was full with our children. Why have we been denied them? It's a question I'd like to put to God directly."

"Maybe even God doesn't have a reason to give us." John brought up a question that Mrs. Mason had asked during one of their interviews. "Emily how will you overcome not giving birth, not breast feeding . . . desires so strong in a biological mother?"

"And remember my response?" Emily butted in quickly. "I said I knew that void could not be filled . . . but the greatest joy is having a child in my house . . . to hold, to kiss, to watch, to love . . . the future is more important. Yes, I longed for the feelings of carrying a baby, giving birth, and holding it to my breast, and you know how painful that longing has been. But the future . . . having a family is more important . . . not how the child comes to us. You do believe me?" Emily said thoughtfully as she continued to move her right hand across her forehead.

"You'll be one heck of a great mother." John remarked cheerfully.

"You can say 'hell'." Emily's light response eased them into a less serious mode, which wove slowly into acts of love.


## 10

It was February 1962, and the Minnesota winter was milder than usual. The old timers quipped, "It'll be a hot summer." Emily was a-buzz, humming and preparing for the early April birth, "I'm praying for twins."

"Emily, remember I'll be gone Thursday and Friday next week, the state pharmacology meeting in St. Paul."

"Yes, I know. I'll be going with you."

"I thought your Dad was coming over. Weren't you refinishing floors?" *Now what do I do,* thought John.

"Oh, that can wait 'til next week. I'm not going to miss a chance to shop in the cities. I can get the last things for the layette, and we can eat at some of our favorite places."

"Why don't you ask Claire to go with us – you'll enjoy shopping that much more."

"You're begging out? Though, it would be fun to shop with Claire. I'll give her a call. Be ready at what time?"

"Ten o'clock will do." *Claire will take her attention away from me. All I need is Friday morning.*

He bowed out of the morning agenda and walked from the Radisson Hotel to the Norwest Bank building, skirting entrances to department stores. He took the elevator to fourth floor and found the Ketchell Agency (established 1954) in a suite at the far end of the corridor. A chime sounded as he opened the door into an empty reception area. A large man quickly appeared from an office on the right. He had two striking features; a baldhead circled by heavy black hair and deep set eyes circled with heavy dark-framed glasses. John thought this private investigator would not do his work un-noticed.

"My secretary is out for a long lunch today. I'm Sam Ketchell. Mr. Strutter?"

John shook the extended hand. "Yes, John Strutter."

"Come on in, John." They walked into an office décor not in accord with John's first impression of Sam Ketchell. A large dark wood desk was fitting; large tiffany lamps were not. A high-back red leather chair sat behind the desk and two blue leather ones were on the other side for clients. An oriental rug of stark colors; green, red, and blue lay over a flat piled carpet of tan and gray. John couldn't identify the personal statement intended, just trusted he had the right man.

John gazed at the large prints of metropolitan cities on the sidewalls. "Are these your favorite cities?"

"In fact, they are. Have you traveled abroad?"

"Wish I could say, yes. I'd like to see Berlin."

"One of my favorites." Sam picked up a pen, "Well, what type of service do you want of me?" With his left hand, he moved a small recorder to the middle of the desk. "Do you mind if we tape this? It's so much better than trying to write all the information."

"What do you do with the tape? I mean, how do you keep it private . . . confidential?"

"Well, trust is a big factor here. Clients ask me to do what they can't or won't do, so they have to trust me. Most of my work is personal and private. But I need all the information you can give and need to hear it straight. It may seem a shady business, but I am not a shady person. How did you end up with my name?"

"Through a lawyer friend."

"Well, are you comfortable with me?"

"Yes, I have to be. Secrets are not my specialties . . . but I guess that is the nature of your business. I insist on total confidentiality – just you and me."

"I understand – not an unusual request. This isn't a divorce case is it?"

"Heavens no," John shook his head, "but could be if my wife found out I was keeping secrets."

"Well, I haven't met a human being who didn't have one or more. Tell me what you want to know."

John explained the pending birth and adoption. "I am following an assumption that knowing who the birth parents are and where their lives lead them may be needed someday . . . can't say exactly why . . . just don't want to be without knowing." John, himself, didn't fathom why he had this unrelenting need to know. "Can we do it?"

Sam nodded his head. "Yes, we can. It's tricky but not

impossible. And, I hear you clearly . . . you want the information kept between the two of us."

"Exactly. Your reports should show the trail of changes and be kept in a place known to just you and me."

"Can do. I'd suggest a safe deposit box. We can decide where. I'll need to know the date and time of birth, sex of the baby and the hospital. I'll go from there. And my costs?"

"Whatever they are – no bills in the mail though – you'll have to trust me on that one."

They talked further about safeguarding reports and telephone numbers. John was emphatic, "Only you working on the case . . . it has to be just us. My trust doesn't go beyond you."

"Got it. And your contact preference is by telephone. Where? I'll identify myself as Sam if I have to. I'll ask for you, or when you can be reached if you're not there."

John had memorized Sam's address and telephone but tucked the number in his billfold. They shook hands. "We'll be in touch."

On the walk back to the hotel, John weighed his actions. *Secrets – they lead to more lies and fibs. Emily would be furious with me . . . seeking information that she wants so badly not to know. I may never need to use it, but I need to know. Maybe, someday, it'll be important for our child. I have to be honest . . . I can't go forward without knowing. And, I blame Emily for having the same desire. Well, first step taken. I'll have to trust, just like the man said.*

# CHAPTER TWO

## *Mothers and Fathers*

### 1

TWO YOUTHFUL FIGURES sit alone on the green bank overlooking a lazy stream. It is a spring day worthy of basking in the sunshine, but the young teenagers are not enjoying the blue sky, warm air, and green grass. They are disagreeing, once again, about the pregnancy they have foolishly conceived. His long body stretches out along side the slender sitting figure, her legs crossed, her head down.

"Adoption is the answer." Her words are firm, lifeless, and serious.

"No, it isn't. It's a baby for us."

"For us? How can we do that? We're still in high school for crying out loud!"

"We can finish school, and. . . ."

She cut in quickly, "And live with parents. No thank you!"

"Maybe your mother won't take us in, but my parents would."

"Oh, dang it, you haven't told them, have you?" She knocked the cap off his head.

"Not yet, but we have to soon. It's two months. You're so little and thin, this won't be a secret much longer."

"Oh, I dread telling my mother. She'll react something terrible.

I can hear her now."

"My folks won't, they . . . "

She shot back, "Sure they're goin' love me – I've only met them twice."

"It'll all work out. They'll want us to keep the baby. I promise it will work." He sat up and put his face close to hers.

She replied in a pitiful voice, "Like the promise you made two months ago? 'Don't worry,' you said, 'you'll be okay.' How okay is this?" She shook her head back and forth, "I'm not backing down! It's adoption."

"Oh, please!" he begged.

"No! No! No! I'm not giving in. I barely like you. How does that fit into married life?"


## 2

John walked through the drugstore looking for his father. "Has anyone seen Frank?" He called his father by his given name when at the drugstore. It was a decision they both made when John first started working the pharmacy -- a decision they hoped would give them equal stance with employees and customers. They wanted to avoid being played against one another, to avoid hearing remarks such as, "Let's see what your father has to say."

John found his father in the back room taking inventory with another employee. "Got a moment?"

Frank motioned for the employee to leave, "We'll resume this tomorrow, let's say early morning." He turned to his son, "What's up, John?"

"Dad, can you handle the store the next couple of days? We just received our call . . . birth has started . . . could be today or tomorrow."

"Are you leaving now?" Frank shook his head, "Dumb question. Of course, you are. Emily will want to be at the hospital. You'd better get on your way." He tucked an inventory clipboard under his arm. "Where do you plan to stay? Want me to call for rooms?"

"No, Emily has called a hotel, one close to Southview Hospital." John moved toward the pharmacy, "I have a prescription to finish. But, you could drive over and pick up Emily for me."

"I'll do that. She's got to be excited. You must be aware, tomorrow is April Fool's day."

"Don't say that to Emily, Dad. I doubt she'd find that amusing. You know, she is still worried about a last-minute change of mind." John handed the car keys to his father's waiting hand. "Be sure you put in my suitcase, grey leather, also shaving kit. It's grey also."

"Anything else?"

"No, Emily has everything under control. She's had her suitcase sitting by the front door for days."

"Well, it's going on three o'clock, let's see if we can get you on your way by four." Frank gave his son a quick, tight hug. "Good luck, John. This is a great day for you and Emily, and I can't wait to hold my first grandchild."

As Frank drove away from the store, he reflected on the day he saw his firstborn in his wife's arms. Helen had been so proud to present him with a son, promising he'd grow to be a healthy tall boy even though he weighed only a couple of ounces over six pounds that day. They had planned on a large family, just as John and Emily had, but there was only John before Helen died of meningitis. Frank never found, nor did he seriously seek out, another woman who he'd let replace the void left in his life. He hoped there was time for John and Emily to adopt another baby. Growing up alone among adults, John grew too old too young.

### 3

Mrs. Mason ushered them into a small office on the first floor of the hospital and said she would return when the papers were signed.

"When can I see the baby?" asked Emily.

"I'll have a better idea about that when I come back. This is an awkward time; the father and his parents are here also. I think it would have been easier if you had waited for my call." Mrs. Mason tone voiced her annoyance. She turned to them from the doorway, "There's a cafeteria down the hall and public telephones, if you need them." She told them to leave a message on the corkboard by the door if they left the room or the hospital. Then she closed the door, leaving them feeling excluded.

"Emily, you must show a little more patience. I didn't think this was a good idea to come before her call. Now that we're here . . ."

"You have more patience then I have, and I couldn't stand waiting in that hotel room." She laid her coat on the arm of a small sofa, "Should I get us some coffee? Maybe a muffin or cookie? Here are some magazines and the Star Tribune." She fidgeted with opening a small leather case she'd carried with her. She gazed at baby clothes and a white blanket knitted by one of the church members. "Why don't you shed your coat?"

"I need to go back to the car for some information for a couple of telephone calls I should make."

"Who to? Can't it wait?"

"Just a couple of old classmates, and I promised Dad I'd let him know how things are going."

"Somehow, I don't recall you being so close to old classmates that you have to call them at a time like this." Emily said sarcastically.

"Suppose you'd remember if I said they are members of the Minnesota Pharmaceutical Association? I need to talk about an agenda for next month. Besides I doubt that we'll be going up to the nursery. I really wish you'd waited for Mrs. Mason's call." He turned his back to her saying, "I won't be too long," and went out the door. He and Emily had argued about coming to the hospital too soon and now he wished that he'd not given in to Emily's pleading. It was obvious that Mrs. Mason was displeased with their presence.

John walked down to the last telephone booth, turned his back, checked the number in his billfold and reached for coins in his trouser pocket. He put a quarter in the slot and waited for a greeting. "Hello, Sam Ketchell here." John liked it when Sam answered his own phone calls.

"Mr. Ketchell, this is John Strutter. We spoke several times in the last month about work you plan to take on for me. I am at the hospital now, here in the city, and will probably be here tomorrow also."

"Yes, I have the notes from our conversation. Has the time arrived? Are you taking the baby home?"

"So far, it looks positive. The baby . . . a boy, was born shortly after midnight and remains unnamed. The mother is still in the hospital; room 2113 is what I overheard. I understand the father and his parents are here also. Mrs. Mason expects to have the signed document by the end of the day."

"Then you want me to proceed?"

"Yes, just as planned. Please call me when you have the information. You have my store number. We'll decide then on where and how to safeguard your reports. I'd prefer not to have anything in writing sent to me. As I stressed before this has to be absolutely private between you and me. I don't want a third party working on this – just you."

"I understand Mr. Strutter, and my suggestion is still for a safe deposit box. If not in your home town, then here in the city."

"I've not thought of anything that looks any better. We might even consider putting the box in your name, but we can discuss the pros and cons of that. I'll await your call, whatever the results. Let's plan to see each other in May, at your office. There's a statewide meeting in the city I'll be attending the third week, on Tuesday and Wednesday."

"Okay. I'll get working right away and I don't foresee any problems. This is doable. I'll call you within a few weeks and I've made a note on my May calendar. Good luck with your new one."

John finished his call feeling he had just committed a sin for which there'd be no confessing. What he was asking Ketchell to do was for his ease of mind and maybe, someday, other's. He quickly placed a call to his father and gave him an accounting of the day, promised to call again tomorrow, and predicted they'd be home by the following day. "Yes, Dad, plan to be at the house to greet your grandson. That will please Emily. She'll be ready to show him off."

Emily looked up when John entered the room. "What took you so long, dear?" said with an edge to her voice. "I was ready to come looking for you." She waited, but John didn't reply. "Nothing's wrong at home, is there?"

John added a fib to his guilt. "No, no, no, no. Dad just had to tell me that Mrs. Lewis was in again this morning with the same questions and complaints about her prescriptions. It's the third time this week, and she doesn't seem to be appeased by our answers."

"Irma Lewis doesn't listen too well, does she? Her constant complaints really upset our church meetings. Claire came close to loosing it with her a couple of weeks ago. Instead, we just adjourned the meeting – best way to handle Irma when she gets on one of her tirades – just find a way to close her off."

"Dad is going to call her doctor and find a helpful response." Lie number two. "Where's the newspaper."

"Right here. I think I'll take a walk to the cafeteria. Want coffee?"

John nodded and turned to read the news.

## 4

The girl's body revealed her youth as she awkwardly held the tiny blue bundle, her arms stiff. Her face showed dismay and bewilderment at finding herself in a hospital room holding a baby. The young boy put his hand on the baby's head. "Please let my folks come in and hold their grandson."

"No, they want to change our minds. Besides they've seen him in the nursery."

"It's not too late. We don't have to sign those papers."

"Yes, we do. We agreed and I'm not telling Mrs. Mason any different. Come on, I'm too young to raise a baby . . . and don't tell me again your folks would." They both became stiff and quiet, he looking at her, she looking out the window.

"You'll be sorry some day." He said softly.

"I doubt it. I want this little guy to have a good, a whole family. I know I can't make that happen. Mrs. Mason told us these two people have a nice home and are a perfect match for parents."

"I know. It's just that we could have done it."

Her reply was defensive, "No, I couldn't have and I think you are kidding yourself. We are kids, not parents." She looked at the baby; "Let's all say good-bye today."

"Okay, I won't push anymore." He gave his assent in a low, hurt voice. "Let me hold him one more time."

# 5

By mid-afternoon, the formal papers were signed and the next morning the baby's future parents saw their child for the first time through a nursery window. His name was to be recorded as Jon Francis Strutter. They choose a different version of John, so as not to confuse the two John's just one generation apart. But the spelling did not make the phonetics sound different; John tended to call Jon, son, and Emily called him *sweetie, precious one*, the *best boy in Witherston*, and often *Jon-son* after he turned his tenth year. PaPo Frank, as Jon called his grandfather said they should have picked another name, "So damn confusing for the whole town . . . there's been old John, young John, and now this Jon. Think I'll call him Jon Francis." And so he did; informally he'd call him Bud.

The baby was forty-eight hours old when Emily first held and fed him. They had a small, private room across from the hospital nursery. She snuggled him carefully into the crook of her left arm, sighed lovingly, and put the nipple of the bottle to his tiny mouth. She repeatedly murmured, "such a sweetie" or "my little sweetie". Her happiness mixed with elation and tears, and John sitting in the opposite corner of the room heard Emily humming. He knew this moment, this day, Emily was born anew. He knew he'd witness an outpouring of love, more than ever before, and that Emily would be a magnificent mother. He also knew he'd have to temper her protection of her object of love so that the young boy would not be smothered and lose his sense of self and independence. John watched the scene before him, wishing that he could magically share her thoughts and feelings.

He might have been surprised if he'd heard her thoughts. Emily wondered if the baby knew from her smell, sound, and heartbeat that she was not the same as his real mother. Her mind reflected on the counseling she and John had with the psychologist, Dr. Dan Green, recommended by Sally Mason. Vividly, she recalled the session when Dr. Green discussed the mother/child bond. He spoke of it as an undefined, unrecognizable, taken-for-granted connection and stressed that the bond begins in the uterus and continues through birth, growing stronger during the following months. Emily remembered how troublesome it was to hear his words, "a separation hours after birth into loving arms of another does not negate, ignore, or diminish that initial nine-month bond in the uterus." But she also remembered his encouraging words, "a strong, supportive, loving environment envelops and develops the newborn baby." Emily surrendered to the fact of the baby's genetic make-up being outside her control, but her son's destiny was to be shaped within her surroundings and influences. Beginning now, in this first hour of hundreds to come, Emily held him, caressed his head, stroked his back, and cooed soft tones to her *precious one*, so he'd feel complete with her, so she'd be the mother he'd come to own.

**6**

Emily was at the hospital each day, feeding, bathing, and caring for Jon. The nurses were pleased at how adept she was without their instructions. Emily told them about the babies she had tended at the church nursery. Today, she dressed him in a blue sleeper, booties and cap, and wrapped him in two blankets, first a soft thin one and then the white knitted. The nursery gave them a two-day supply of formula, and the Strutter family headed for Witherston Thursday afternoon. Jon was four days, 12 hours, and 23 minutes old.

"John, I want to plan a welcome gathering for our family, friends, and church members. Like maybe in the church basement, after his baptism. Everyone will want to see our son." John heard a new softness in Emily's voice.

"Maybe. Only it must be without gifts. I won't be comfortable with the town showering us with presents. Why not have something at the house instead? Just our family and close friends. Choose a time when your father can drive over. Wouldn't you like to have him stay a few days?" John urged her towards a smaller celebration. Having a large party seemed to put an obligation on the community that did not suit him.

"Dear, are you trying to rein me in?"

"Yes, I suppose so. First, let's set a baptismal day and match it up with your father. I'm sure my aunts and a few of your friends would like to prepare the food. Let's keep it simple, low key."

"Okay, okay. I guess I can be glad warm weather will be here in another month. I'll walk him every day to show him off."

"I know you can't wait . . . the proud mommy."

After a few miles of humming, Emily said sadly, "How hard it must be to give up your baby. I wonder how she felt as she held him for the last time? Does she have regrets? Did she not have a home to take him to? Does she think of him? I couldn't have done it, but if she hadn't, we wouldn't have this sweet, precious boy."

"Well, Em, those are things we'll never know. Think about how young she was. Would you have kept a baby at sixteen?

47

I know, I know, you wouldn't have gotten pregnant. But not every Catholic girl remains so pure. A pregnant teenager poses a problem for families . . . that's why there are adoption agencies."

"Wish he didn't have to know about his adoption. Can't we somehow find a way not to tell him?"

"Em, that's not rational. All of Witherston knows we adopted a child. How do you think you can silence a whole town? Remember what Dr. Green recommended, 'do it sooner rather than later.' We have a few years to prepare for the day. Maybe we should talk with him again." He looked over at Emily and the baby. "Let's just enjoy whatever Jon brings us each day. We need not solve every issue this very moment."

"You're right. I think I'll continue a rosary novena for the young mother. I hope Mrs. Mason assured her that this young guy has come to a loving home."

"That would be nice, Em."

# 7

"I appreciate you giving me your lunch hour." John said as he shook hands with Sam Ketchell. John was taken again by Sam's solid, strong presence.

"Heck, I can eat lunch any time of the day." Sam patted his ample waistline, "You can see I have some extra to go on. How's the little one doing?"

"Quite nicely – not too much disruption to the household. But he has made it different, in a very good way." As John seated himself, he asked, "Have you come up with anything?"

"Yes, though not the complete background for both families, but here's the story." Sam pushed a green folder across the desk towards John. "They're from Colorado."

John opened the folder to a typed report and a clip of documents. One page gave the facts: Nora Paulsen from Denver; stayed with an uncle, Lee Paulsen and wife Ellen in Minneapolis until she moved into the Catholic Charities Home for unwed mothers in October

1961 (probably to continue schooling). Stayed with the uncle and aunt for most of the summer of 1962 before returning to Colorado. Lives in small community on outskirts of Denver with her mother, Marianne Paulsen who is an executive and part owner in a local accounting firm. No information on Mr. Paulsen. Nora attends Northeast High as does the young man, Tim Parsons. She's a junior, he's a senior. No background on his parents yet. Nora's birth date: October 29, 1946. Tim's June 10, 1945. The baby's birth certificate was recorded as Tim Alan born April 1, 1962 at 12.43 a.m., before re-recorded as Jon Francis Strutter for the final certificate.

"I don't know if I should have expected more for seven weeks, but it seems you've made a good start. We know the names and where they live, and we have the beginning of a trail. I have to admit, I am curious about the methods you use to find this information, but on the other hand, I don't want to know either."

"You won't have to worry about that, John, my sources and methods are my business. It's better that way." Sam picked up a small piece of paper and leaned across to John, "Here's the signature card we'll both sign for the safe deposit box I've rented in the Norwest Bank in this building. We'll both have keys. I thought having the box here close to me facilitates securing the reports. That makes it easy for me and private for you."

"Seems like a good arrangement . . . I find no fault with it. Can we take care of it now? I have about another thirty minutes before I need to leave."

"Great. Let's take the elevator to first floor. I plan on giving you updates by phone. I'm sure to have more in a couple of months. Then you can always read them in full when you visit the cities."

Before they left the office, John reminded Sam, "Remember, I don't want bills mailed to me, or any other thing with your name. Let me pay now in cash and I'd like to continue that way. I'm in the cities three or four times a year. Will that work with you?"

"It will. I have no reason not to trust you. I doubt that you have ever reneged on an obligation – you just don't seem the type."

John laughed, "You probably checked my background also."

"Good conclusion, John." Sam added with his own chuckle.

# THE STRUTTER FAMILY

# CHAPTER ONE

# *Pre-School Years*

## 1

J ON'S GENETIC HERITAGE showed in his blue-green eyes, a match to his birth mother and different from the ancestral brown or hazel color of the Strutter's. When friends in town commented on the unique color, Emily would be quick to interject that the Knowland family had a history of blue eyes some three or more generations past. She so wanted Jon to belong to her.

Barbers would cuss the cowlick at the nape of Jon's neck, a swirl of hair the size of a fifty-cent piece that refused to go any other way than clockwise. He would never know this was a distinctive feature of his birth father.

At full growth, Jon would be five feet, nine inches. His slim torso and short legs were typical of most of the ancestors of both birth parents. His short stature would lead to selective sports – he became a star with the freestyle on the summer swim team and a cheerleader for basketball and football versus being a player. Two other genetic inclinations would not be known until later.

Emily was intent on surrounding the baby with love. Her touch was soft, sure, and soothing. Her words were spoken in light, happy tones and she often sang or hummed as she held him. Jon was quite fussy the first couple of months, crying sharply and randomly, waking up often during the night.

"Em, might you be responding too quickly to the baby's cries?" John suggested, as he saw how Emily went immediately upon hearing the slightest whimper. "I remember my grandmother saying that a baby had to exercise his lungs."

"John, I'm not worried about his lungs. I want this little fellow to feel he can be happy . . . no, more like secure with me. I want him to know my heart beat, my voice, my arms. I want to help him make his way from his birth mother to me."

"Might he not like to hear my voice, feel my arms? Don't you think he should know both of us?"

"Why, John, are you jealous?" Emily said quickly as a tease.

"Hadn't thought of it that way." John peered over his glasses. "While I've not been accused of being the demonstrative type – other than by you -- I still want to be a part of this parenting."

"I guess I have been selfish. I must admit, I've held him to myself . . . like I don't want him away from my presence. Maybe I still can't believe he's here. Are you saying you want to share the night sessions? That means interrupting the sleep you need for work."

"Emily, as if I'm sleeping when you are out of bed. I hear Jon's cries, feel you get up, and wait for you to return. Surely you've noticed my pats when you come back to bed."

"Yes, and I curl up and sleep in peace. John Strutter you are a dear. I love you more than you'll ever know." She moved to his lap and snuggled into his shoulder. He kissed the top of her head and stroked her thigh.

In a few moments John whispered, "Shall we?"

"Yes, before *little one* is awake." Emily hummed like a purring kitten as John carried her from the living room to the bottom of the stairs.

Later when the passion had been satisfied, John suggested, "How about we both take the first call tonight? I'll hold the baby, you can warm the bottle . . . and change the diapers."

"I'll let you off this time, but that's part of parenting. You can't just do the parts you like," Emily murmured as she curled into his body to sleep.

## 2

Emily humming softly, opened a white box, lifted the tissue paper and the baptismal clothes Jon would be wearing this day when she would present her son to the congregation. She wasn't sure she wanted to cover his straight, well-formed legs, but she'd been taken with this outfit of soft blue cotton. The blue and white top attached to the solid blue bottom had tiny white buttons around the waist and up the front. "Oh, you are going to look so precious. Won't he Mom?"

Since Jon's arrival, Emily found that she missed her mother more than ever. She continually spoke to her, sharing her love for the baby. "Do you see how he does this or that?" or "Look Mom, how alert he is." And always "Isn't he beautiful?" Emily was saddened that Jon would never know the presence of a grandmother. Her mother had died when she was in her teen years, and John lost his mother when he was only five.

Emily was still humming as she put the soft blue booties on the baby, unaware that her husband had been standing in the doorway. He watched as she lifted their son. "Looking pretty handsome, eh? The outfit matches your blue eyes." He crossed the room to put his arms around Emily's waist. "And, the mother is quite beautiful herself."

"Oh, John I didn't hear you come up. Look he's smiling at us." She snuggled her nose into his chin. "I am rather excited."

"Yes, I bet you are Em and rightly so. It's like a debut. I hope Jon will enjoy the attention and not be too fussy. Is everything ready in the tote bag?"

"Yes, you can carry that – pick up his bottles as you pass through the kitchen. Oh, hand me the blue and white blanket over there. It's the one June knitted. Isn't he darling, John?" Emily gently wrapped 'her precious one' in the blanket and left the nursery still humming.

The first four rows of pews were reserved this Sunday for the Strutter family: aunts, uncles, and cousins. Emily's father, Carl and the Knowland family took another row. Emily felt a bit smug when Father Wentz acknowledged the occasion from the pulpit. "Today, we baptize Jon Francis Strutter and offer our prayers for his journey from babyhood to adult. We ask that God guide him through the many steps he will walk and bless those who will teach him with love and patience. Welcome Jon to St. Anne's and congratulations, John and Emily."

Many of the parishioners stayed after Mass to join in the happiness of the Strutter's. They crowded into the baptismal nave of the church as the baby was christened with holy water and gave their congratulations during the reception that followed in the parish hall.

Emily proudly held her son in her arms, without blankets, so people could see the beautiful body clothed in blue. Like a miracle, he fussed very little with the voices and movement around him. Emily nodded a hello to a tall sprightly lady approaching her. Mrs. Kinney prayed in the fifth row pew every Sunday directly in front of Frank Strutter and knew the family for the fifty years they'd attended St. Anne's.

"He's a beautiful boy," the elderly lady said as she touched the baby's arm.

"I tell him that every day," Emily replied.

"I suppose we'll be seeing him in church more often?" Mrs. Kinney moved her hand to feel the soft layer of hair.

Emily shrugged her shoulders. "Not for a while. He's prone to cry quite often, so John and I are coming to mass at different times for now."

"I suppose babies have to get use to their new surroundings . . . he certainly seems at ease with all the commotion today. I can tell Frank is pleased; his first grandchild." Mrs. Kinney touched the baby's hand before slowly walking to the coffee urn, stopping to talk along the way – everyone was her friend.

Emily looked up to see a smiling face. It was June, her co-chair for the nursery program. "How lovely you look, Emily. This is a nice way for all of us to see you and meet your son. May I hold him?" June could sense a bit of reluctance as Emily murmured about Jon being sound asleep.

John leaned towards June, "Emily's an over-protective mother. That's probably natural for a new mother who's waited so long." Emily gave John the hurt look of a small puppy but did not relinquish the baby.

"We've missed you, Emily." June said attempting to ease the awkwardness. "Will you be coming back to the nursery soon?"

"Yes, I thought I'd drop in this week. Since the weather is still warm, we walk every day. I'll show off Jon, of course, wrapped in the blanket you knitted for him." They both silently watched the baby. "We haven't had a new baby in the nursery for a while, have we?"

"No, not since little Jenny Vigil."

They turned when they heard Claire's voice. "Emily, when are you going to let me take care of Jon? Certainly you have to go out sometime."

Emily smiled at her best friend. "Thanks Claire, but Frank has been there for now. He stops by every other day right on the button around feeding time. It's really cute to watch him. He's so gentle when he holds Jon."

"Well being his first grandson and all. I can only imagine what great buddies they will become. Now how about me?"

John watched Emily as she struggled with this offer. He knew her biggest fear: to be seen as less than perfect. She had persuasive powers, along with drive and determination, to structure her world as she wished it to be. John knew he'd have to counter, and with gentleness, to keep young Jon from being smothered by his mother's code of perfection.

John leaned towards his wife, "Emily, didn't I hear you mention that you need to go shopping. Mightn't that be a good time for Claire and Jon."

Another hurt puppy look, but Emily relented. "We could do

Wednesday or Thursday? I have errands and shopping to do; I'd only be gone an hour. You could do Jon's afternoon walk." Emily didn't tell Claire about the stories she told Jon during their walks, of birds, dogs, flowers. Even though it was just sounds to his baby ears, it was her voice he was hearing.

On the other side of the room, the interest in Jon's presence continued. "Well, Frank, your first grandson. Bet he'll replace us old guys at the café?" To which Frank replied, "Not all together – when he gets old enough, maybe Emily will let him join us."

In his heart, Frank wanted to make up for the hours he had missed in his own son's young life. He'd been so busy at the drugstore during the baby years and then aloof with grief after Helen died. Frank saw the same doting mother in Emily as he'd seen in his wife, and instead of taking a background role as he'd done as a young father, this time he wanted his grandson to have lasting memories like those John had for his grandfather.

"You know you old farts could go to the park with us – you know, play in the sand box. Buy an ice cream for the kid."

"How about we wait until he can fish? He ought to be able to hold a pole by three, wouldn't you say Frank?" Their gibes made no dents, only chuckles; their friendships went back to school days.

The Toohey twin sisters, who'd worn identical attire every day of their sixty-two years, approached John dressed in lavender wool suits, large pearl buttons on the jackets. "John, we are so happy for you," they said in unison. "You and Emily will be such good parents."

John smiled and took their hands, "Thank you for saying so. Emily is training me in baby care."

The three of them laughed. "Well John, we can't think of anything you wouldn't be good at."

Father Wentz extended his hand to the tall man who stood apart from others. "You're Emily's father, aren't you?" The man took Father's hand and said, "Yes, I'm Carl Knowland. The baptism was very nice . . . I liked the way you explained each step. And quite a crowd. Seems like everyone was waiting for a Strutter baby."

"Is this your first grandchild also?"

Carl held up four fingers. "No, my two sons have two each. Jon swings the number of grandsons to three, and he'll be the youngest one by eight years. The two girls are over with Emily," he pointed. "They can't keep their hands off the baby. I've noticed Emily can't either." He wished her mother were here. He'd raised a teenage daughter alone, and it had taken a lot of devotion. He was pleased with what he saw.

Frank Strutter rang a small bell as he moved to the front of the hall and turned toward the crowd. John and Emily looked at each other with questioning glances as Frank spoke. "It is a proud day in many ways. One, a child for John and Emily, a happiness in which we all are privileged to share. Second, your presence blesses this occasion for our family, and we are proud to have your friendship. Third, your generosity for this celebration."

He looked directly at his son and daughter-in-law, "Frank and Emily, everyone respected your wish for no presents," and then he looked around to everyone and, with a chuckle, said, "Emily had the baby room full before Jon arrived home. What could we've added?" His right hand brought out an envelope from his jacket pocket. "To share in your joy and welcome your son, your group of friends are giving a contribution to the church." He saw John shake his head. "The ladies' altar society, with Father, is to make a purchase in the name of John, Emily, and Jon Francis."

Frank walked towards Father Wentz, handing him the envelope, "Father here are the gifts from the friends of our family. The envelope holds $1,000." They all heard Emily gasp, as the respect for the Strutter family had once again been affirmed.

## 3

Jon's environment shaped traits of wonder, awe, simplicity, and trust. The world around him, primarily parents and two grandfathers, would animate his curiosity and wonder throughout his early years. His emotional needs were never left unfed. His mother sang songs when she held him, which was often. She stayed with him as he went to sleep, with her hand on his body wanting him to know how wonderful he was. As a baby, he was "beautiful and happy." When he was two, she added 'kind'; at three she added 'strong'; and at five he was "happy, kind, strong, and smart." Jon began humming before he was even two years old.

Grandfather Frank stopped by every other day to be with his grandson. He was pleased that Emily trusted him with Jon and his bottle and solids, when the time came. Jon called his grandfather PaPo Fank until he started school and, PaPo came to call his grandson Bud. They would come to be the best of buddies; PaPo taught Jon how to roll a ball, build tall stacks with wooden blocks, and recognize pictures of dogs, cats, squirrels, and rabbits from picture books that had belonged to Jon's father. Grandma Frances had kept her grandson's books, wooden blocks, and toy cars; the boxes were found labeled with John's name when the family home was dismantled after Frank's parents died. Frank had kept them in his attic waiting for a grandson to be born. When Jon Francis was two years old, Papo devoted a morning each week for their special time. They'd go to the park to play on the swings, the short slide, and Jon's favorite, the teeter-totter. As Jon aged, they would plant vegetables, share nature walks, and learn how to recognize the signs of animals that lived in the woods.

Grandpa Carl, Emily's father, drove the hundred miles to Witherston every other Saturday to stay a day and night with his daughter and family. He was their weekend baby sitter so Emily and John could join with their friends for a dinner, at a card table, or in church activities. Young Jon came to love the camping trips with Grandpa Carl and later, the time in the workshop where they made toys and furniture.

Jon's earliest recollection was his hospital stay three months after his third birthday. Enlarged tonsils had made breathing difficult and caused too many infections along with too many episodes of choking during sleep. Jon remembers waking to strange surroundings – a big bed and a white room absent of his stuffed animals and toys. His eyes searched the room, past the strange lady who was at his side looking at something in her hand, to the foot of his bed where his father and mother stood.

"Hurt, Mommy." Emily quickly came to his side and leaned over to kiss his cheek.

"Where, Jon?" He pointed to his throat. "It won't be for long, sweetheart."

"She put something on my face." Jon said in a wispy voice.

"Yes, Jon, but it's gone now," the nurse said at the same time that Emily said, "you were a brave boy."

"Hurts."

"It will go away soon," said the nurse. He made no response to her question, "Want some ice cream?" She brought a straw to Jon's mouth. "Let's take a swallow of water first"

He clutched his lips together. "No. Wanna go home."

"In a couple of days." Emily put a hand on his head. "You are such a brave boy. Let's take a sip of water . . . you like using a straw."

"Wanna go home." Jon began crying.

"Sweetheart, Mommy will be right here with you. See my bed is right over here. I wouldn't leave you all alone. Now let's try a sip. There, that's a good boy."

Tears rolled down Jon's cheeks. "Hurts Mommy."

"I know, I know. It'll be better tomorrow. You are a brave, strong boy. Daddy and Mommy are proud of you. So is the nurse." Emily turned to her and asked, "Can he have ice cream now or maybe ginger ale?"

As the nurse left the room, John came to the side of the bed opposite Emily. He held the tiny hand in his and said, "I'm proud of you son. The hurt will go away and get better if you swallow and drink water. Mommy will help you." He waited while Jon took a sip and scrunched his eyes as he swallowed. "That's good,

Jon." He looked at Emily, "You want me to stay the night?"

"No, just until evening, when he is feeling more comfortable. I need to be here. John, he's so little. He doesn't understand."

"He'll be okay." He looked over his glasses into the small face, "How about this son? When you get well, we'll go pick out a dog. Would you like that?" He watched his son's eyes light up and they smiled at each other. "So you think tonight what you'd like to name your dog. Can you do that?"

"Yes, Daddy."

## 4

"John, you promised him a dog . . . in July, and now it's the end of September. He keeps asking . . . don't you think it's time to come through with your promise?" Emily scolded.

"It's not like I've ignored it, Emily. I've told him the doggie house hasn't any puppies. I know, I know, you are going to say I'm telling my son a lie. Yes, it is a bit of a stretch from the facts, but they haven't had a good batch of dogs to pick from. You know, once I take Jon in there, I'm not going to get him to leave without a dog."

"Well, then go buy him one from a kennel," Emily said harshly.

"Why are you so upset about this, Em? I don't see Jon in tears, but you are certainly close to crying about this. What's this all about, really?"

Emily put her head down and rubbed her forehead. "I don't think you should've said it, if you were going to wait so long. Jon should be able to trust us. It's not a good example."

"Emily, Emily, are you trying to make life perfect for Jon? What are you afraid of? Doesn't Jon need to learn patience? Trust comes from a fulfillment of a promise, not on a time table of gratification." He waited for Emily to look at him.

"You asked him while he laid on that bed in the hospital to pick out a name for his dog. He did so – and he still doesn't have his pet. Poor showing!" She stood up with a huff, "Think about it. I'll wait ten days and then I'll get the dog."

John knew he was being pushed to be a perfect parent for a perfect childhood. It was a scenario that would recur as Emily pressed to make a utopian life for Jon. Would it have been different if the child had been hers or if there were more than one? Later he called Pat Harris, the local vet, asking where else he might find a dog. Pat suggested a pet clinic over in Anthony, just thirty miles west of town. He said the clinic screened their animals and specialized in smaller dogs.

Pat added, "You ought to call first to see what's there right now. If you bring one home, let me know if we need to schedule shots. It's a good learning for youngsters to see that dogs have to get shots too – I like to think it helps them see that shots are okay."

The following Saturday morning, Jon was standing by his dad's bedside when the sun had barely lightened the sky. He pushed his fingers into his father's arm several times wanting him to open his eyes. Short on patience, the boy tapped his cheek. He saw his father squinting at him.

"What's wrong? Do you need help?"

"Help dress me. I wanna see the dogs"

"Son, it's too early. If we leave now, no one will be there to let us in. Come on, climb in next to me and let's watch the sun come up."

Jon was quiet for several minutes and then asked his father, "Will the dog come home with us?"

"Yes, son. Today you adopt a dog to bring home."

"What's dopt?"

"Adopt means you choose a dog to come live in your house, cause the dog doesn't have a home to go to."

"Why not Daddy? Doesn't he have a mommy and daddy?"

"Yes everyone is born to a mommy. But, maybe this mommy didn't have a home for her baby."

"Will he like my house?"

"To adopt means we have to make a good home for the dog. You can do that, can't you?"

"You help me, Daddy?"

"Of course, son. We can do it together. Grandpa and Mommy will too"

Dad and son drove away from the driveway at mid-morning; Emily watched from the porch, waving with a forced smile. John knew she was torn between wanting Jon to have a separate and special time with his dad and being with her son to select his first pet. She'd hinted about having a family outing, but John purposely ignored her remarks. Rather, he'd brought paper and pencil to the breakfast table for Jon and Emily to make a list of items to buy for the dog -- feeding bowls, leash, bed, toy, collar, treats – and set an expectation for their fun visit to the pet store.

As the car turned on to the highway, John felt his son's quietness and looked over to see the boy's eyes slowly close. *"Good,"* he thought, *"who knows how early he was really awake this morning -- excited and ready to see his dog. A little nap will do him good."*

John reflected back to the afternoon his grandfather had taken him, hand in hand, for a walk to a neighbor's house. It was a Saturday also, and the young couple (faded from John's memory) took them to their back porch where John saw a black and white dog snuggled into blankets with five little puppies. One was to be his, his grandfather told him and he had first pick. Every day he walked the three blocks to see the puppies until his puppy, the littlest one, was ready to leave his mother. Pepper was his first lesson of being responsible for another living being. Grandpa expected him to take total care of the dog and had John write out a list of chores he was to do for Pepper. Grandma helped on the sly – or so we thought – John doubted that anything escaped his grandfather. John wanted to have the impact on his son that Grandpa had had on him and intended that the dog would be the start in framing lessons of responsibility.

Jon sat up quickly as soon as the motor stopped. He rubbed his eyes. "We here, Daddy?"

"Yes, son. It looks like a nice place. Let's go meet the people and the dogs. We have lots of time. We don't have to hurry and, remember, you can take only one dog home."

"I know Daddy. I have to go potty."

After a young man in a red shirt showed the visitors to the restroom and drinking fountain, he waited to take them to the wing of the building where the dogs were in separate, clean pens. He led them past barking dogs toward a hallway door to show them an outside yard where they could have playtime with a dog. He knelt down to talk with Jon. "Is this your first pet?" Jon nodded up and down. "Do you have a name for your dog?" Jon nodded, "Shorts." "That's a great name. How old are you?" Jon held up three fingers and his father added, "plus six months."

The young man stood to talk with John. "The dogs with a white ribbon on their doors have screened the best for children. It's a clue that helps in finding the right dog for someone young. Let us know when you want to go outside. Just ask for me, Andy, or Susan, over there in the red shirt."

Jon took his father's hand as they started down the aisle. He stopped at every cage, calling out to each dog. First he talked to a little black one who stayed back against a wall. Jon moved his hands and called, "here, here." The dog looked but didn't move.

"Maybe he's shy son, look here's a yellow one." The dog pushed at the cage when Jon came to look at him. The dog wanted to nip and Jon jumped back. When Jon moved toward the cage, the dog lunged again. His father noted that there were no white ribbons for these two dogs.

Next, Jon watched a brown and black dog running back and forth, but it didn't seem to catch his interest. He did stop to talk to a little white poodle that licked his finger when he tried to reach between the wires to pet it. "He's pretty," Jon said. He came back to this cage a second time.

"Jon, let's see all the dogs." He'd noticed one more ribbon down from the poodle.

There they saw a light tan dog with a broad black face sitting in the middle of the pen, tail wagging, swishing across the floor and when Jon approached, it greeted him with two 'arf's' as if to say hello. The dog stood up when Jon waved to him, and then sat down when Jon squatted in front of the wire door. The dog gave another friendly bark, and Jon poked his fingers through the wire mesh. The dog came over to sniff his hands, sat down and arf'd again. "He likes me, Daddy. Can I hold him? I like him, Daddy."

"Yes I see that. Look when he stands, Jon, his legs are short – just like the name, Shorts. Should we take him outside?"

"Yes. I want my ball."

"I have it here in my pocket. Let me get the young man to help us."

With the freedom of outside, Jon and Shorts took to each other like a fairy-tale match. The dog ran with the boy, stayed close when Jon stood still, licked his hands, watched the ball, and displayed a happy disposition. Jon rolled on the ground and Shorts pushed into him without biting or nipping. Jon held him and giggled as the dog licked his face.

They played for twenty minutes until Jon tired and crumpled to the ground, the dog stretched out by his side. Shorts had a long body, John guessed maybe eighteen inches, but was small in stature, maybe ten inches high. He was glad that Shorts was beyond puppy stage and behaved as if he'd been well treated. When Andy showed the little boy how to put a leash on the dog, Shorts held still. John was pleased with what they'd found and finished the arrangements for taking Shorts home, including picking out a carrier for traveling. It was difficult getting the child to understand that it was best for the dog not to be loose in the car. "I ride in back with Shorts," he said as they opened the car doors.

Later during the ride home, Jon asked, "Where's his mommy, Daddy?"

"I don't know, son. She must live someplace else."

"All those doggies had no mommy?"

"None of those doggies were babies anymore. Mommy dogs have a lot of puppies. She can't take care of all of them. They have to go to new homes."

"That's why we dopt Shorts."

"Yes, Jon, now Shorts has a home with you."

"Can he sleep with me?"

"We'll see."

## 5

The next three summers were immensely happy ones. Young Jon played at the art of growing flowers, in pots and from seeds. He was four when Emily painted a small tool bucket and watering can yellow with his name in large red letters. She placed a yellow sign with J O N in red letters, in a plot for him, extending beyond her's to the end of the garage. The bucket held a child's shovel, rake, trowel, and she taught him how to use each of them in putting plants and seeds into the ground. To a small boy playing in the dirt was the best fun, and Jon and Shorts did a lot of digging. A few flowers survived and a few were replaced with new plants. Jon took his dad outside one morning, telling him, "Look, flowers gone."

"Yes, I see Jon. Looks like the rabbits made a dinner of your flowers."

"Not nice to eat mine. My garden not pretty."

"True son, but outside belongs to all creatures. My grandma told me we all have to learn to live together. Maybe you and mommy can get some more plants today and PaPo can put some wire around them to keep the rabbits out."

"I want red and yellow flowers."

Jon took a liking to gardening, and after a couple of years of flowers, he became a summer buddy with PaPo to plant and tend a vegetable garden, which was much larger than his mother's flower beds. Grandpa Frank patiently answered the barrage of questions:

"Why do we put pieces of potatoes in the hole?" "How do carrots get long?" "Can't peas stand up?" "Do rabbits eat onions?" "How does this little seed make a radish? " "Can Shorts and I play in the water?"

Shorts was by his young master's side, day and night, except when Jon played in the tree. Grandpa Carl had made a wide-rung ladder for Jon to climb up into the branches of a small sturdy apple tree in the back yard. Emily was apprehensive.

"Dad, this is not a good idea. He'll fall, scrape himself . . . and . . ."

"So what, Emily. That's the norm for little boys, even little girls," he chided. "He'll break a bone, I bet is the next thing you are about to say. Emily, the branch is not that far from the ground . . . besides we can't coddle Jon away from doing what little boys love to do."

"Wow, it's rough keeping you three grown-up males in tow."

"It takes three of us to help you unleash Jon."

"Dad, that's not a kind thing to say. I have to watch over him . . . after all he is only four years old."

"And, five months," replied her father.

Emily put out the ladder only when Jon made a fuss. She'd try to dissuade him but gave in when she saw Jon tighten his lips and back away. Over time, she lengthened tree time from fifteen minutes to twenty minutes, but never more than thirty and all the time keeping watch from the kitchen window. Faithful Shorts watched from the bottom of the tree, joining in Jon's fun with an occasional bark. Emily noticed that Jon dutifully sat on the same branch (the only one she permitted) with his back against the tree trunk. He'd begin a pantomime -- moving his lips and hands, shaking his head up and down or back and forth. She didn't hear his words but heard his laugh rush out in a spurt of giggles. She thought he was carrying on with Shorts.

"Jon, what do you tell Shorts when you are in the tree?"

"Nothing"

"I see you talking . . . or are you singing?"

"Sometimes."

"You mean, sometimes both?" Jon nodded his head. "To the birds and squirrels?" Emily asked.

"No, to Mikey. He's my friend."

Her eyebrows squeezed together in a frown and with a question. "Your friend? I don't see another boy in the tree."

"No, Mommy, he comes to see me. Shorts likes him too. He doesn't bark when Mikey is in the tree."

"Honey, what does Mikey look like?"

"Like a boy. He tells me about animals. He likes bears the best. He says clouds look like animals. He showed me a duck."

"He sounds like a bright boy. What else does he tell you?"

"He lives in a tent and plants corn with his father. Just like me and PaPo."

"Are you sure you see this boy."

"Sometimes, just his voice. We play games, make funny sounds. He can hum now – just like us."

"Sweetheart, let's tell Daddy about your friend when he comes home."

"You won't make Mikey go away."

"Sweetheart, I don't think we can."

<hr/>

Three weeks later the ladder disappeared. Jon begged his Grandfather Carl to make another one.

"Emily, what happened to that ladder? What did you do with it?"

"Dad, why do you immediately blame me?"

"Come on, Em, no one else was as against Jon in the tree. Why have you made the boy so unhappy?"

"Oh, Dad, I wish you'd never made the ladder. I told you I was not for it but you insisted. I had no choice but to take the ladder away."

"Okay, why? Better be a good reason."

"You would have done the same thing. I told you about his

imaginary friend, Mikey. Well when Jon told me that he was going to fly like a hawk with Mikey, that was alarm enough for me. I tried to tell him that only birds can fly, but Jon kept insisting that Mikey would give him magic. He was quite excited.

"I stood under the tree the next time, but Jon cried saying Mikey wouldn't come if I was there. That night I told John to take the ladder away. Jon believes that some one stole it."

"Emily, for Christ's sake, loosen up. Can't you play along with a child's fantasy?"

"No, not when it's my child. Forget it Dad?"

## 6

1968 was a year of emotional headlines: Two assassinations -- Martin Luther King and Robert Kennedy; a monster crowd protested the Viet Nam war at the Chicago Democratic convention; Richard Nixon won the presidential election by 500,000 votes; seven Jesuit priests entered Maryland Selective Service records and burned hundreds of 1-A classifications; John Lennon and Yoko Ono appeared nude on the cover of a newly released album -- it was banned; and Johnny Cash sang his biggest hit, *Folsom Prison Blues.*

In Witherston, the Mayor and two city council members were accused of accepting kickbacks from contractors bidding on the new City Lake Park. John Strutter agreed to serve as interim Mayor until the investigation was complete and ready for legal action. Even though the citizens of Witherston implored him to be their permanent Mayor, he turned a deaf ear and did not enter the mayoral race.

It was an eventful year in the Strutter household, Jon celebrated his sixth birthday April first and would start first grade in September. That summer John told Emily that no matter how reluctant she was it was time to tell their son he was adopted. They were enjoying a late summer evening on the back porch; the afternoon rains had made the air cool and the sky clear for the stars and a quarter moon. Jon and Shorts had gone up to bed early – they'd spent a lot of energy playing in the rain, and Emily reported they were 'dead to the world' as she folded her legs beneath her on the cushioned chair.

"Seems a shame to have to burst the bubble. Think of all the questions that will need answers. He'll feel different . . . I won't be his mother any longer," Emily said with sadness. "Wish we could avoid this . . . seems tragic to upset his life."

"Em, I wish you could take a more positive perspective," John said firmly. "Tragedy doesn't seem to linger in our family . . . Jon is a happy, well-adjusted, confident young boy. What other mother's love has he known? You can't really believe he won't want more of the same, do you? That he'll turn away from you? Hardly. Em it's the HOW . . . how we tell him . . . how we assure him . . . how we make it natural rather then an oddity, an affliction, or a crushing tale."

"How, how, how," Emily retorted sharply. "It isn't going to take away that he has another mother. Oh, I'm sorry John, and another father."

"Em, come on, let's get real. We've been fortunate that no hint of this has come to Jon before now. Either our friends or members of the church have been overly cautious, or purposely closed-mouthed, for none of his young friends have mentioned the word adoption. But, with him starting school, that's asking for a miracle." John peered over the rim of his glasses, even though Emily would not notice in the darkness. "Remember Emily, Dr. Green told us to talk about adoption around his fifth birthday. Maybe we ought to seek help from him, if he still has an office with Catholic Services."

"Well, John, maybe you'll give me points for having made some preparation. I've been in the adoption section at the library several times to look for some *how's* that you spoke of. And, Claire and I have shared some thoughts about *how* to do it."

"Good for you, Em, and what ideas do you have?" John asked, ignoring the hint of sarcasm in his wife's words.

Emily left the lounge to walk the porch. "Well, there is a children's book that tells a story of a pair of Canada geese that wanted a gosling to hatch from their eggs. It never happens and each year they become sadder and sadder because they have no family. They fly to a different lake one day and find another pair of geese with too many goslings to care for. The story goes on with how the parents can't tend to all their children and ask other pairs of geese on the lake if they would want to take a gosling. Of course, the childless say 'yes' and promise to love it as mothers and fathers should. They take two to their nest and help them grow to adult geese."

Emily leaned on the railing across from John. "I thought we could use it as an analogy of how we waited for God to send us a baby and how lonely it is living without children. Then we too found a baby who needed a home and a mommy and daddy. And, we chose to bring him home . . . to be our little boy, Jon . . . something like that. We'd have to help him understand the word adoption or adopted, as that's what he's likely to hear, if he hears at all." Emily paused, then said, "Well, how many points do I get?"

"Enough. Using a story probably makes the message clearer. He might remember that he adopted Shorts, and how he chose him from all the dogs who needed a home and a boy to love him."

"Yes, Claire thought of that also. She also thought we ought to talk to Father Wentz – he might have connections for us. Remember the Wagner's – they've moved to another parish – but they had adopted children."

"Yes, and it's possible, he might know of an adult who was adopted. Hearing their story of how they were told might have insights for us. Let's ask him out for dinner this Saturday. Isn't this the weekend your father comes?"

"I'll give them both a call tomorrow," Emily promised.

7

Instead of advice over dinner, Father Wentz recommended a psychologist, Dr. Catherine Hawley who had offices in the medical clinic building. John had heard about her from a couple of the store customers, nothing out of the ordinary, just that she was new in town. They made an appointment for Thursday morning and dropped young Jon off at Claire's house. She had butter cookies on her kitchen counter for Jon to frost, and then they were going to draw flowers with colored pencils.

Dr. Hawley was standing in front of her desk when they entered her office. She extended her hand to John. "Welcome. I'm so glad to meet you. Father Wentz spoke highly of you and of the esteem the town people hold for the Strutter family. The drugstore has been family-owned for a long time, I understand."

"Yes, two generations. It began with my great grandmother . . . she started helping sick people with natural remedies. Guess she was quite well known in the county." John was surprised that Dr. Hawley was young; he guessed maybe not much older than he and Emily. Her auburn hair was ear length and held back on both sides with clips, and her grey eyes looked directly at him assuring him she was an intent listener. Not often, he noted, had he seen so many freckles dotting across a person's nose; her make-up could not disguise them. "I'm surprised we haven't met before. How long have you been here?" John asked.

"Almost sixteen months. After the university in Minneapolis, I did all my graduate work and thesis at the University of Indiana. I returned to Minneapolis for private work until this offer from the Clinic. I've been pleased, as it provides me more of a lead role on the staff and in the community. In fact that's how I met Father Wentz. We are members of an advisory board for mental health."

Dr. Hawley directed her attractive grey eyes to Emily. "And, Mrs. Strutter, Father tells me you are quite involved with many of the church programs. I am of another faith, but have admired the beautiful structure of St. Anne's." She motioned to a sitting area, "Please have a seat."

John and Emily sat on a small divan and Dr. Hawley seated herself in a chair opposite them. Emily felt a bit distracted by Dr. Hawley's good looks and her youth.

"Please call us John and Emily, Dr. Hawley. I'd be more comfortable." Emily leaned forward, "As I explained on the telephone, we have an adopted son, Jon, who is six years old and is about to start school. We were told when we adopted him that three or four years old is not too young to talk about adoption with him. We've not formally done so yet, and my husband feels we should not wait much longer. I want to do it right, and we are looking for professional advice."

"Well, like most things, there are different points of view on this matter. I am in the group that subscribes to beginning at a young age but in a less direct manner."

"What does less direct mean, Dr. Hawley?" John questioned.

"I like to think of telling the adoption story in a building block fashion, little by little. It's a complex concept and the child won't grasp it all at once. Make it an on-going topic rather than a one-time, full detailed story . . . tell the child what he is ready for and answer the questions he might have. Starting in this way avoids the traumatic aspects and gives the child assurance that he can talk about adoption when he has a need to know. Questions come from unexpected sources and pop into children's heads at the oddest times."

"The only time we've used the word, adoption, was when Jon," Emily pointed at her husband, "not this John, our son, Jon. I know it's confusing. Anyway, we likened his picking out a dog at the kennels to adopting – that is, making a home for some one who didn't have a home. Nothing really has come up since then."

John picked up the rest of the story. "Emily is worried about saying the wrong thing or not having a right answer for his questions. So we've not brought the subject up ourselves and surmise there has been no cause for him to do so either. But, I'm not comfortable waiting any longer."

Dr. Hawley mused for a moment and turned her gaze to Emily. "You have apprehensions?" She paused before asking, "What troubles you about telling your son?"

Silence filled the room. John kept his gaze down, focusing on his hands. Emily looked to the right, away from John and Dr. Hawley and then hesitantly began, "I want to be the mother, the only mother. Having to speak of another mother will pull him away to think of another mother. His questions . . . how will he understand a mother who didn't keep him? I don't want to tell him. The idea of two mothers is threatening, I guess."

"Why?" asked Dr. Hawley.

Emily replied quickly with, "I want his life perfect. I want it to be just us."

Dr. Hawley caught John's eyes with a quizzical glance. John lifted his eyebrows as if to answer, 'so you see how it is'. He reached out to Emily, but she moved her hand away. "Emily, we'd be living a lie if we keep adoption a secret from him. Think of how imperfect it will be if Jon finds out when he is older. He could be upset, disappointed in us, not understand, and question why we kept this from him. And, his never finding out is an unrealistic expectation. Too many people know he is adopted."

Silence filled the room again. Dr. Hawley broke it by describing a possible scenario. "We, by 'we' I mean our profession, have seen more question and wonderment and anger from adopted children who didn't know before their teen years. If this is when the news reaches them, they get the concept, but also will have more issues with their identity."

"Like what?" asked Emily.

"A lot more questions at a time when their own sexuality . . . their identity is appearing. Who am I? Where do I belong? Why did she give me up? What was wrong with me? Why didn't she want me? It comes as too big of a surprise – like an intrusion from the adult world a teenager does not want."

"Ugly!" Emily shot out.

Dr. Hawley took note of how John jerked his head as he lowered his eyes. *A patient man waiting for his wife's acceptance.* She kept a tender and compassionate voice as she continued, "That's why I prescribe to the building-block method. It keeps adoption natural, an on-going topic, not a big issue, words heard in a warm environment of love, a sharing in a positive, caring manner. Most important is the natural aspect – it does not make it into a 'big deal' as teenagers would say. The key is to make it comfortable, an environment you and your husband have already built. Pre-schoolers tend to think in simple terms, tend to trust you and take you words literally. That emotional level of trust is key. Can you see this, Emily?"

"Yes, up here," she pointed to her head. "Down here it's harder." She pointed to her heart. "But deep down, I know we have to tell him."

"Emily, tell Dr. Hawley about the Canada geese story. That could be our beginning." Emily related the essence of the story.

Dr. Hawley's kind smile was meant to denote praise. "Now, that's a building block. With a picture book in front of you, it helps to diffuse the emotions you might be feeling. Young children interact through emotions and will pick up on yours – positive or negative. So a picture story is good to use. I know of several other good books, that way you'd be building the concept."

"How do you tell him that he is adopted? That's the hard part for me. It's one thing to speak of the concept, another to tell the real fact."

"I suggest that you do this together and maybe your husband could begin the story, about the hospital, seeing him as a baby. Emily I can imagine that you would sound joyful in describing how beautiful he was, the excitement of bringing him home. Tell him. Liken it to his bringing his dog home – Shorts, was it? Help him remember how happy he was. He'll get caught up in those emotions. And don't be afraid of telling him that you did not carry him in your tummy. Has he ever seen a pregnant woman?"

"Not that he's noticed. But Nanci who works with me in the church nursery is just in her fourth month."

"Here's where you might use the coming of her baby to explain that all children are born of a woman who is the birthparent. One of the books I suggest for you is about a couple that adopt a baby. It's written in a very simple and straightforward manner. What's helpful is that the book is there for your son to pick up and look at. His questions can lead you into further explanations."

"I like the idea," said John. " It keeps the discussion low-key and the trauma out of it. And if we stay aware, we will probably pick up on other ways to mention adoption."

"Yes, that's true. The most important thing is that your child feels comfortable talking with either of you about adoption and birthparents. When he gets to be older, he will probably have more questions. Often they want to know how the adoption was arranged and if you saw his birth mother. Show him his birth certificate – that's assurance he belongs to your family. And, at some point, the child typically wants to know why."

"I've gone to the library," said Emily, "and have some answers one might make to that question, and think I'd opt for saying that we don't know what problems his mother faced. We do know she was fifteen and maybe she was not able to handle being a parent so young."

"Certainly, a teenager or older child can empathize with that." Dr. Hawley affirmed. "I think Father Wentz could be of help in some of the issues you might have and seek out a professional when needed. I sense that both of you have provided a loving, safe environment for your son. That alone has the biggest impact. Have trust in your love."

"Our aim is to raise a well-adjusted adult; we are both very committed to that," said John. "I believe I understood your advice is to aim for a happy medium – many babies are born and many are adopted. I understand the importance of Jon hearing about adoption in positive ways – the books will do well in that aspect – and to keep any sad regrets out of our talks. Answer questions

when Jon has them and make no judgments on the birthparents."
His re-cap was more for Emily's ears, to dampen her reluctance.

"That's the essence. Never skimp on telling him how happy
you were when you received word about the adoption. It was a
time of celebration for you and it's okay for your son to know that."
Dr. Hawley looked into Emily's eyes. "Are you more comfortable
now?"

"Yes, our discussion has helped." Emily turned to John and
took his hand. "It's really what you have been trying to tell me.
I'm going to help to do this as perfectly as we can, and forego
being perfect myself."

"I believe you can, Em," John said softly with a smile. And,
then to Dr. Hawley, "Father was right, you've given us the help we
needed. Now, if you'd write down the names of the two books,
we'll go plan our next steps."

"Mrs. Strutter . . . Emily, perfection is not the winning prize
of life. Perfection tends to shut out other experiences, other ways
of learning and growing. Trying for perfection, for itself, is very
limiting. Your true story is that you have each other."

⟩━┥◆⟩━O━⟨◆┝━⟨

"Did you see a lot of babies, like with the dogs when I picked
Shorts?"

"No, Jon, we waited for you in the hospital where babies are
born."

"Did that other lady like me?"

"Of course, Jon, but she was too young to provide a home
for you."

"Why did she have me?"

"Best we can know, Jon, is that she and the young boy did not
intend to start a family at fifteen. Can you imagine your cousin,
Laura being a mother?"

"No, because she still likes to play with us." He picked up one
of the books, "Will you read this story again? I want to tell PaPo
about the geese and their babies."

"Yes, we will read it as many times as you want."

As Jon snuggled between his parents, he said, "I'm happy you took me home. I love you."

With tears in her eyes, Emily hugged her precious boy. As John savored the scene he thought, *too bad we didn't bring twins home.*

Emily's earlier fears proved ungrounded. The adoption subject did not upset the family emotions and relationships. John and Emily never embellished a birth mother story; thereby, not seeding any fantasies to be born. They extended Jon's blanket of security by sharing with his grandfathers how they were going to talk about adoption and insisted they also read the books. Jon's serious questions about his birthparents were asked later when he was a teenager.

## 8

"John, you had a call from Minneapolis this morning." Frank informed his son. "Said his name was Sam. Do you know him? I asked if he wanted your home number, but he said no, it wasn't that urgent. Said something about a meeting in Minneapolis. Is this about the next state meeting?"

"It might be dad. You know I like to keep us in the loop. I'll follow up with Sam and see what's on the agenda."

And, he thought of the secret he was keeping from Emily and how uncharacteristic it was of him. Was it only his curiosity? Was it because he didn't like voids? He had no inkling of how the information would be needed or used, and he knew it had to be tucked away in the safest of places.

Sam's report: Female still attending University of Colorado and rooming with another female. Same address. Male is construction worker in southern California. His family now permanent residents there. Report filed. $450 due.

# CHAPTER TWO

## *The Young Boy*

### 1

AN OUTSIDER LOOKING in on the Strutter family would have exclaimed, "Perfect." A few might conclude that the young boy of the household was overly cared for, particularly by his mother; others might extol the opposite – saying the intricacies of his mental and emotional tapestry were being woven with extreme care.

Emily's number one watchword was *be happy* and she guarded against the household being shadowed with low spirits. Jon heard her promptings when a conflicting opinion loomed or he was bent on having his way. She'd say, "Make it a happy day." "Let's be cheerful." "Happy is better." "Show me a happy smile." Jon, always sensitive to what he thought was criticism, would retreat within and give a smile.

"Now isn't that better?" His mother would say, and she would tousle his hair or tweak his nose. And, she never failed to say, "I'm so proud of you, Jon-son." And, he bent to the strong influence of praise and his aim to please his mother grew. Her affection for him was happiness itself.

Emily lived her watchword, making chores and duties seem light-hearted and easy. She guided her boy, in cheerful and firm ways, in mastering his tasks: keeping toys organized, planting flowerbeds, grooming Shorts, sweeping the porch and sidewalks, mailing notes to Grandpa Carl.

Now and then Jon would ask, "Would my other mother be proud of me?"

"Yes Jon, I believe she would like that you are a happy boy and can do so many things so well. I bet she'd be proud of your flower garden."

## 2

"Daddy, why do we call this your office?" Jon walked into the room where his father sat at an odd-looking desk. When closed it was in a curved shape and when opened Jon saw many slots and drawers. Much different from the flattop desks his teachers had.

"Well, son, I need a quiet spot to do paperwork for the store and work for the City Council. Not things a young boy would understand . . . some day maybe you will be sitting here doing the same."

"Can't I work in here with you now?"

"What would you work on, Jon?"

"Draw pictures of my flower garden. Look at my books. Build a house with blocks."

"Jon, when I am in my office it must be quiet . . . I have work to get done."

"I'll be quiet Dad."

"And Shorts?" Young Jon shrugged his shoulders.

"Let me think about that, son. Maybe you and Grandpa Carl could make a small desk. We could put it by the window."

"Okay."

Jon's early experiences with his father assured him he had a steady pillar of support. When adult, he fully realized why his father was treated with unshakeable respect in Witherston. Jon came to accept that his father was unruffled by events; neither excitement nor agitation drew him away from a calm manner. His father had a patient, listening ear and an ability to ask the right questions to draw out the right things to be considered. A discussion with him always seemed, more often than not, to end in right decisions. The son also learned that his father rarely changed his mind after a decision was made. Not that it was rigidity, more that it was his nature to be loyal – to ideas, responsibility, people.

One-on-one talking time for father and son mostly happened when they walked to Reed Pond, just five blocks from the house. They'd rest on a bench, watching the birds; other times Jon brought his fishing pole and they'd sit on the pier. This is where his father encouraged patience as Jon trained Shorts to stay, sit, roll over, and fetch. Jon would remember these times as the closest hours with his father, and whenever he needed advice or to talk out a difficult situation, he asked: "Got time for a walk to the pond, Dad?" The answer was always "Yes."

It was late September and Jon had started third grade instructed by Sister Mary Rose. He and his dad were walking around the pond, picking up the first colored fall leaves.

"Dad, we have a new girl at school. She's telling us she has two mothers."

"Hum. What did she tell you about her two mothers?"

"One lives in another city and one lives here with her father. I asked her if she was adopted and she said no."

"Jon, that's not really polite to ask right away if she is adopted. You should wait for her to tell you. Did she understand your question?"

"She isn't adopted, but has two mothers. I have two mothers and adopted. But I only see one mother, she sees two."

"What's her name, Jon?"

"Ellen. She just moved here to live with her dad."

"Well, maybe this is how it is for Ellen. Her mother who lives in the other city and her dad who lives here are birth parents, but her dad has remarried and Ellen maybe thinks of her father's wife as a mom also."

"Will the wife adopt Ellen?"

"No, only if the birth mother gives her legal right to do so. Remember the birth certificate you have? It tells whom you legally belong to. In the case of a divorce, which seems the case for Ellen's father and mother, legal rights stay with the birth parents."

"Will I ever see my birth mother or father?"

"Not too likely, son. They were very young and have gone on with life, where we don't know. Guess you'll have to be satisfied with Mom and me. We're glad you are our son." He put his arm around his son's shoulders and gave him a squeeze.

During dinner, Jon had more questions about adoption. "I was born in Minneapolis, wasn't I? Is that where they lived?"

"You mean your birth parents, Jon? We don't know. As I said this afternoon, they were young and we don't know where they live."

"You two were talking about what this afternoon?" asked Emily.

"Well, Jon was asking about a new class mate that has two mothers, and he was wondering why she knows them both. I assume that it is a divorce with a re-marriage for the father," replied John.

"Did you see my mother and father?" Jon looked to his mother. "Didn't they get to see who was taking their baby? Why didn't you talk to each other?"

"No, Jon that was not allowed."

"Why not? What did you have to do to take me home? Why couldn't they see me again?" His father looked to Emily and waited for her to answer.

"John-son, adoptions make a clean break with birth parents and information is kept very private. That is the law. It's for the best, less confusing for the child. It gives the little boy or girl one home, one mom and dad, as a normal life should be."

"Can they find me? Can we look for them? Maybe, we'd be friends."

"Son, those are good questions but not too probable to be answered with a yes. As your mother said, laws have been set for adoptions. And, by law the adoption files, records, are closed."

"Maybe, some day those laws will change," Jon snapped. "We don't know what they look like."

"No, son, we don't. But, we know who we look like, and I'd say we're a pretty good-looking family."

"And happy," added Emily. "Hey, I've got your favorite chocolate cake for desert. How about with vanilla ice cream? A sweet dish for my sweet boy."

"Ah, Mom, you've got to stop calling me sweetie – I'm ten years old. You make me sound like a little kid."

"Well, you'll always be my precious, my sweetie, the best boy in Witherston."

# 3

Grandpa Frank, who was PaPo until Jon was nine, transferred his love of soil and animals to his grandson. Frank introduced Jon to the two Strutter's stores and, task-by-task, Jon learned how to clerk in either one by the time he was sixteen. Grandpa Carl instilled in Jon a love of nature and camping. They read from guidebooks about trees and birds when they hiked in the woods. Jon also learned to work with wood in Carl's workshop; sanding, oiling, staining as Grandpa refurnished old pieces of furniture. Jon's bedroom boasted the pieces he'd worked on, and Shorts had a doghouse built by the two of them.

Jon asked of each grandfather, "What was Grandma like?"

Grandpa Frank told him, "Grandma Helen was a beautiful girl, a lot like your mother. She loved flowers also and made cookies every week . . . the best I ever ate. Here's a picture of her. She was very young when she died; your father was only five years old . . . he knew her for only a little while. It was hard for a little boy to lose his mother, but he was with his Grandma Frances who gave him a lot of attention. Grandmas are special, and I wish she was with us. I still miss her, Bud."

"Me too, Grandpa."

Grandpa Carl told him, "Your Grandma Ethel was a hard-working woman. She grew up on a farm in a large family and had a lot of chores to do. Milked cows, cleaned barns, weeded gardens, and learned to bake bread when she was fifteen. But, she loved to dance, Jon. That's how I met her, and we danced every Saturday night when a band was in town – if not, she'd want to dance at home. One Christmas, our family gift was a phonograph and records. When the boys came and later your mother, we all danced. Ethel always thought that all that music started Emily's humming."

"Mom has a picture of Grandma on her dresser. She remembers a lot of things."

"When Grandma died, your mother was in high-school. Her brothers were older and out of the house, so Emily and I went it alone. Grandma Ethel was a good woman, and so is your mom."

"That's what she says too."

The family noted that Jon used his left-hand for eating, playing, fishing, woodworking, planting, drawing and writing. They mentioned only once, "Jon is the first left-handed person on either side." Privately they knew it had to be a genetic trait from the birth parents.

# 4

"Yes, it is. Yes. What do you have?"

"She's still in Denver and at the same job. She has moved to new address, a larger apartment, and a male now lives with her. Both names are on the mailbox. His name is Ben Allen."

"She'd be in her late twenties by now. Keep a close check, they may get married."

"Yes, we'll know if there's a change of name or address. Follow-up on the birth father indicates he was killed in action in Vietnam."

"So, we are down to one. I wish I'd known more about the

young man. You'll deposit the report then, and what's my bill up to now?"

"It took a bit more this time, I'll need $650. I'll let you know when the situation changes."

"Yes, do that. Thanks for your report."

# 5

As was their Sunday custom, the Strutter's attended nine-thirty mass at St. Anne's. This Sunday, all the Strutters – uncles, aunts, cousins, and grandfathers – would be sitting in the up-front rows to the left side of the main altar. Today was Jon's entrance as altar boy.

"Remember, Jon-son, to lift your cassock before stepping up to the altar."

"I know, Mom."

"And keep your eyes on Father." Emily fussed. "You don't want to miss his cues."

"Mom, we practiced all week. I know what to do."

"Well, it's your first Sunday," Emily patted his hair in place. "I know you don't want to make a mistake."

"Mom, you don't want me to make a mistake. Father Stern says it'll be just fine. I just have to follow Max, he's been an altar boy for two years."

"I know, I know. This is an exciting day for all of us. We're all so proud."

"Emily," John walked into the kitchen, "let's be on our way. Carl, are you ready?"

"I've been ready for thirty minutes. I think we ought not to sit up close to the altar, Emily. It'll make Jon more conscious of you and your fussing." Carl showed his concern for the effect of Emily's over-protective behavior on his ten-year old grandson. What he saw once appropriate for the little child looked limiting for the young boy.

"Now, Dad, Jon will be okay. This is our red-letter day. Right?"

She asked with a smile at her son.

As they went across the lawn to the car, Jon kept close to his father's side. "Dad, can I sit up front with you?"

## 6

"Dad," Jon said with an up-tick, as if a question.

His father looked up from the papers spread out on his desk, where he'd been engrossed for the last part of the afternoon. "Yes, son." He spread his hands over the papers he'd been intently working on.

"Dad, I need to talk."

"Okay, right now or later? How urgent?"

"Do you have time to go down to the pond?"

"Son, I always have time . . . what's up?"

"Well, can't say here. It's, it's sort of private."

"You mean your mother shouldn't hear?"

"Sort of Dad . . . I just want to talk with you."

"Sounds serious. Is it?"

"Yeah, sort of."

"Sort of sounds like you are sort of serious and sort of need time soon." John attempted to lighten his son's somber look. "Are you sort of in trouble, son?"

"No, Dad. I just need to talk about something."

"Well, how about you give me another thirty minutes here and then we'll walk down to our spot by the water."

"That'd be fine, Dad. I'll be out back with Shorts. Trying to teach him to stay when I throw the yellow ball."

"How's he doing with that trick?"

"Doing better. He's getting the difference between the two colors. See you in a bit."

"You bet." John watched his son turn away and wondered if Jon was going to bring up that topic which they had touched on briefly a month ago. Ten year-old boys seem privy to new information about girls and start to talk about their body parts and the sex stuff. He laughed out loud when he thought of how he had asked his father, "What is my penis suppose to do with a girl?"

Thirty minutes, on the nose, John came through the kitchen. "Em, Jon and I are walking down to the pond. We'll take Shorts and the training balls."

"That's nice. Watch how he's made progress with Shorts. Cute trick – stay on the yellow, fetch on the orange."

"Supper as usual? At six?"

"Yes, that gives you two a good hour. Just a casserole dish, it can wait if need be."

Emily felt supremely pleased as she watched her husband and son turn the corner of the driveway. The trust between father and son was seen as a blessing and gave her a sense of pride. John should have had more children. His even temperament, his patience, his silent watchfulness, and his rock-solid presence were traits a child could admire in a father. They'd applied for a second adoption, but with fifteen to twenty couples waiting for every newborn, their chances had been slim. Mrs. Mason had encouraged adoption of an older child but Emily always held out for a baby. Five years ago, they were third on a waiting list, but the mother changed her mind after she held the baby. Emily saw the absence of a large family as a punishment, and unbeknown to others, it tested her faith.

"Your mother says Shorts is doing good with your new trick."

"He's funny, pop. I hold the orange, he barks, ready to run. I hold up the yellow, he bends his head and sits down, with a sad look."

"When are you going to show him off?"

"At our summer picnic."

They were nearing the lake property, the south half recently bought by the city (as a council member, John had been instrumental in heading the drive to purchase the land). Now the city owned all the ground around the pond and plans were laid out to enlarge it into a lake and make an official park for picnics, lawn games, fishing, and paths for walking and cross-country skiing. It was the end of April and the winter snows had melted and moisturized the large plot of ground. There'd be green grass, beds of flowers, and a sidewalk soon. They headed across the short end of the plot towards a bench by the water – Shorts running out in front, looking back at Jon quickly, just like best pals would do.

"Tell me, Jon, what sort of problem do we have today?"

"Dad, this is serious."

"Yes, I sense that. Is it school? A friend? Have you done something wrong?"

"It's a friend. He's telling me a strange story."

John's inner flag went up. "Stories about who . . . what?"

Silence, except for Shorts who was barking to get Jon's attention. "Shorts, sit!"

"I'm waiting Jon. What's the story?" John paused. "Which friend, son? I guess it might be Jeff." No acknowledgment. "Steve?" No response. "Alex . . . Matt?"

Jon looked up at his father, blinked his eyes twice to hold back the tears. "It's Matt. He's going to stop being an altar boy. His father is really angry. But Matt says no, he won't do it."

"Hum, that's strange. Is it the Latin responses? You said some of the boys were having a hard time learning them." John waited for an answer but only got a slight head nod. "Son, is there more to this story? Do you know why Matt doesn't want to serve at mass?"

"It's sort of like things you talked with me about. Things that are about . . . you know what."

"You mean about boys and girls, Jon?"

"Yeah, sort of."

"Which is it? . . . Girls? . . . Boys?"

"A man, Dad." John watched his son keep his head down, avoiding a direct look. His second alert flag went up.

"Son, are you trying to tell me a man is doing something

that's not normal with Matt . . . something you've not heard of before?"

Jon looked up, a wetness to his eyes. "Yeah, he's sort of scared . . . doesn't know what to do."

John was now in full alert. *The rest of the story is going to connect with being altar boy somehow.* "Are you the only one who knows?"

"I think so, Dad."

"And, you want to help him?"

"Yes, he's my friend, my buddy."

John put his arm around his son's shoulders and tightened his fingers. "Tell me what's happened, son. What has the man done to Matt?"

"He kissed him on the mouth, Dad."

"Once?"

"He tried to do it a lot."

"At one time?"

"No, all year. He doesn't like it."

"What else has the man done?"

"Took him into a room and took off his pants."

"Matt's pants?"

"No, his. He said he wanted to show Matt it was okay to see each other."

"Then what did Matt tell you?"

"He wanted him to touch him." Jon whispered, "Matt wouldn't take off his pants." His emotions were in his voice, in his throat; he was shaking his head. "Isn't that wrong, Dad?"

"Yes, son, it is. How did Matt get away from the man?"

"When he grabbed him and tried to make him sit on his lap. Matt yelled, 'No, leave me alone,' and ran away."

John was puzzled, overwhelmed and shocked. *I'd not expected something this serious. Go slow. There is more yet to hear.*

"When did this happen to Matt?"

"I don't remember. The man wants to talk with him again in the back room."

"Back room of where, Jon?"

"At church. It's bad isn't it, Dad?"

"Jon, tell me who this man is."

"Dad, it's the priest." He dropped his head back on the top of the bench. "I feel sorry for Matt. I'm scared too."

"I can see why." John said, struggling with his own emotions. He was nauseated, a heavy queasy glob anchored in the pit of his stomach, anger was enveloping his being. A sickness arose, from his remembering the whispers he heard one year when he was an altar boy. Fear kept him from asking the older boys why they played 'hide and seek' with their parish priest. He'd overheard their words, such as, "I'm not going." "My father wouldn't believe me." "Let's stick together." "What'd he say to you?" The commotion ended when the priest left the parish, re-assigned to a new parish; he'd left without a farewell party. John was only twelve at the time but had honed in on a secret known by the boys four to five years older than he.

"Son, do you think Matt has told his father?"

"He's afraid. He said his father won't believe him. He'll be punished for lying. But he's afraid of Father Stern too." Jon waited and then added, "Matt didn't want me to tell anybody. He might be mad because I told you."

"Son, you've done the right thing to tell me – we have no secrets – that's how we learn to trust others. For now, maybe we keep this to ourselves until I can think of how best to handle this and help Matt. I'll have to tell mother."

"Don't get Matt into any more trouble. His father is already mad at him."

"No, Jon, I especially won't do that. I want to help Matt, just like you do. But, I think you ought to let Matt know that you told me. That mustn't be a secret."

"I already told him."

"Jon, I'm sorry this has happened to your friend. It is not right for a priest to do such things, and I can't give you any reason now why he did. What's important is that he doesn't do it again. That's what I must work on. For now, tell Matt not to go with Father alone and neither must you. I wish we could talk with Matt's father."

John could understand why Matt might be afraid of telling his father. He'd been witness to Steve Sledgling's hot temper and ugly language. Mr. Sledgling had made nasty scenes in the chambers when he'd brought his views to the City Council. Once was over a re-zoning of corner property on his street ("We don't need any damn business and more fucking traffic in our neighborhood.") The next one about leash laws not being enforced ("I'll kill those dogs who leave shit in my yard.") The last was really nasty. He'd received a fine for keeping three inoperable junk cars by the back alleyway. ("A lot of guts fining a property owner." He held up the paper, "I'm going to make it disappear," and put his lighter to it, dropping the flaming sheet to the floor.). *Thank God, he's not been a member of the parish groups. He's hard to deal with. Poor Matt, scared of the priest and scared of his dad.*

"Thanks, son, for bringing this to me. We'll talk again about it, later. Now, why don't you show me how Shorts does the ball trick? He's been a good dog, lying quietly."

# 7

Father Patrick Stern had been at St. Anne's for barely two years. He'd replaced Father Thomas Wentz who'd been the parish priest for eleven years and before Father Tom was Father Michael Swanson who'd served at St. Anne's for seventeen years. John had grown up from age twelve to twenty-nine with Father Mike. Parishioners had written the Bishop both times about Father Swanson and Father Wentz, asking that they remain at St. Anne's. The Bishop denied the request, responding at the time that Father Swanson was needed in the diocesan office (he became Chancellor of Education – all schools were under his guidance), and later the Bishop replied that an older church within the diocese needed the leadership of Father Wentz.

The parishioners understood why Father Wentz was sought out, for they knew his gifts: developing work teams for parish projects, expanding the parish youth program to include summer missionary work, beautifying the grounds (Emily had chaired the committee and Jon had been a junior landscaper). Father Tom had turned a strong, viable parish over to Father Stern. The church members watched closely to see if Father Pat would disrupt or change the successful aspects built by his two predecessors. Much to everyone's liking Father Pat kept an on-going schedule of personal visits to parishioners, particularly those families experiencing hard times, in the throes of serious illness, or infrequent attendance at church. He was a hands-on supervisor of the youth programs, enhancing the Bible classes and recreation events. *My God, how convenient that was!*

John and Frank Strutter, through the Knights of Columbus, knew many male parishioners from other Minnesota parishes who typically shared information, but since Father Patrick Stern came to St. Anne's from a small, rural parish in Ohio, he was unknown except for the background announcement prepared by the bishop's office. *I think I know why we got a priest from another state.* John mused. *It's not a common practice. We got a pedophile. He probably was moved from parishes more than once. How can I find out?*

John recalled a story told by an attendee at a Catholic male retreat several years ago. It was about an older priest serving at St. Boniface in Whitney . . . transferred to new parishes every three to four years . . . finally given permanent duties at the seminary. Rumors hinted at sexual misconduct but lacked details. The suspected target was teenage boys . . . lot of youth trips to bigger cities, weekends at cabins, fishing, golf outings. *God, we have Father Sterns supervising the youth programs. What an opportune set-up.*

John wondered what would have been the reaction of his father, if he had brought this tale to him. *Dad's not an assertive person and shies from confrontation, more a supporter than leader.*

*The loss of Mom so early in life must have made the difference.* John was certain his grandfather would have taken direct action. He'd push people to be responsible for their mistakes and decisions. Grandpa John would have sat face-to-face with the wrongdoer; attempt to get the sinner to admit to his deed; and argue good reasons why corrections must be made. That might involve an apology, a return of stolen goods, or retraction of a slanderous rumor. Grandpa had been the stalwart, the principal, and the consciousness of the community. His deeds and examples set the standards and few citizens grumbled.

John knew his grandfather would've been direct. He would have gone to the priest, uncovered the story, pressed for correction, and kept on point until the situation was resolved. John would speak to Father Stern this week, and then to Emily.

# 8

Every other month, members of the Stewardship Council met on the third Thursday; eight people who raised, recorded, and tracked incoming dollars for the church building budget. The meeting started at five thirty with opening reports followed by a catered dinner and then a formal agenda. The members hung around afterwards for informal discussions and were typically on the way home by eight thirty. John lagged behind as the rest of the men left, helping Father Pat clean up the meeting room. As the chores neared completion, John asked, "Father, could I have more of your time tonight?"

"Sure. You want to sit here at the table?"

"I'd rather it be your office."

As they locked the meeting room and headed for the rectory, Father Pat inquired, "What's our topic tonight?"

"A serious one," replied John, "an issue that needs immediate resolution."

They were at the steps of the rectory, "Why not sit on the porch, it's a cool evening. Have a seat."

"No, not tonight. I'd prefer the privacy of your office."

Father opened the door to his office, lit by a Tiffany lamp on the large mahogany desk across from the door. Father motioned left to one of two high back chairs that faced each other. "Let's sit here John. Would you like a scotch?"

"No thanks, not tonight."

"Now what's so serious? Trouble at home? . . . Though that seems unimaginable. On the Council? I thought the discussion for capital spending went well tonight."

"No, it's closer to you than the Council, Father." John had decided to come right to the point. "I've been made aware of your actions with one of our young boys."

"In what manner are you suggesting?"

"The kissing. The touching. The displaying of yourself." John kept his eyes on the priest, his tone of voice subdued and even.

"Those are very serious accusations, John."

"I'm very aware of that Father."

"Boys tell stories . . . often hard to decipher why . . . one needs to . . ."

"I don't take these as idle tall tales," John interrupted. "I believe them to be true."

"Are you making charges? If so, are you sure you can substantiate them?"

"Not yet. Though I am asking for a cease and desist."

"Your words sound like a threat. What are you intending to do?"

"No more threatening than your behavior on the soul and character of young boys."

"John, this is a senseless conversation . . . one I'm willing to forget."

"I'm not willing to," John quickly interjected.

"What is your intent then?" Father raised a clenched fist to rub across the bottom of his chin.

"To safeguard our young sons. You either stop these pedophilic advances, or I shall bring in outside . . ."

Father retorted sharply, "John, your accusee is admitting no wrong. I'm afraid you've been listening to wild tales."

"Father Stern, maybe you don't know me well enough . . . I would not be here unless I believed I had true and real facts."

Silence filled the room and the two men stared at each other. John saw hardness in Father's eyes; hardness from fear more than anger, and a tightness constricting the lower portion of his face. John felt a similar tightness in his face. In a deliberate voice, John continued, "Father, I assure you that any further misconduct will not be secret. Correct your behavior . . . seek help through the bishop, and . . ."

"John, I think you've said enough."

"No, let me finish, one more thing. The outing you and your priest friend planned for a small group of boys must be cancelled. Two days at a cabin by Lake Ustice, with no other parent or chaperone is out of the question."

"You are making accusations against Father Pratt also . . . someone you don't even know."

"No I don't know him, but I do know of your behavior and a private weekend with young boys in a secluded area does not sound wise. Cancel it!"

"And if I don't? This is part of the Youth Program, a lot of planning has gone on, parents have made arrangements."

"Cancel it or I will!"

"John, you surprise me . . . that you would ruin a celebration for eight boys."

"You surprise me, Father. How in good conscious could I condone this, knowing what might happen to those eight boys."

"John, you have put a lot of work into this parish, don't mar it by acting precipitously."

"Father, I am asking you not to mar our parish by continuing behavior unfitting to the faith or the robe of a priest."

"John, I do believe we are at the end of this conversation."

"Father, I believe we understand what's at stake here . . . let's do no more harm."

"Goodnight, John. I trust you keep this story contained."

John walked the seven blocks to his house reflecting on the last hour. He thought Father Pat too cool for this being a first-time accusation. *Does that indicate he'd been able to disenfranchise the accusation before, or had there not been a direct accuser? His mild defenses, lack of anger, and righteousness were not solid assurances that this would be an easy fix. John wondered if more visibility must be made – the Bishop – that might be too fast an escalation – besides the Bishop may already know Father's history is studded with young boys – maybe the reason for the move from Ohio – where before then? God, do the bishops protect these priests?*

By the time he walked the last block, John decided his next step would be a drive to Minneapolis to talk with Father Swanson who he'd known since he was twelve. Father Mike had been like a replacement for Grandpa John, always there, always listening, always a mentor, always open to discussing hard decisions one was facing. John could always count on those two men to do the right thing, in the right time. *I'll call Father Mike. Maybe drive up for lunch. Emily would want to go along. Emily. Telling her is not going to be an easy task. Emily's well-defined guidelines, priorities, standards – her logic defining what is right – and certainly the morality of a man of cloth, particularly her Catholic priest -- this will ram into that structure like a naval destroyer.*

He wasn't ready and went another block past the house to further weigh the consequences. *She's too intuitive; she'll smell something's up, my visiting Father Mike. Jon might say something about Matt . . . hardest is to speak the first time, easier now that he's told me, and I told him I'd tell his mother. Worse would be her finding out I kept this to myself, about her child . . . the damage to our trust and marriage – unthinkable. My task is to keep her from escalating it too fast.* Final decision, "best to handle her reaction up front, delaying it might be more than I want to handle." He gave a heavy sigh before opening his front door.

**9**

John followed the TV voices to the den and found Emily humming and engrossed in a jigsaw puzzle. He doubted she was listening to the late news but she did sense his presence. She looked up, lifting her face for a kiss, as John walked towards her. "Hi, you're a little late. Was the meeting long or did you men just gab longer?"

"Nothing out of the ordinary. I think we have a good start on the drive for capital expenditures. It's going to take a bit of extra work and an earlier start to raise the seventy-five thousand by end of next year. Did you and Jon get a start on his project?"

"Yes. At least scoping it out. Quite naturally, he is thinking of a landscape for his diorama. Since he wants plants and flowers, the southwestern desert or a rain forest appeals to him. Here is a sketch he drew and a list of materials he'd need. Shall we place a bet on which one he'll do?"

John looked at both pieces of paper and said, "I'll place my money on the rain forest."

"Me too. It'll call forth his creativity. Dad will be coming over next week. I thought he'd be a great help with Jon." Emily patted the edge of the table, "Sit down and help me with this puzzle. Find this piece here. I've been looking for the last hour."

"I can see why . . . so much foliage . . . almost three quarters of the picture." John pretended to search among the hundred of pieces laid out on the large wooden table, an antique he'd found at an estate sale for Emily's 40th birthday, a perfect size for her puzzles. "Emily, we have a serious situation to talk about. This is a good time, with no interruptions."

Without looking up, Emily said, "Oh. What's up?"

"Em, it's a very sensitive issue and one we'll have to keep to ourselves right now. It's important it stays between the two of us. Promise?"

"John, I'm not a blabber mouth, or one to spread gossip. This sounds serious. Is it something that happened just tonight?"

"No, it came up the other day."

"When you and Jon went off to the lake? I suspected something serious. Jon left quite sober and you came back that way. Well, don't keep me in suspense. Is Jon-son in trouble? Has he done something wrong at school?"

"No, it is about one of his friends. Matt Sledgling. He shared a secret with Jon, one involving Father Pat." Emily sat back in her chair and gazed up at John, holding a puzzle piece still between her fingers. "Matt's story as related to Jon indicates that Father has made improper, let's call it what it is, sexual advances with Matt."

"What? That can't be true, John." Emily threw the puzzle piece on the table. "He's a priest. Matt's a young boy. Why would he tell such a story?"

"Emily, Jon's words and actions gave me no reason not to believe the validity of Matt's story." John repeated the discussion by the pond. He could see the shock in Emily's eyes and the retreating of her body. "I know, it's hard to digest."

"My God, John! Has Father done anything to our son?"

"No, but I have to wonder who else besides Matt."

Anger glowed in Emily's eyes and her arms were locked tightly across her chest. "John, how could a priest do this? Be so base . . . so untrue to his calling . . . hiding behind the robes of the church. He's a . . . he's a . . . "

"Yes, his behavior is that of a pedophile." The word, spoken out loud, sounded evil and like its menace brought heavy silence. Emily sat motionless, head down, nodding back and forth. John stood up and paced the room.

The silence was broken by Emily's question, "What is Matt's father going to do about this?"

"Matt's father doesn't know. Matt is ashamed and scared to tell him. He says his father won't believe him." John came back to the chair across from his wife. "Listen Emily, I want to take the action that will be the most effective and least harmful to Matt, and any other boy, if there are others. Raising a big commotion will just bring a lot of talk without an answer."

"We could drive him from the parish."

"So he can be a pedophile in some other parish? Besides, there'll be others like Mr. Sledgling who'll not believe a young boy's story. People don't want to hear that of a church, of a priest. And, what a division that would cause in the congregation."

"John, you can't just do nothing – that's not the man I know you are."

"You're right Em. The first thing I've done is talk to Father, that's why I was late. I want him on warning that someone knows of his behavior and then I want to discuss this with Father Mike. I need to hear what action the church will take. This can't be the first accusation of this type they've heard."

"You are suggesting that this is a common occurrence?" Emily raised her voice.

"Hard as it is to swallow, my dear, I doubt that this is the first time a diocese has been faced with accusation of sexual misconduct."

"Please John, shut up! I feel slimy. Priests playing with little children! My God. He ought to be strung up." Emily's anger shot her body up from her chair. She turned to John, "I certainly can't go to church knowing this. To see that man say mass. To go to him for confession. To have him lay the host on my tongue. No, never, never!"

"Emily I know how hard this is for us but promise to keep this between us. Don't bring it up to Jon unless he does. Let's keep it private, and that includes our family, until we see Father Mike. Can you do that?"

"John, I have no desire to spread this news. I want him gone. When can we see Father Mike?"

"Next week, I hope. I've left him a message and should hear from him tomorrow. Any day good for you?"

"Any day will do," Emily said dejectedly.

It was a restless night. Emily lay quietly, oblivious of John's tossing and muttering. Her mind kept producing the image of a small boy being fondled by a man in clerical dress, his hands upon the boy, his mouth seeking the small lips, his genitals on display. *Why must my faith be destroyed in this manner? Who can I turn to? God, I trusted in you, in religion, the words from the pulpit, the good works of people. Guess I'm naïve, stupid . . . human beings make human errors . . . but sins under the guise of religion. I feel like I've been violated.*

John woke to an empty spot next to him. He went downstairs and found Emily sitting at the kitchen table with a cup of tea. He stood behind her, placing his hands around her shoulders. "I'm so sorry Emily. This is hard on us, our church, our faith."

"I want to strike him, John . . . hit him . . . stand up and denounce him. He's taken away something precious to me. He's a hypocrite. He makes fools of us."

"I know, I know, but we must be strong. We have to make a difference, but I'm not seeing how just yet. I suspect it will be step by step and require our courage and patience."

"Father Mike will have to have some good answers for me," Emily spoke harshly, "and a solution."

## 10

"How's my young man, this morning?" asked Emily as she placed a plate of scrambled eggs and sausage on the table. "Here's your favorite breakfast."

"Can I stay home from school today?"

"Are you sick? Let me feel your forehead. It doesn't feel hot."

"I'm tired."

"Well honey that's not reason enough. You completed your homework, didn't you? You weren't really late to bed."

"But woke up a lot"

"Why was that?" Emily thought about the conversation he might have overheard.

"Oh, just dreams and noises."

"Bad dreams?" Thinking of her own images of last night.

When Jon responded, "Yeah," Emily said, "Want to tell me?"

"No, Mom . . . better eat fast . . . my bus will be coming."

"School looks okay, then?"

"Yeah, it's the religion class today. Father Stern is teaching it, and . . ."

"I know son, your father told me . . . You know . . ."

"Got to go, Mom." Jon said in a rush, gulped his milk and grabbed his school bag, "See you later."

"Hey, I get a hug, remember." It was a quick one, and off Jon hurried with Shorts barking behind him.

Emily thought about the burden of Matt's revelation. She presumed young boys talk about their physical bodies, at ten it wasn't much different from girls, just different parts; but the thought of a priest touching one of them, suggesting sexual acts, exposing himself brought anger to the surface again. Disbelief lingered with Emily. She kept trying to find a plausible answer for why a priest, under the protection of the church and his collar, felt he had the privilege and right to molest a young boy. She'd heard family members hint at affairs between priests and church secretaries, or a woman from the congregation, but never a child. *Betrayed.* Emily doubted she'd face or talk with Father Stern again. She doubted if she could attend services.

John called at ten thirty. "We'll be seeing Father Mike next Monday; it's his most open day for the week. He has all morning and up to two thirty free. We could leave around nine giving us a couple hours before lunch, and we'd be home by five."

"What about Jon? Should I call Claire?"

"No Dad is going to pick him up at school and bring him to the drugstore. He'll put him to work stacking shelves. Dad was curious about the trip. I didn't tell him we were going to see Father Mike, just said you'd been wanting to go to the city. That seemed to satisfy him."

## 11

Father Mike answered the door himself. It was as if he had their two-hour trip timed perfectly. "Welcome, welcome. Good to see the two of you."

"I know, it's been too long," Emily said, reaching for Father's extended hands.

Father placed his left hand on John's back while still holding on to Emily's left hand and headed the three of them through the foyer and waiting room. "Let's go into my office."

It was Father's sanctuary, his private office, three doors down the hallway of open-door offices meant for diocesan business. The outstanding piece, when one walked into his space, was his personal desk, a family heirloom dating back to the 1850's. The second noticeable feature was the French doors opening into a small patio enclosed by an ivied brick wall. A magnificent Japanese maple awash with burgundy red leaves stood opposite a small green leafed tree shaped as an umbrella over a glass table and cushioned chairs. Inside, shelves well stocked with books, pictures, and religious icons lined one entire wall. The three of them sat in tapestry chairs to ask and answer opening questions about parents, work, and recent trips. On a sideboard were a silver coffee urn, plates and utensils.

"John, your request for a quiet private discussion hinted at a serious matter, so I asked cook to fix lunch for us here. She'll be ready when we are. Hope that's okay."

"Very perceptive, although I thought we could make a reservation for one o'clock which would give us two hours . . . though I see we have already chatted away twenty minutes."

Emily added, "You know how much you like the ambience of DeVito's, Father."

"Another time, Emily. Somehow, I sense our time needs to be here in this room. Coffee before we get started?"

"I've had enough today. Been cutting down on caffeine," John replied. "Emily drinks more of it than I do."

Emily stopped Father from getting up. "I'll get it. How about you? Cream isn't it?" Emily walked to the sideboard. They waited until she had placed the two cups on the table in front of them.

"How's the boy? What's he doing?" asked Father Mike.

Emily searched for pictures in her purse as she told Father, "Oh, he is so full of life. He's training his dog, Shorts, new tricks and riding his bike and fishing with my father. He really has gotten into gardening with me, as well as Grandpa Frank."

"Sounds like a normal, healthy young lad. Still waiting for another baby?"

"Disappointment there," said John. "The baby we were waiting for was born last fall. It was a girl, just what we hoped for."

Emily butted in, "The mother changed her mind when she saw the baby, so we are back in the queue. We are past forty now, so it may be too late," she said sadly, "and besides there are so many on the waiting list. Mrs. Mason has asked us to consider an older child, but I'm reluctant."

"It's no doubt a better chance for adoption is in that older group. I know you want a baby, but you two could give so much to a child of any age. You are both fine parents. You could do so much to help an older child. Well, I don't mean to preach, I'm sure that you and John will make the right decision." Father turned to John, "Well, what's the issue?"

"Not a pleasant one, Mike." John relayed the afternoon talk by the lake.

Father Mike sat still, listened intently, with hands clasped together in his lap. He nodded his head, "Have you spoken to Matt's parents?"

"No, I haven't and don't think I can, particularly since Matt is afraid to do so. I can imagine why, as I have witnessed unpleasant behavior by Mr. Sledgling. At this point I don't want to betray Matt's confidence in Jon."

"Isn't Father Stern the priest who came to your parish from another state via northern Minnesota?"

"Yes, what do you know of him?" Emily asked with interest.

"I've only met him once, even though he's been here almost two years. Right?"

"Yes," replied Emily. "I notice that you don't visit our school on your rounds."

"Regretfully so, as I do miss the parish, but the larger schools have had needs that take more of my time and attention. We do a lot of our interactive work with the smaller schools through group conferences – parish priest coming here rather than me going there. My personal interaction with Father Stern has been in those settings."

John had watched Father carefully and remarked, "You seem not surprised by my story. Are you making light of it? Or do you have some background on him that you wish to withhold?"

"Only speculations from two other priests on the circumstances of his move from Ohio."

Emily couldn't contain her reaction any longer, she pleaded, "Father Mike, how can this happen? What privilege, what freedom does a priest have to taint a child?"

"They don't, Emily, but I fear there are ugly-looking human qualities even in men of the cloth."

Emily rushed on, "You mean there are others? This is common?"

"No, but it does occur."

"Dirty, rotten, evil," cried Emily.

Father leaned forward in his chair, reaching for Emily's hands, which she drew away from him. "Yes, it is all those things, Emily."

"How can you be so calm? Aren't you angry?"

"Yes I am, Emily. As a priest, it is one of the worst scenarios I'd wish to hear. The two priests I mentioned, with me, make a group of three who keep these accusations in constant visibility with the Bishop."

"What headway do you make?" Father caught the icy tone in John's voice.

"Slowly I must confess. These are delicate issues for religious leaders to address."

John interrupted, "Swept under the rug, relocate the perpetrator, is that the Bishop's answer?"

"So, it might seem to you. The church has thought that therapy, penance, condemnation, a second chance would . . ."

John interrupted again quickly, and Emily saw an anger in John never seen before. "Mike, this is pedophilia! It's a crime in the eyes of justice, the law."

"I know, I know, John. We do take these accusations seriously, and they are studied within the context of the church. There's a world-wide reputation to care for, consideration of the legal counsel offered, the faith and trust of millions . . . as I said . . . delicate, very delicate."

"So, as a Catholic parishioner of St. Anne's under Father Stern, I should be patient and look the other way. Or is that turning the other check?" John said cynically. "Should I hope that a group of three will change the Bishop, or the church dramatically? That's living in fairyland." John's body slumped back into the chair, a sign of defeat to Emily. Her heart sank, for John, her faith, and the perplexity rising within her.

Father waited, without reward, for John to bring his eyes back in line with his and finally said, "John, I don't have an answer or solution of the church to give you, but surely we have a course we can take to safeguard Matt and . . ."

"Mike, John went face-to-face with Father Stern," said Emily. "What if that threat of exposure does not cure his behavior, nor make him cease? The threat to my son or other sons is terrible. You are asking us to back-up the church by protecting the boys. Something is terribly wrong here! Terribly wrong!"

A heavy pall hung in the room. John remained disengaged; his body in the same slumped position, and Emily sat as if in silent mourning. Father Mike sat on the edge of his chair waiting – for what, he did not know. He broke the silence, "What are you thinking?"

Emily was first to respond. "I'm not sure that I can go to church and, if not, what will I say to my son, family, friends? How do I mend my broken faith? Or can I? I have only John now. I feel violated, betrayed, isolated."

Slowly John leaned forward and looking directly at Father Mike, said in a very sober voice, "We came to you to find hope versus excuses, a champion rather than a defender. I can see that I was wrong to expect a direct line to the Bishop, a promise of action to remove Father Stern, and to see consequences for his behavior, his character flaws.

"What have you given us – 'this stuff happens, the Bishop is made aware of it,' punishment is soft-pedaled. Now, in reflection, I've never heard of a priest being defrocked. Their secrets are kept hidden. They get second chances to repeat the behavior. They remain a minister to congregations and a menace to young boys. The perpetrator continues to wear his collar and retain his place in the church. That doesn't match my ethics.

"Father Mike, it will be a sorry day if we leave here with these perceptions. I am very disappointed, all the way around."

"Disappointed?" Emily added, "I am shattered." She and John sat silently waiting for Father Mike to offer a solution.

"John, we can bring this case to the Bishop, but it must be with a written charge by Matt and his family. The church can't bring formal action on anything less – you would need the same if you took this accusation to other authorities. Could you get an affidavit? Will Matt and his parents come forth?" He waited for an answer that didn't come. "No, I suspect not. Well . . . John, Emily, I will see what pressure I can put forth in discovering Father Stern's time in other parishes. Maybe he can be transferred elsewhere."

"Into another parish and other boys for Christ sake?" Emily shot out.

"No, hopefully into the seminary where he'll enter therapy. I regret that this answer is not the one you'd hoped for. John, I encourage you to see how you might help the young boy's parents to make a formal charge with Bishop Wallinger."

"Like you, Father, I can't promise anything. I do intend to talk with Matt, with Jon, to coach them in how to stay clear of Father Stern. You do what you must do; I'll do what I have to do."

The three sat in tense expectation, as if a divine answer was forthcoming. Father finally broke the awkward silence, "Shall I let Emma know we are ready for lunch?"

"I think we shall pass on your offer. My appetite just isn't there. Emily, how about you?"

"I think it best we go on. I really don't know what our lunch conversation could be, Father. This is a tough dilemma for three old friends."

"I understand how unpleasant this is, but we have to give it time to work itself out. Be assured I shall not stay idle. I will visit with the Bishop as soon as possible this week. And, I know John, you will be vigilant at St. Anne's. And, Emily, don't let your faith in God go easily. He is always our answer; let's pray for his guidance."

"Oh Father," Emily sighed, "you make it sound simple." As they walked toward the door, she said, "We'll do our best."

## 12

The silence within the rectory stayed with John and Emily until they were beyond the city headed down Highway 60 towards St. Peter.

"Would you like to stop for lunch, Em?"

"Would you mind doing take-outs and going to the college park. There are nice shade trees and lovely flowers. I think we need the fresh air and beautiful surroundings."

Before they opened their sandwiches, Emily rested her elbows on the picnic table, cupped her chin into the palms of her hands, looked directly at John and asked, "We can't let a little boy be a victim of the dark side of religion. What's your plan, John?"

"To protect Matt and Jon first, and get Father Stern out of our parish. I'm thinking that Jon should have Matt over this weekend. Maybe you could work it out with his mother for an overnight stay. Thought we'd take the boys to the city baseball game and afterwards I'd take them out with baseball and mitts while you cook supper."

"Are you setting that time to talk with the boys?"

"Yes. I want Matt to feel comfortable in telling me his story, so we can talk again. I'd like to see if I could get him to tell his father or mother. We need them, just as Mike said."

"You say Mr. Sledgling is very hot headed. No telling what he might do. Seems you'd have to be with Matt."

"I realize that, but first Matt has to tell me. I want to help him stay out of another situation with Sterns and let Matt know someone, me, is watching Father. Step by step. How well do you know his mother?"

"Not too well. She hasn't joined with the churchwomen on any project. But, if I go to her as the mother of her son's best friend, the invitation should have a chance. This is Monday. I'll call her tomorrow. Maybe our invitation should include Friday and Saturday night . . . gives Matt more time to get use to being with us. On second thought, we'd better ask Jon first, I can call her on Wednesday or Thursday."

"Emily, I'm still not inclined to tell anyone else. I can't quite see how just our family can oust Father Stern. I could depend on Jack Harris and Tim Brandt if I brought them into the story. I know I could trust them and they're respected in the diocese. Let's take the first step this weekend and see where we'll go from there. Okay?"

"I know you want my promise to keep this quiet. That will be easy enough. I'm rather ashamed even to tell Claire. I'm confused . . . bewildered . . . too angry to even attend church." John remained silent, knowing it best to let Emily talk this out. "I can't reconcile God . . . church and little boys . . . my faith is battered . . . I can't forgive." She spoke in a spiritless voice.

"What happens if you're not in church? How do we answer the obvious questions so many will ask?"

"I don't know! I don't care! I can't see that man, hear his voice, his words! Such a farce . . . a mockery of all I believe in."

"I know Em, the imperfection of it all is very hard." He took her hand, "Why not play sick this first Sunday. Hopefully, you'll be able to keep appearances, until . . ."

"I can't if that terrible person is still at the altar!" Emily sobbed into her napkin.

John's plan moved slowly. Matt was too hesitant, and too fearful, to tell anyone else. It took another sleepover before John gained Matt's confidence. No progress was made toward Matt telling his parents, and Matt wanted to believe that Father Stern would not bother him again. John thought that was probably true, since Father no doubt knew John had Matt under his wing. The best news came two months after the visit to Father Mike. The Bishop sent out an announcement that Father Patrick Stern would be transferred to the seminary to fill a teaching position and Father Thomas Wentz would be returning to St. Anne's. John called Father Mike to say thank you.

"How's Emily doing?" Father asked.

"I can't say for sure. Her only words still are angry ones. Her religious belief has been badly shaken, shattered really . . . don't know if she can forgive the Catholic Church. She goes to Sunday services for Jon and maybe to hold on to her trust in God. It's delicate."

"I'll make a visit to St. Anne's when Father Wentz arrives to particularly see Emily. I'd like to help her."

"Well, Father Mike, we both need help."


**Emily**

*This is the last time I'll sit through his sermons. I hate him . . . never want to see him again. Listen to him; 'give ourselves to a higher authority' . . . (he thinks God approves of him, what he does) . . . 'He does not condemn' . . . (he believes he's above punishment) . . . 'but He guides us' . . .(I hope he guides him right into hell!) God! Listen to me . . . will I never release this anger? Can I ever have faith again? I'm one of your children. What do you do with this? How do you forgive?*

## 13

The Altar and Rosary meeting had an agenda item that the members would not have expected. Emily Strutter announced her resignation from the board after ten years of holding one position or another and, when questioned, gave no reason other than 'it's time for others to lead the group'. When questioned further, Emily said she would still be giving time to the day care and children projects. Claire, Emily's closest friend within St. Anne's, was more surprised than others. Emily was a natural leader and a self-starter, energetic and full of ideas with enough enthusiasm to motivate others.

As they locked the basement door, Claire suggested they have a cup of coffee. "Oh, maybe another time," Emily replied. "I should be on my way."

"Come on, Em, I think it's time we had a heart-to-heart talk."

"About what?"

"About changes in Emily, that's what. I've noticed a lot less enthusiasm and a pulling away from your church friends. It's like you've cooled off. Something has to be up. We've been friends too long for me not to be curious and concerned."

"Are you trying to show me how perceptive you are?" Emily said lightly.

"Maybe – as a way to start the conversation. Come on over to the house. I'll make some coffee and you'll be home before school is let out." Claire put her arm through Emily's and headed them down the street towards her house. "We've shared so much of our lives and thoughts, we certainly can handle this also, can't we?"

"Oh Claire, I wish it was that easy."

Claire's kitchen was the center of her home and the largest room. As they walked through the back door, Emily suggested, "Let's have tea, Claire. I've had enough coffee, at breakfast and at the meeting."

"Sounds good to me. Herbal or regular?"

"Either one. I'll get the tea cups from the cabinet."

Claire granted no space for small talk. She went right to the question. "Emily what has happened? And, please don't tell me 'nothing', cause I won't believe you."

Emily looked at her friend and then closed her eyes, as she said, "I promised John I would not speak of this with anyone."

Claire was more direct. "Does it have to do with Father Stern?" She waited. "Well, does it?" and waited again. "Look, Emily, we both may know something we've kept quiet for the protection of St. Anne's. But those of us with doubts are concerned for our young boys. And, you are too, I suspect. Particularly for Jon."

"What do you know? You share first."

Claire's story was not much different than what John and Emily knew. Claire spoke of hearing about altar boys who no longer wanted to serve mass. One parent believed his son was being abused by Father Stern but couldn't prove it. Several parents made light of the boys' comments and the rumors that followed. Claire herself said she'd been skeptical, as it was unthinkable behavior for a priest. But after Father Stern was re-assigned, her skepticism had weakened.

"Some people seem very glad that he is gone, in fact too much so. Can it be true? I asked myself. I figured it was, for the boys are now back at the altar . . . rumors have quieted, but I've noticed that your interest and enthusiasm has waned. So unlike you!" Claire paused before asking, "Emily, was Jon one of the boys?"

"No, but one of Jon's friends was, and his parents were never told. He said they wouldn't believe him. It's all so awful, so hideous. A priest. A man preaching the message of God, using his honored role to do horrible things with young boys. I can't let go of the thoughts. I can't forgive and I certainly cannot forget." Emily's words rushed on. "I can't be Catholic anymore. Father Stern couldn't have been the only priest . . . I imagine, others have too. I hate them." The barrage of words silenced Claire. "Yes, Claire, I've changed. It's hard for me to go to church, mass, communion, and I'm only doing so because of John's family. But, if I can find a way out, I'll take it."

"I'm so sorry, Emily. To give up one's faith . . . it means so much to me. I have to believe that the church would not allow children to be harmed without punishment. They have removed him from parish assignment."

"Yes, but he's still has the role and title of a priest and all his wrongs remain invisible. Well, now you know Claire. I'm doing the best I can but forgiveness is not there for me, if it ever will be."

"I'm truly sorry, Emily. It isn't a perfect world, is it?"

# CHAPTER THREE

## *Teen Year Scenes*

### 1

T HE CALL FROM Sam in 1977 reported a change in name and residence. "She's now married and lives with her husband, Ben Allen, in a condo in Denver. She still works as a medical technician and he as a sales manager for office equipment and furniture. He is thirty-two, one year older than she." John sent a money order for $700.

### 2

"Hi, Gretchen. We'll be by to pick you up at seven. My father is driver tonight. We're picking up Ken too. Matt and Mary are walking to the gym. They said they'd 'trick n treat' along the way."

"Can't wait for you to see my costume. I'll need lots of room in the back seat for the full skirt."

"Mom is just finishing my tunic. I'll be green all over. Guess what I'll be?"

"The Green Hornet?"

"How would you know about him?"

"My older brothers have the comic books."

"Good guess but wrong. Too bad you only get one."

"You can have one guess of who I'll be."

"The fairy godmother from Cinderella. Bring your wand so you can turn a pumpkin into a carriage for a ride home."

"Wrong, Jon. See ya at seven."

Jon was a freshman and this was his first big school party – an all-out Halloween night planned by the parents. He would have liked it more if he didn't have to depend on his father for transportation, but he had another five months before he could test for a driver's license.

Shorts sat with head cocked as he watched Jon put on a green jumper, large floppy shoes and barked when Jon covered his entire head with a green cap.

"Shorts." Jon croaked and leaped at Shorts. The dog ran out into the hallway and crawled back to sit in the doorway. "I'm Froggy, Shorts. Mom, where are the gloves?" Emily was twirling them as she came into the bedroom, looked at her son, and adjusted the green cap.

"You'll do fine, Sweetie. Hope I'm standing by when you shed the green suit and become the handsome prince. Gretchen should love that act."

"Hope I don't get too hot wearing two layers."

"We're going to keep the hall cool, knowing that you'll be generating heat, playing games in costumes. Don't know how you'll dance with those floppy feet."

"Good reason to get out of dancing."

"Now, Jon. You have to learn to hit the dance floor; girls don't want to sit out. Maybe we should have practiced more this summer."

"Okay, okay Mom. Maybe I'll make my transformation early in the evening."

"What's Ken's costume?"

"He's superman, but not turning into Clark Kent. Gretchen is not telling me her's. Though said she has a large skirt."

"Almost seven." They heard from downstairs.

The Strutter car pulled out of the driveway with a bright green frog and Maw and Paw hillbillies. They stopped two blocks later for a ballerina in a tutu and six blocks further for superman in a flowing red cape. Emily said gleefully, "We are in high feathers tonight," a saying of her mother's when it was a happy occasion and spirits were jolly.

## 3

Jon was five months from being fifteen and exhibited the traits that would strengthen as he grew older. He was thoughtful, straightforward, hard working. He had a serious attitude towards life, not unlike his father, shouldering responsibilities other children might find burdensome. He took care of the yard, summer and winter, and under his mother's watchful eye planted the flowerbeds. He took pleasure in making new variations of designs and colors. His Grandfather Frank knew his grandson would start preparing the garden plot in the spring without his asking. Being the center of attention would not be important to Jon, being in the center of what was happening would be.

Every morning when Jon opened his eyes, he'd find Shorts ready to start the day - he'd be sitting on the floor by the head of the bed, eyes glued on Jon's face. The morning Jon awoke and found Shorts curled up under his bed, he felt uneasy.

"Dad, Shorts is acting strange. He's under my bed and won't come out. I even held out his favorite dog biscuit. Something's wrong, Dad. He's still there."

"Hum, not like Shorts. Let's see what's up."

They moved the bed to get next to Shorts. He was listless, didn't attempt to get on his feet, but wiggled his tail when Jon put his hand on his head. John felt his nose -- very hot – and looked at his eyes, which were milky and without recognition.

"Son, he's dying, from what, who knows. Let's put him on his cushion and take him to the vet. You get him ready, I'll call Doc Stevens."

Shorts died in Jon's arms as they drove to the vet. "Let's go back, Dad. I don't want the vet to take him. I'll put Shorts in the back yard."

Jon stayed apart from the family all day. He made a box for Shorts, wrapping him in his favorite plaid dog blanket, and placed his written good-byes inside along with the yellow and orange balls. Alone, he dug a hole under the apple tree, and planted flowers on top of the grave. It was late afternoon when Jon came inside and looked for Shorts' items.

"Mom, where are the toys, his dish, his leash, his cushion?"

"Sweetie, I put them away. Thought it would be easier for you not to see them."

"Mom, Shorts was mine. You have no right to take his things. Keep out of it. You can't make this a happy time! Where are his things?"

Emily had never felt Jon's opposition so strongly before, and it startled her. "I was just thinking of your loss, wanting to make it better."

"Sometimes you can't make it better. Just let me have his things."

Jon dedicated a shelf in his bedroom for Shorts' playthings and pictures as a way to keep him by his side for the rest of his teen years. The cushion indented with Shorts' body remained on the floor right below Jon's pillows.

# 4

Jon and Gretchen finished putting up the last decoration for Jon's sixteenth birthday party. They'd worked with Emily all morning hanging banners, blowing up balloons, hiding items in the neighborhood for a treasure hunt, picking out the music for dancing, and decorating two cakes, one chocolate and the other lemon. Gretchen suggested they put eight candles on each cake and have two blowouts. "That way you'll get two wishes." To which, Jon replied, "April Fool."

After eating Emily's chicken salad sandwiches and tomato soup, Gretchen and Jon went down to the City lake for a sprint around the trail. The sun was bright, making an exceptionally warm day for so early in the spring.

"I think I'm too full to be sprinting. Coach always says, 'No running on a full stomach.' Let's just do a slow walk."

"The ground is dry, let's play our 'when I grow up' quiz," suggested Gretchen.

"Okay." They stretched out on their backs, the tops of their heads touching. Jon started the first question. "What place in the world would you like to see?"

"The Taj Mahal. The story is so romantic and the pictures I've seen are too. To think he built that place just for his love. It would be beautiful to see in the moonlight. India has a romance about it. What's your place?"

"The Northern Lights from the farthest point north."

"Brrr . . . go north to the Pole? Oh, I suppose the lights could be romantic. Your next question?"

Jon was ready. "What would be your best vacation spot?"

"Easy," said Gretchen. "Hawaii or maybe Tahiti – the dreamy islands, blue ocean, beach, sunsets. Oh, la, la. Want to go with me?"

"This is a hard one for me," answers Jon. "It's either England or France for the beautiful gardens. To see Versailles would be awesome, but the villages in England are said to be charming. Every house has a garden. Guess if it had to be only one, I'd go for France."

"Well, it would be more romantic to be in Paris. Japan has beautiful gardens too and you could visit Hiroshima. Next question: What do you want for a career?"

"I want to make beauty with flowers, plants, trees, grasses, and even rocks. My dream would be the head of an arboretum or my own business designing grand landscapes for big homes. Bet you want education."

"Right on, Jon. I want to be the head of a university department or president of a small college. My father says that's quite ambitious for a woman. Makes me doubt myself."

"Gretch, we can do anything we want if we set our minds to it. Don't give up your dream because of someone else. Ken has a practice he likes to do . . . of what he wants. He draws images in his head . . . keeps a mental story of how things can be. He believes in that stuff about, 'what you think is what you get'."

"That's just day-dreaming. Jon, if you could be anything . . . . live a far-flung dream . . . a craziest thing . . . what would that be?"

After a bit of reflection, he said, "I would love to have been one of the explorers of the Amazon. To see, to walk, to listen to the rain forest before others. To be the first to see new plants, strange insects. That had to be awesome. It would be like being at the beginning."

"Well, I'd be far from that. If I could have my wish, I'd be a princess in a small country, like Grace Kelly. She had a magical life and everything was beautiful."

People had walked past unnoticed by Jon and Gretchen who were lost in their images of what could be. They'd heard each other's daydreams, their inner desires without noting that their interests were poles apart.

Gretchen wondered out loud, "I think about what will be my best age. Forty, I think . . . enough experience to be smart, young enough to enjoy life, and still have time for dreams to come true. How about you Jon?"

"Hadn't thought about age. Maybe fifty or sixty. It seems wisdom comes later . . . as it is with dad and my grandfathers. I'm not sure what age would be the best. Maybe it's always just where I'm at – sixteen seems pretty fantastic to me right now."

"Sweet sixteen and never been kissed."

"April Fool. Hey, don't our kisses count?"

# 5

"Do you want black side or white?" Jon asked Matt as they set out the chessboard and men. "Did you read the book I gave you?"

"Some of it. Enough to know which way the pieces move. If I don't remember, can we refer to the book? You know I play checkers well, beat you most the time, but chess isn't just jumping over pieces."

"I'm not that good either. Dad wins most games so far. I get five or six moves before he checks me. Of course, Dad should be a master, his grandfather taught him. They played chess a lot. So, black or white?"

"Give me white. King/Queen in the middle, then the bishops. Right? Then the knight and what's the last piece . . . oh, yeah, the rook. Can't we turn on some music?"

Listening to a Beatle's tape, they settled on the floor, opened cans of soda and Matt made the first move, pushing his white Pawn in front of the King's Bishop two squares. They discover later that this is not a good opening move. Jon moved the Pawn in front of his King two squares. Matt studied before deciding not to capture Jon's Pawn. He toyed with the chess piece, moving it back and forth before making his second bad move, which he soon saw.

"Not a good move," Jon quipped, as he captured Matt's first white Pawn.

"Okay, I'll capture you." Matt took the black Pawn off the board without seeing that he'd exposed his King to a lethal attack. Jon moved his Queen quickly and checked the white King. Matt had no man to capture the Queen. "It's checkmate – game's over."

"Man, what did I do wrong?" moaned Matt.

"You played the game like checkers, one move at a time. In this game, you have to think two to three moves ahead," answered Jon. "In chess you can't neglect the safety of the King. Rule number one, lug head."

"Okay, smarty, so you've played a game or two with your father. Give me time. I'll learn and I'll whip your butt."

As they re-set the board, Jon told Matt. "Dad says that Father Sterns is not at the seminary teaching any more. He's hasn't found out yet where they sent him. You suppose he exposed himself with the students?"

"Well, they'd be older than we were," replied Matt. "Do you suppose he likes boys of any age?"

"He might. Sort of sick, eh?"

"Wonder why men want to play with their own sex? Ugh, seems gross. I was so shocked when Sterns put his hands on me . . . I remember I couldn't move at first. And, why did he pick me?"

"Maybe there were others - they just never told anyone. Or maybe he thought you'd give in. Or maybe he knew your father wouldn't back you up. Who knows, it was weird, eh? Wonder who he made his confession to." That episode left an indelible mark on both boys. It was a secret they kept between the two of them, a secret they seldom pulled out to examine.

"Don't know what your father did but he saved me. Okay, this time I'm going to protect my King." Matt moved his King's Pawn up two squares. Jon did likewise. Then Matt moved his Bishop on the kingside and Jon played Queen's Bishop. Next Matt moved his Bishop in position to capture Jon's Knight. The game played longer than the first and Matt made a bold move of moving his Queen forward to capture a Pawn, leaving a pathway open for Jon's Bishop to capture a Knight and check the white King.

"Wow, didn't look ahead for that move. Well, at least we went eight plays instead of three. Think your mom would let you drive over to the pool? We could practice our flip dives."

## 6

Jon was five foot seven and would grow another two inches. His body was slim with short legs, long torso, narrow, trim chest and strong shoulders. His striking features were his unblemished skin, bright blue eyes —- a shade darker than a robin's egg – a strong forehead topped with thick light brown hair, which turned blondish under the summer sun. To his mother's disappointment, Jon was partial to only one sport, swimming. He was a member of the summer swim team; although he liked the breaststroke his specialty was freestyle. His speed showed well in the last leg of relay competition. Emily was an enthusiastic fan and lane timer. Jon could hear her shouts even with the water splashing around his face.

Matt swam for fun but enjoyed baseball too much to give it up for his friend's sport. Jon's other close friend, Ken, was on the swim team, excelling in the backstroke.

"Hey, Jon have you heard?" Ken yelled into the phone. "We've earned enough points this summer to go the state swim meets in St. Paul. Great, eh?"

"Wow, are you sure? It'll be Witherston first time. How'd you find out?"

"The coach told Staley and he started the chain of telephone calls. Guess we'll find out tomorrow morning at practice. Whoopee!"

While Matt and Jon had been classmates and buddies since third grade, Ken's close friendship started when they were seventh graders. Math was their weakest subject, so they did a lot of studying together, sometimes with personal instruction from Jon's father. They decided to keep the challenge going and were planning to take extended math courses in their junior and senior years.

They had a lot of similarities; curiosity for nature, sensitivity to criticism, loyalty to their ideas – often bordering on stubbornness in debate – and a drive to excel in their undertakings. The most notable difference was in their artistic expression; Jon's in gardening and landscape design, Ken's with a charcoal pen and paper. Their conversations were about them and their ideas, so different then those with Matt, whose talk centered on sports and girls - and more girls.

"Jon, aren't you interested in any other girl besides Gretchen? I know Ellen Cummings and Nan Kubrik are dying to go out with you. Mary could set up a double date with us," Matt suggested.

"Gretchen's been a good friend since she moved into our

neighborhood three years ago. I'd have to ask her."

"Jeez, Jon, why? She's gone out with other guys. In fact, Dave Cross has the hots for her right now and is making a move for her."

"If she wants to date Dave, that's okay . . . we aren't going steady."

"All the more reason to go out with Ellen or Nan. How about movies this Friday night?"

"Maybe next week." Jon knew his low interest in girls was a puzzle to his friend, but Jon couldn't explain it, not even to himself. After Mary, Matt dated Sharon and Julie and Karen while Jon went out only with Gretchen – they were a steady couple in other's eyes, particularly his mother's.


# 7

It was the middle of August when they headed off to the St. Paul swim meet. The parents made reservations early at the Uptown Motel within walking distance of the large community pool. Ken's parents, Jan and Greg, drove their camper and it provided a kitchen during the two-day meet and beds for the boys at night. Both sets of parents had volunteered; two of them would be lane officials and two of them time keepers.

"We are up against tough competition," offered Coach Simmons. "Luckily we'll have equally matched teams for the first two relays, but we'll have to be strong and fast to top Whalen or Jefferson, if we get that far."

"Coach, can we practice at night?" asked Jon. "I'll do better if I can swim those lanes ahead of time."

"You bet, sign up for times. There'll be security people on the grounds all night, but I don't want you swimming any later than ten o'clock. Check in when you turn in for the night. My camper is three down from yours. Meet at the pool at eight o'clock tomorrow for sign in."

Jon and Ken were filled with high expectations when they

locked the door of the camper at ten fifteen. They flopped on the couch with lemonade and a bag of chips.

"Let's create our win for tomorrow," said Ken.

"What do you mean?" asked Jon.

"I'll start a story about our relay, when I stop you pick it up and keep the story going. Only rule is that the story must be only in the positive, ending in a win for us. Ready?"

"This is your positive thinking? You start, you're the first one in the water."

"Okay, close your eyes," Ken directed. "See all this happening. Ready?

"The shot of the gun jump starts the relay, I'm poised in the water and move forward with a strong back stroke. My arms reach out and pull me forward. My legs churn the water and move me in a rhythm that propels me with a new power. I feel I am moving with ease and speed. The cheers of "go Ken" are loud. I keep pace and turn the corner two seconds ahead of lane two. My turn is smooth and fast with a strong push-off. I pull ahead of lanes two and four. My arms stretch overhead and propel me through the water. I hear from the shouts that it's me and lane four. My finger tips hit the wall and I see a body spread out into the water."

Jon picked up the story line. "You touch the side and Tad dives in ahead of lane two and four. His arms reach forward in a strong butterfly stroke and pulls through the water pushing him forward to gain a three second lead. Tad's turn is quick and powerful as he pushes back to the finish line. His hand touches with the last stroke at the same time as lane four. Weasel enters the water."

Ken continued, "Weasel quietly glides through the water with arms in motion before him, fingers pointed to cut the water, providing the flow to push his body forward. We watch as he glides, stretches, pulls back, turns one second ahead of lane four and heads back to the starting lane. He's gaining inches, seconds, and touches poolside two seconds ahead of lane four. Go Jon!" Ken pushed a fist out.

"I stretch out and launch into a lead. My feet go into motion and thrust me through the water. My arms curve above my head and push a path for my body. I am gliding without effort and I increase the speed of arms. I make an easy turn without breaking stride and am on my way home, my head turns just enough to gather air, wasting no extra energy. I spurt ahead, I am winning. My fingers touch the pool tile. I win! We win by four seconds!"

Jon and Ken clapped each other on the head, gave each other a hard body clasp, shouting, "We are winners! We did it!" They pumped their arms for the victory.

"Okay, Jon, that's our dream for the night. Rehearse it again when we wake up and we shall live it out tomorrow. This is the technique that the coach was suggesting. I read about golfers who use this same mental rehearsal."

The boys hugged again and Ken kissed Jon on the neck, which Jon ignored but didn't push away.

Jon kept that picture in his mind as he fell asleep, but his dream was of Ken. The sexual aspect of it was stimulating but puzzling. It seemed too comfortable.

>-•→•-O-•←•-<

The team finished seconds ahead, mostly because Ken gave the relay team a five-second advantage. Jon held strong and added another second. As the team celebrated with towel snapping, Ken winked at Jon, "We could make anything happen for us. Wanna try?" Jon shrugged his shoulders.

# 8

"Grandpa I have to write a paper on an aspect of World War II. I know you were in battle and Grandpa Frank wasn't."

"That's right. He was exempt because he was missing those two fingers on his right hand. Pretty hard to handle a gun. How are you suppose to write this paper?"

"Our teacher wants us to interview someone. If we don't know a veteran, then we're suppose to search in the library. I think I'd like to write about what it was like as the war ended. Where were you?"

"Well, I was with the divisions that landed in Italy and drove on through to Germany. We'd left a little village called Bolzano and were headed towards Innsbruck when we heard the announcement over the loud speaker that the Germans had surrendered. The shooting didn't stop immediately, as the word to the German troops lagged behind the announcement to us. When they did know it was true, the German soldiers came towards us with white flags and their hands on top of their heads."

"How did you feel when you saw them, Grandpa?"

"It's eerie, Jon. One moment you are shooting at them with a gun and next you are dishing up food for them. How we turned from hate to compassion amazed me. It was in that one instance that I saw the falseness of war. Nothing but destruction is gained from warring, and when the fighting is over, the people have to work together to bring a sane semblance of life to the world. One wonders why we don't start with the working together first. Of course, that wasn't possible with Hitler."

"But, Grandpa, wars have been in history forever. The latest is Vietnam. Why do we like wars so much?"

"Well Jon, don't know that we like them as much as people like the power of conquering others lands and ideas and to rule over others. Man has in him the need to be king of the world, to have his particular ideas be honored more than another's, to be proven right through their might. Our leaders say 'we'll fight to have peace.' I don't subscribe to that concept anymore. Fight brings destruction until one side gives up; in their losing, war ends but does peace really come? I think not. It just means that men lay down their arms, for a while."

"But, Grandpa, when war ends and there is no fighting, that is peace."

"Not really, Bud. Does a loser go away happy? Does the loser feel no revenge? Does the loser not want another chance to prove he or his country to be right? Consider a fight on your school grounds – not with guns, but with threats, fists, and arguments of who's right and who's wrong. So one guy is bigger, stronger, has more guys on his side and comes out the winner. Does the other guy, the loser, end up happy? Do you hear him say to the winner, 'Thanks for letting me be a loser. I go away with no hard feelings.' I doubt it. What do you think is the human reaction?"

"Well, I think the loser walks away wishing he had won, hoping he could have shown that he was right. If it bothers him a lot, he may plan to come back again for another fight. The loser doesn't usually forget."

"Right you are, Bud. And there lies the dilemma for the human race. When do we decide that it is wiser to collaborate, to work together, to find a win/win solution versus a win/lose? From the looks of us, as a whole, I'd say we are a long, long way from that scenario."

"Your thoughts would make for a different paper. Suppose you could help me find some noted political figure, or philosopher, that draws that same conclusion?"

"Ha! You don't think Carl Knowland's quotes will carry enough weight?" Grandpa asked in a teasing voice.

"Oh, Grandpa. Don't you know that a paper has to have several ways to support the theme? Can you help me?"

"Yes, I think I have some help on my bookshelf. If not, we'll get to the library."

"Grandpa, how could you be a soldier if you didn't believe in it? You could have been a conscientious objector. Isn't that what it's called?"

"Well, when you are young . . . let's see I wasn't thirty years old. Young with a whole lot of patriotic zeal. Going off to war for your country was an honor. The right thing to do. You followed your leaders. I don't have my head in the sand, even now. I know that young men and women will go to war again because their country asks them to. It's just, well, Bud . . . it never is the solution, for the time in between wars lasts such a little time."

Jon compared this win/win proposition to his father's way of handling conflict and realized how carefully his father resolved issues so that both parties saw themselves as partners versus adversaries. He could see the merits of win/win and would look for times to put it in practice. Jon grew to be a trustworthy competitor versus having to win at any cost. He would learn that people need their dignity and self-esteem and that being heavy-handed or one-way was like a punishment.

## 9

Emily and Jon were preparing flowerbeds, spading, raking peat and fertilizer into the ground and roping off sections for the summer garden design. They'd started early that morning and were now having lunch of chicken sandwiches and milk on the back porch. It was the second weekend in May and the sun played hide and seek behind white billowy clouds.

"Oh Jon-son, this is my favorite time of the year. It's always a new beginning. The trees in bud, our perennials peeking up, dirt ready to nurture seeds. Mother nature coming alive and I feel renewed."

"I wish Shorts was here. Remember how he liked digging the dirt as if he was helping me. His snout would be covered with dirt and sometimes he dug so deep, like he thought he'd find a prize." Jon started laughing, "Remember the time he saw the snake? How he jumped back and ran around me twice as if encircling me with protection. The snake was so little; Shorts tossed it up as if it was a toy. Then he carried it over to the far flowerbed and buried like he did with bones. He was a smart dog. I still miss him."

"Jon, we've had such blessed spring plantings – our golden moments – some of my happiest times."

"And, Mom you do like happy times. You think life can always be one happy moment."

"Why not? Only we can make it happy or the opposite, and who wants unhappiness."

They sat quietly for a while. "Just think sweetie, you'll be off to college in another year ready to carry on the family tradition of being a pharmacist. It's a proud thought, isn't it?"

"Mom, don't you hear me saying that I'd like to be a landscape architect? My interest is not in pharmacy."

"But the store is family history . . . it's important to carry on the tradition. Your grandfather's, your father. You don't want to be the one to break that . . . it would shock the whole town."

"Mom, you're trying to make a perfect picture again. Maybe I'm not perfect. You know I have more than the Strutter tradition in me."

Emily quickly retorted, "Jon, perfect is not the issue, it's what is the right thing to do in the family. Besides you are perfect in our eyes and always will be. Your life is here. Family. Gretchen. A business ready for you. Your home. Our flower gardens."

"Mom, I want to be me. But I don't know who that is yet. Can't I go explore?"

"Of course, Jon. But you'll find that this is where your heart belongs. Nothing is better than here."

"Guess, I'll want to find that out for myself."

"Jon Francis! That borders on disrespect."

Late Sunday afternoon, Jon suggested a walk to the lake. He was bothered by his mother's pressure about his future. He felt obligated to the family but also knew tradition could be carried by several of his cousins. In fact, Uncle Lyle's youngest daughter was graduating from pharmaceutical college in two years. He'd been constrained to Witherston and Strutter's for seventeen years and yearned to experience other avenues to life. He was torn. How to do so without hurting his parents, particularly his mother?

"Dad, are you okay with me not being a pharmacist?"

"Yes, son. Why? What's up? Thought we'd agreed you'd go for another career."

"Well, I did too, but Mother hasn't bought into it. She hit on the issue again yesterday . . . playing the family tradition song . . . suggesting how the family would be hurt. Hinting I'd be disrespectful. How am I gonna win her over?"

"I'm not sure that you can. It's best not to look at this as a win-lose game. I suspect that the underlying alarm is your leaving home and Witherston. You have been her pride, joy, and happiness for the last seventeen years, and she probably wants the same for the years ahead. Not that I wouldn't like to have you here also, but if it's not your calling then I'm afraid none of us would be really happy."

"Tell me, Dad, how do I get her to accept my studying architectural landscaping. Who knows, maybe we'll start a new Strutter business. Would that be so bad?"

"Best not to promise that before you know that Witherston is where you'll end up. Why not think of it this way, son . . . bring your mother along to your interests. After all, flowers and gardening have been a love for both of you. Maybe you can get, or school can help you get, the type of studies you'd have to take. Maybe botany. Design. Grasses, or whatever. Talk it over with Mom. Plan it out. Once she gets excited about the possibilities, she'll let go of the pharmaceutical idea. Either Minnesota or Iowa State would suit your degree, neither of them being too far from Witherston. We'll plan to visit both schools."

"But, Dad, she'll start planning a landscaping job for me here. Maybe, I'll want to go to another city."

"Whoa, son, step by step. First wean her from the pharmacy to another line of business. *Where* that happens is the next step. You don't know where that might be. Who knows it could be here, in the cities, or wherever. Don't fight her Jon; bring her with you in your interests. And you know I support you in what you want to do. Ha! Providing it's not off the wall."

"What would that look like, Dad?"

"Anything that keeps you from a college education." John punched his son's arm and then turned to a more serious tone. "It's time to begin planning your trips to Minneapolis and Ames . . . and it's time we include this in more of our dinner conversation. Let's start tonight; our first step to helping you set your college plans and major. The more we discuss and plan, the easier it will be for Mom to accept. Remember, Jon, she is very attached to you . . . you are the love of her life."

"Ha! That's what she says of you." Jon punched his dad's arm, "Dad, you are the great guy. Thanks. Will you wait for me while I sprint around the lake? Clock me," he yelled over his shoulder.

John would miss his son in the drugstore. He had to secretly admit that he'd looked forward to having a similar close working experience such as he had with his dad. Jon had work at one or another Strutter store during high school, as did most of his cousins, working up from being a stocker to cashier. Jon caught on to inventory control quickly and, during this summer, had managed the ordering and invoicing processes. He'd enjoyed Jon's time in the store during his high-school years and was proud of how he took charge naturally, but he suspected that Jon was looking beyond Witherston for a life.

John watched his son's jogging stride as he came around the last bend in the lake trail. How could he help Emily let go, to give Jon his full independence to decide his future, his fate, his own experiences? *Keep talking the issue. Assure her that Jon needs his own life. It's not a denial of the family. We've all been too close, he's given us too many good memories. She needed more children, her forever lament.* Jon's absence during the upcoming college years means also the absence of his friends to fill the house. *She'll be lonely. Fill the hours with children; maybe a project she could spearhead, organize and direct. Maybe a city start-up . . . better yet, a Strutter project -- day-care or an after-school program for creativity. Maybe apply the junior achievement concept for students to develop fundraising projects or youth groups beautifying the city streets. They could grow the flowers and other plants from seeds - plan spring planting days. Yes, yes, I'm on to something here. This time I'll be the manipulator. Ha! I've had a good model.*

As his son came to a stop, John pointed to his watch. "Timing was 15 minutes, 13 seconds. Two seconds slower than last time."

"Gee Dad," Jon panted, "you ought to jog. Makes the bod feel so alive." He dropped to the bench they shared. "Wish Shorts was still here, He always was a yard ahead of me, no matter what my timing. He held his tail as high as his head. Such a show off."

## 10

Ken and Jon were headed towards Mankato with their cross-country skis mounted on the rack top of Ken's Jeep. It was a clear, bright sunny February day without the typical Minnesota winds. Temperatures promised to be in the twenties and the snow on the golf course would be the right depth and consistency for easy gliding. Emily had packed sandwiches (salami instead of chicken salad), chocolate brownies with walnuts (Ken's favorite), and a thermos of milk. It was calm and sunny, a perfect day to eat at the picnic tables that the groundskeeper kept on the course for winter skiers.

"This may be our last cross-country, old buddy. I plan to be downhill skiing in California next winter. Up in the Sierra's or Tahoe. I wish you'd go to California with me." Ken said looking over at Jon.

"You mean drive out with you?"

"No, dumbbell. To live. You could study horticulture there just as well. Your mother isn't still hung up on pharmacy, is she?"

"No, I can't and no she isn't. I doubt that I could expect another concession from her – like being five states away. It's hard to get parents to understand, and Dad says it works best if I take one change at a time. Your parents had three kids, which makes a difference. I'm the only one and Mom's life stills revolves around me."

"Yeah, that's pretty plain to see. We've got to have our freedom though. I want to have the say for my life. Parents seem not to understand but bet they wanted the same."

"Weren't your folks against California?"

"Yes and no. I need the art schooling and a community that

supports me."

"What do you mean?" Jon hesitated before asking, "It's more than art, isn't it?"

"Jon, you know I need to find guys similar to me. I figure I need to be far from family for that. Mom and Dad suspect but aren't ready to accept."

"Do they think I'm one too?"

"One what Jon? Say it."

"I can't. I don't know that it's true."

"Come to California with me and find out. We have so many eyes on us in this town with no known homosexuals."

"If I can't explain horticultural over pharmacy, how the heck do you think I can explain guys over girls. You've got to be kidding!"

"We could find out ourselves."

"No, I can't."

"You haven't had sex with Gretchen or any other gal have you?"

"No, not yet."

"God, Jon, you're in as tough a spot as I am. All tied up in a Midwestern town, parents controlling your life, and Catholic authority oozing through your veins."

"Let's drop it. Okay?" Jon said with an edge.

"Okay, old buddy." A few seconds later, Ken softened his tone, "You are my best friend Jon. These last years would have been harder if you hadn't been there."

"I know. I like you too."

"Well, thanks. You can always change your mind. California and me."

Jon grinned and shook his head.


## 11

March 1981: Jon's senior year, his national test scores were high, he was accepted at the University of Minnesota, owned a '74

Chevy Impala, and had gained his mother's reluctant acceptance of his plans for architectural landscaping. He knew she still held an image of her son returning to his hometown to start a business. For now, Jon looked forward to April first, his nineteenth birthday, and planned a bigger party for it than for graduation.

Gretchen, Jon, and Emily had spent the morning decorating the downstairs and removing the rugs for dancing. Gretchen helped with food preparation while Jon shopped for drinks. The three of them ended with Emily's famous chicken salad sandwiches for lunch, followed by broken chocolate chip cookies that had not baked perfectly.

"What's with the cookies, Mom? Where's my cake?"

"Being decorated elsewhere. You'll see it when you blow out the candles. Look, I think we are ready for tonight. I'll clean up here; why don't you two go off for that walk you mentioned earlier?"

Emily watched them head for the lake. *Imagine nineteen. How fast it goes. It's hard to see him grow up. I wonder if she thinks of him on his day. Does she have regrets? Is she lonely? I couldn't have shared him with her. The next four years will be lonely with him gone. I've got to keep his interest in coming back here to work.*

Jon and Gretchen kicked up the dead leaves along the wooded path, talking about the coming year. "Jon, it will be lonely next year, being left behind to finish my last year without you. I'll miss your personal tutoring for my science class."

"Time goes fast in that last year. You'll be picking your college and enjoying the senior fun times."

"I'll be dating someone else for the games, prom, senior day. Won't that bother you? I hope-a, hope-a."

"Did it bother me when you went out with Larry this summer? No. Or Greg last year? Even Matt asked you out. High school should be fun and be shared with more than one person. We've been good friends since you moved here and I know I'll miss our friendship. But, I'll see you over the holidays."

"Big deal for a girl to hear! Friendship! I'd like to be your steady. You haven't gone with anyone else . . .Well, maybe a couple of dates that Matt talked you into. Everyone looks on us as a steady couple. Why can't we play it that way?"

"Oh, Gretchen, not again," Jon moaned. "We are steady, we go to the parties together, we double-date with Matt."

As Jon hesitated to find another example, Gretchen cut in. "No Jon. I want more than holding hands and a peck on the cheek or a once-in-a-while romantic kiss."

"I kiss you every time I take you home," Jon protested.

"And, yeah, that's about the only time. Other couples kiss and even make our a little. Not us."

"I guess I'm not the hot, romantic type. And, I'd have to tell Father in the confessional." John tried to beg off.

"I'll bet not everyone confesses their sexual fun, and those that do . . . what? You suppose they'd have to say an extra rosary. Doesn't seem like a big deal."

"Come on, Gretch, our group has had a lot of fun times . . . but guess you have to say I'm an exception."

"And, somewhat of a loner." After a few more steps, Gretchen asked cautiously. "Jon, are you one of them? Is that the group you want?"

"One of what?"

"Well, you know . . . you must know that a lot of kids think Ken is one of them. And, you spend a lot of time with him."

Jon stopped and pulled Gretchen around to face him. "What are you saying? What's being said about Ken?"

"Oh come on, Jon, he's different. Kids call him 'Kennie' behind his back. He seldom dates . . . tries to be friends with all the girls . . . it's plain to see he prefers your company or Mick's . . . he's taken to art, school plays . . . and just isn't like other guys."

"So? What's bad about art?" Jon said defensively.

"Jon, let's drop it. Sorry that I brought the subject up. If we continue on, we'll ruin your party. Forget I said anything." They resumed walking and Gretchen said lightly, "Think I'll jog home. See you tonight . . . It'll be a great party." She turned and waved as she began running.

"So, do they call me 'Jonnie'?" he yelled at her.

Jon, head down, walked back to the bench by the lake. *It is confusing, not being sure who I am. I like Gretchen, but not all girls. I like being with Ken, but not all boys. I'm still a virgin . . . that's confusing. I get off with my sexual fantasies – sometimes females bodies, sometimes male bodies. Which am I? Not something I can ask my dad. First subject we can't come to the lake to discuss. Maybe it's time to have sex with a girl and forget about confession. When I get to college.*

## 12

Jon opened the screen door to the back porch where his parents sat reading the *Sunday Star Tribune* delivered every week from Minneapolis. They looked up as he rested his body against the porch railing.

"Want the funnies?" His mother held out the colored sheets. "The sports page?" asked his father. Jon took them both and lifted his backside up onto the railing.

"You have a pensive look," his mother noted, "as if you are about to ask a favor. No? Then what's up?" She added as Jon shook his head,

When Jon started with "Mom . . . Dad . . ." his father lowered the paper and looked over his glasses and his mother titled her head to look straight into Jon's face. He heard them both say "Yes?" in unison.

It took all of Jon's courage, although he didn't feel brave, to say, "Mom . . . Dad. I want to know my birth parents."

John folded the paper into his lap and looked over at Emily whose face turned ashen and stiff. John knew what he had heard was no casual comment. "Well, this takes us as a surprise, but I suspect that you've been wondering for some time. What is it you want to know, son?"

*How can I help them understand I want to connect with my root*

*parents – to fill in all parts of me – to know who I am?* "I want to know who they are. What do they look like? What do they do now? What did they grow up to be?"

"Jon Francis," his mother broke in, "that's not possible." Her voice stern, tight from holding back emotions.

"Wanting to know birth parents is not an uncommon wish of adopted children. But why is this important right now?" his father asked, wanting to ease away from any burst of harsh words from Emily.

*How do I help them feel what I feel? Incomplete – a portion of me that has no images, no history. Did he like boys and girls?* "I know about you, the wonderful people you are, the home we live in. You are my real parents, now and forever. But, two other people made me. It's like carrying a mystery around inside, and I want to solve it."

"Why now?" Emily asked, her voice cold and hard as ice.

"Mom, I'm nineteen, an adult. I want to feel like a whole person."

"So, we haven't done that for you? What didn't I do to make you feel 'not whole'? Tell me. I want to know."

"Mom," Jon moaned.

"Em, Em." John's voice held a warning.

"Go on, tell us." Emily snapped.

"Mom, you didn't do anything wrong. I have no emotional hole to fill. You and Dad have given me a perfect life, home, family. There's no neglect, no hurts, or anything like that. It's just that if I know all my parents, I know my complete story. You know stuff comes from genes – heredity - ancestors."

John could hear that his son had thought about this request. He could tell that he must have rehearsed his words, his thoughts, his rationale.

"Then it's just curiosity? Who suggested this?" Emily grilled.

"Sure I'm curious, and no one is behind me. I can live without knowing if I have to. But, how much better to take away the mystery? I don't want to always wonder."

"What do you wonder about?" Emily said. "We never told you any stories about the young boy and girl, because we never had the facts, except for their ages. There are no records, no trail to follow . . . when we took you home from the hospital, the files were closed. And, forever, let me add."

*Now's not the time to tell her I've done research at the Library. We could approach the agency. Maybe they are looking for me.*

"What would you do son, if you knew where they were?" asked his father.

"See them — talk with them — find out what they do." He knew better than to say, 'are there other children?'.

"No, Jon. That's not to be. I'm not interested in extending our family. We are a happy family, a good family. I won't be subject to disruption of our happiness. She may not to be interested, either." Emily paused before adding, "You show no evidence of health issues. So you have blue eyes and write left-handed. What else is there to know about ancestors?"

Jon shrugged his shoulders, "I guess I just wanted to know." He moved to the porch steps, "I think I'll jog around the lake."

As he disappeared around the corner, Emily said, "I don't want to discuss it. I will not agree to a search."


## Emily

*After all this time, I felt I was safe. His words struck like a blast. I went dead — frozen like an iceberg. Why? Why now? Something — what could it be — triggered this. He'll never tell me . . . maybe his father . . . not me. Maybe if there'd been more children . . . brothers and sisters. We should have adopted those older children . . . he wouldn't have been alone. Was I selfish to hold out for babies? If so, I'm being punished for that selfishness. John told me I'd focus too much on the boy if there weren't others. So, what was wrong loving just one? His life has been full, happy, without hurts, pain. It's going to be lonely without him in the house. I want him home again . . . wonder if he doesn't return to Witherston? Yes, I should have filled my house with children. Oh, Jon don't open the door . . . I don't want to know them now. She gave you up for good reasons . . . leave it at that. Let's keep our happiness. God, don't take this from me too.*


## Jon

*Scrap that idea. I knew Mom couldn't do it. Took Dad by surprise . . . maybe I played this wrong . . . should have talked with him first. Wish I could explain it to them. I'm not sure I want a relationship – Mom's thinking that I do. I just want to see them, hear them. I have this need to know them . . . without revealing myself. Could I hold my tongue and not give me away? Like Mom says, maybe she wouldn't want to know me – it's too late – too upsetting.*

*Shit, I can't even describe to myself what I want to know . . . is the big question, my sexuality? Pretty dumb to think I could find that out just by seeing them. No, it's more than that . . . I want a picture in mind what that girl and boy looked like . . . even a photo would help. Mom is my mom, no replacement for her, and I really hurt her today. It's a family Mom wants, more children. I'll date a lot of girls in college . . . find one I can love. And Mom will have grandchildren. I'll visit the agency too . . . when I'm twenty-one . . . maybe I can get something on my own. I want to know what they look like – who they are.*


## John

*And I have the information sitting in a bank. Em would hate me – never forgive me. Jon would be excited. Not surprised his wanting to know – surprised he hasn't mentioned before. He likes his life to be neat, tidy, in order . . . not unlike us. I have a sense that there is something specific behind his asking . . . maybe we should have more one-on-one's. We haven't sat on the lake bench for a while . . . if we go too soon, Emily will suspect us. Dear, dear Em. I should have pressured for more adoptions . . . . she could have spread her love . . . with more family.*

*Maybe it's time I go see . . . Brandeis is just across into Illinois. How could I drive there without arousing suspicion? Maybe ask Sam for a more detailed background check. Maybe. And I need to know where Jon is on this – how important is it, and why? It'd be risky to let him know her whereabouts.*

<h1 style="text-align:center">13</h1>

"Sam Ketchell speaking."

"Hi, Sam. John Strutter here. Got a minute?"

"You bet. How's everything going? I haven't anything new on your couple in Brandeis."

"Well, that's what I am calling about. I want more personal information, like their credit standing, reputation in their business, photos of them, their house, business."

"Hey, what's up?"

John explained. "Well, I often wondered if my son would want to know of his birth parents. He does. He's asked. Not sure, yet, how I'm going to play this out with him. Of course, you realize, that only you and I know what we know. In any case, Jon wants to see them – not so much to build a relationship, he says, rather a need to know what they look like, what they do, where they live. Says he needs to know about the 'rest of him'. Seems natural to me but not to his mother."

"So, John, what do you have in mind?" Sam quizzed. "A personal visit to Brandies?"

"My preference would be to personally take the trip, but can't determine how to do that without arousing suspicions here at home. That's the last thing I want. Could you go?"

"I'm pretty well tied up with two rather involved cases right now. What precisely do you want to know?"

"Just what I told you, a picture of what their lives are like."

"Since you want answers right now, I could send a reliable young man who works for me. He's good. Low key. He's come through on several delicate assignments for me. I trust him and think you can too."

"Yes, well, if that is the only way it can be done. Wonder if we wait a couple of months? Jon isn't insisting right now."

"Wouldn't help me that much. I can vouch for Curt – not too worry."

"Okay Sam, my trust hasn't been pinged yet in eighteen years."

"Yeah, I'm eighteen years older too, into my sixties."

"Don't quit now Sam, you're too good."

"Well said Mr. Strutter. I admire your fine judgment."

The following month when John was in the cities, he visited the bank and saw and read the results of Curt's visit.

Nora and Ben Allen  --  1081 Highland Vista Drive  -- Brandeis, Illinois

Ben is 36 years old. Nora is 34. No children.

The home is a rambling one story stone-wood house on the Highland golf course in Highland Heights, a closed community. Market value is $325,000. Members of the country club; Ben is on the Board. He plays golf regularly; she does tennis. (Photos enclosed of house, country club, and personal pictures from the monthly newsletter.)

Allen Insurance Agency, started by Ben's uncle is very successful. Office is in historic brick house owned by the Agency. Second floor offices are given to Steffen Financial, a tax and bookkeeping service owned by Eric Steffen, CPA. A staff of twelve. Clients as far away as Quad Cities and Chicago. Ben is the key out-front man. Stellar credit rating, no debt except for small operating loan with local bank. Could not ascertain salary numbers. (Photos of business front enclosed.)

Nora is owner of an upscale print and frame shop in downtown Brandeis. Outstanding loan of $75,000 with local bank. Business now three years old; staff of two; Nora is active manager. Nora owns two horses stabled at Highland Heights stables. (Photos of business and horses enclosed.) Nora is a member of Chamber of Commerce and well acquainted with the town people

Credit rating at high range of scale. No mortgage. No outstanding balance over sixty days with credit cards. Two cars (presumed paid). Ben drives a late model BMW (presumed owned by agency); Nora drives a two-year old Volvo station wagon. They have a ski home in Crested Butte, Colorado and a time-share condo in Kauai.

Nora is of slight built: maybe 5'4", trim and slim (would guess no more than 105 lbs.), brown hair, blue eyes. (As witnessed in the store, photo enclosed – unable to get up close shot.)

Ben is sturdy, muscled body (as one that visits a gym regularly), six foot at least, dark hair and eyes. Observed him in coffee shop talking with two other men. Laughs a lot, everyone seems to know him, stopping at his table and talking with more than a hello.

Waitress indicated that everyone knows Ben Allen, "best thing Brandies has going for it."(Photo enclosed, arrow points to Ben.)

John looked again and again at the photos. He felt an uneasiness and wondered if he might someday regret his request of Sam Ketchell.

## 14

"Emily, before Jon heads off to college, I'd like to know if he's still determined to know his birth parents." It had been several months since that Sunday morning conversation on the back porch. The subject seemed taboo among the three of them.

"No!' was Emily's firm reply.

"Don't you want to know what he is feeling, thinking . . ."

"No!!" Emily stopped his words in a higher harsh voice.

"It's better to talk, to know, then to leave him isolated in his own thoughts." John tried to make an artful argument.

Emily turned on him sharply, "Then you do it. You be the good father. But I'll never consent to a search. Why must our family life be violated? They are strangers." And then Emily pleaded, "Please John don't let this happen."

John placed his argument. "Em, these are hard stands you

143

take. We are Jon's mother and father. We've been there during all of his formative years . . . the most important ones -- baby, young boy, teenage. Jon has been well loved, has had perfect attention and care. Nothing can replace our being his parents. There can be no other home but this home."

"I don't want to test any of that. I can't lose Jon or I have nothing left." Emily's voice dropped to a whisper.

"Emily that is quite a sad thing to say. What are you afraid of? Lose everything? What do you mean?" Emily shook her head, saying nothing. "Talk to me, Emily."

"All my life, things are taken from me. My mother just when I needed her. Three babies, wanted and longed for. Then another adoption canceled with a last minute change of mind. My religion reduced to just formalities by a sinful priest." Emily rubbed her forehead, "And you question why I'd want to jeopardize my only son."

"I've realized that Father Stern turned you against the church. Yes, yes, I know that you still attend out of respect for the family, but your heart . . . your belief is not there. You've become cynical, expecting the worse. Faith is more than a church."

"Oh, how easy and forgiving you are. John. You who preach and talk high principles and then can overlook the black marks, as if they don't matter. Such a façade, dishonest really."

"No, I didn't turn away from St. Anne's. It is a community of people who trust each other and come together to join in prayer. A church is of people who care about other people, religion brings those people together under one roof, but God is more than a church or a religion. You may have lost faith in church but don't lose faith in God, Emily. Without that you lose trust in yourself and others."

"Well if God is not religion, then I don't need to go to church just to keep the family in good stead. I can find God any place, in the garden, on a walk, when I go to sleep, when I wake up."

"You are angry, aren't you Emily? With me? With God? Is that what eats away at you?"

Emily put her head in her hands crying, "I don't like being afraid."

John enclosed her in his arms, quietly – silently. When the sobbing eased, he said, "Let me help you Emily. Your pain is hard to live with, and I've missed your humming." With that, he tightened his embrace and kissed the top of her head.

## 15

It was the end of a hot August day as father and son walked towards the lake. In a couple of weeks, John and Emily would be moving Jon into a dorm on the Minnesota campus. They would be driving two cars packed with clothes, books, bedding, and enough home-made goodies to last a couple of weeks.

"Well son, a new chapter about to begin. Excited? Nervous?"

"Oh, some of both, Dad. Learning my way around campus and getting use to a roommate is the first hurdle. I've never had to share a room and bath before, except with Shorts. I hope he won't be some jerk."

"You're bound to meet a few of those along the way, let's hope it's not the first room mate. Too bad Matt or Ken didn't choose Minnesota." A few steps later, his father added, "Remember Jon to call your mother often and I do mean *quite often* the first weeks and months. She'll be wanting to know you're okay, what your doing, eating – you know those things mothers worry about."

"I will, Dad. I'm going to miss both of you. I'll be popping in for weekends. It's good I'm only just a few hours away. And we can see each other when you come to the city for your meetings."

When they came around the final curve of the lake, John said, "Let's sit here awhile. I want to re-visit a subject with you."

"Okay, what's the lecture about now, Dad?"

"More of an interest than a lecture, son. I wanted to know how you were feeling about the wish to know your birth parents. Our discussion on the back porch a couple of months ago shut down too quickly. I felt we hadn't closed it off properly. Did we?" He asked as he turned toward his son.

"I know mom was upset, and I should have talked with you first. She made a bigger deal out of it than I thought would happen. It doesn't seem strange to me. I wasn't looking to getting a whole family relationship going. I just want to know who they are. Can't you understand that?"

"Yes, Jon, I can understand that curiosity would be there in an adopted child. Making that happen easily is not a viable possibility, what with the laws being as they are. And your mother is very protective of you and our family."

"I know Dad. I don't want to hurt her, and I guess I'll never make her understand what I want. It's not like I want us all to be buddy, buddy friends. It's just that a part of me seems to be a mystery."

"What if you disliked what you found? What if they aren't who you want them to be? You can't be free of having expectations and you could be very disappointed."

"Yeah, but the mystery would be gone."

"Son, explain what you mean when you say you want to see them. You want one look? Do you want to talk with them? Do you want them to know who you are? What are your expectations?" John waited for an answer, which didn't come immediately.

"Look Dad, this is not a big deal. I don't think I'd want them to know who I am – to begin a friendship or anything. I just want a look-see. I don't want to be curious anymore. God – oh, I'm sorry Dad – I'm happy being with you and Mom . . . can't imagine being with anyone else . . . nor not being with you here in our home. I'm not out to mess that up for Christ sake – of, sorry again Dad. Let's just forget it. Maybe some day I can find where they live on my own and trust me, I won't let Mom know. I love her and her perfect life. Don't you?"

"Okay son, I think I understand what you're after. It's not big deal but important in it's own way. Am I right?"

"Right Dad. Don't worry about it, but thanks for asking."

When they got back to the house, Emily was in tears and packing bags. Her father, Carl, had just had a heart attack and she wanted to get home. It was a sad, tearful drive to Cross Center and even sadder when her father died the next day. John noticed Emily's early tearfulness changed to a repression of emotions by the end of the day; she was passive, wrapped in a silent cocoon. Her responses came in cold single words. He realized she must be feeling the pain of yet another loss – a precious item taken from her life, right before her son was leaving home for college. For the first time during their married life, John felt he had lost touch with his wife – she seemed to be beyond his reach.

Jon stayed off to the side and let his mind drift back on his many times with Grandpa Carl: their walks in the woods, the overnight camp-outs. He thought about the workshop where they'd built bird houses, a house for Shorts, his desk in Dad's office, book cases for his room, and all the Christmas ornaments. He remembered Grandpa's love of forest animals and the feel of wood in his hands. Jon knew he'd learned the beauty of both along with patience under Grandpa's teaching. There was now a void that wouldn't be filled, and his sense of family strengthened. He realized, for the first time, that death gave a person's life more meaning.

## 16

The high school friends had one last summer party in Stutter's back yard. Boys and girls ambled in and out, and a few parents dropped by. Everyone had left by ten o'clock and Jon and Ken said their good-byes under the oak tree. Jon would be heading for Minneapolis on Friday and Ken was headed for California the following Wednesday.

"How we goin' keep in touch?" asked Ken.

"I'll get your address from your mom. You can always write to my home address. Mom can send it on to me or I'll be home again at the end of October."

"Wish you were coming with me. A little scary all by myself,"

Ken whispered.

"Think your jalopy will make it to California?"

"Oh yeah. Dad and I had it all worked over and got new tires. You make it sound like an old piece of junk. It's only three years old, dodo."

"I thought your Dad might drive out with you."

"Well, because this is my decision, I think they are going to let me sweat it out by myself. They did give me a gas card and $500 to help get me started. If I can find an apartment to share with others and any kind of job the first week, I'll be okay. I don't have to start art school right away . . . I want to settle in first."

"I hope it all comes out the way you want it, Ken. I feel like you are walking into a new world. California lives a lot different than we do here, and it's like a long way away. Let me know when your pictures are shown in a gallery. I bet you're playing that in your mind already, eh?"

"When I show in a gallery, you have to fly out. I'll want to show off big time."

They sat silent for a moment, until Ken reached out his hand and put it over Jon's. "You've been my very best friend, Jon. I know that you stood up for me when others made fun of 'Kennie' and I love you for that. If I could have my thoughts come true, you'd be going with me."

"I know, but I'm not ready to leave this kind of life yet, if ever. Guess you have more courage than I have."

"You'll always be my best friend," Ken said. He paused and than added quietly, "My first love."

JON

# CHAPTER ONE

# *Freshman Year, University of Minnesota*

### 1

MOM, DAD, AND I were catching our breath after bringing up the second load to my dorm room on third floor when my six-foot roommate and his father brought in their first boxes. "I'm Jay," the stocky guy with red hair said. "And, this is my father Glen Huxley." He pointed to the logo on his T-shirt. "Alexander, Minnesota. Where you from?"

"Witherston, just south of The Cities. This is my father and mother, John and Emily Strutter, and I'm Jon – J o n."

We eyed the room, bunk beds stood against the far wall, individual desks on each side of a lone window. There were a miniature refrigerator and microwave by the doorway and a large closet with defined space for two. Dad flipped a coin for choice of the bottom bunk. Jay called tails and lost the lower level for the first semester although he insisted he liked the top bunk. On the second flip of the coin - tails again - Jay took the left side of the room and I the right side. My beat-up red beanbag, my favorite spot for studying, fit scrunched into the corner by my desk. Mom thought it needed a reading lamp and said we'd find one after lunch.

I felt squashed with my five-by-five space. I'd never had to share before. I'm confined to a cage with a magpie for company. Jay's a talker; usually nothing of importance, just a monologue on guys, classes, girls, food, sports, brother, sisters, cars and more girls – unending. He'll never know me, I thought; he can't shut up long enough to listen. During the night I could hear him muttering, sometimes yelling out loud or laughing. A hard poke into the underside of his mattress and my words, "Jay, stop it" was usually enough.

I sought out quiet spots to study – open lounges on each floor of the dorm, the library, student union, and I'm still looking. Other than the chatter, Jay honors our imaginary boundaries and tends to be orderly; he doesn't crowd into my space. At first I longed for my spacious room at home, Dad's everyday interest, and Mom's meals. But the dorm room became only a place to dress and sleep, as I became acquainted with the rest of the university.

I slipped into campus life easily, a community of like ages intent on getting across campus to classes. I may take up Dad's offer of a bike. Getting used to large class size and different teaching styles was a bit of a challenge, and so it seemed a good choice to get all the prerequisites done the first year. It suited me that Jay and I ended up having no common classes.

I now saw the merit in my high school courses: Math, Social and Natural Sciences, English Comp and Literature. As I registered for a BA in Landscape Architecture, I knew I would need more math and earth science classes, and I looked forward to starting graphics and drawing next year.

Mom called several times a week, "just to hear your voice" she'd say, and I told her the feeling was mutual. How I've bristled in the past at her over-attention; but I know that it's because she has a real, genuine interest in me –'her only precious boy'. Matt used to tease me that I'd never get away from my mother hen, but I'm not sure that I want to go too far. It's nice to be special, maybe even perfect, in someone's eyes. *Ah Mom! What a mother you are!"*

On her last call after all the questions of how I was, how was school, did I go to church, did I miss her, she reported, "Gretchen was seen with Rob Stevens – a date I suppose."

"Probably. Look Mom, that's okay. I'm sort of surprised though, Rob and Gretchen don't seem date material."

"Jon, she's probably lonesome. Why not call her. Can't you urge her to wait?"

"For what Mom?"

"You."

"Mom, I can't do that. She has a senior year to enjoy. I urged her to do that. I'm in school for four years and she will be too. Besides Mom, you don't even know if it was a date."

"They came out of the movie house together."

"They could have had single tickets, you know. Let it be Mom. Gretchen and I are free to do what we want."

"Have you met a girl?"

"Yeah, lots of them."

"Oh, Jon, be serious. Have you gone out on a date yet?"

"No, Mom, and I promise you'll be the first to know. Hey, where's my box of chocolate chip cookies?"

"On the way, you should have them tomorrow. Hope they won't be in pieces. You're still coming home for Halloween weekend, aren't you? Do you want a party?"

"With who? All the crowd's gone."

"Not Gretchen."

"Okay, you have the last word. Gotta go. Say hi to Dad and Grandpa. I miss them. And, you too."

## 2

Into my second month I made my first visit to the student hangouts in Dinkytown; ordered a beer and watched the crowd rather than mixing. On the second beer, I joined in with the lively cheers – led by a boisterous cheer leader -- for the Big Ten game tomorrow with Illinois. The students were in high spirits. Was it the game or the beer?

I hesitated about sharing my time on a sport, but couldn't resist trying out for the swim team and saw more good swimmers than I'd expected. I qualified for the third team, and one of the coaches said he thought I could make a higher team with workouts. I wondered if swimmers were beer drinkers.

I like this independence and freedom and at the same time, I miss home. I thought of Matt, who went to South Dakota on a football scholarship, and wondered how Ken was making out in California.

## 3

"Hey, Jon." First the voice and then Jay appeared at the door. "Some of the guys are going to shoot pool. Come join us."

"I've never played."

"Well, good time to start. I'll be your partner."

"Are you good?"

"Not bad. Bring your wallet, we put a dollar on the table."

"Each game?" I asked and he said, "Yep." I grabbed my money and hurried after him. There was time for minimal instructions and any balls I put in the pocket was like, by accident. We lost three games.

Jay shrugged, "You've got potential but it'll take a lot of practice."

"I'm a great chess player," I told him.

"Well, this is more fun than staring at a board. You gotta stick with the action, pal."

## 4

Dad and Mom had not intended that I take on a job my first couple of years, but a posting on the bulletin board caught my interest. The work was in the greenhouse, which was located in the agriculture fields about five miles off campus. I drove over that afternoon and easily found the superintendent's office, two desks, one person.

"Hi, I'm Jon Strutter. I'm looking for Mr. Deaver who needs helpers for his greenhouse." I held out my application.

"Glad to meet you Jon, and you've found the right person. I'm Walt Deaver." He extended his hand across the desk. "Yes I'm hoping to hire nine students, and you're the sixth one today. Tell me, have you had any experience in growing things?"

"Yeah, since I was four years old -- flowerbeds in our yard and vegetables at my grandfather's. I like working in the soil and plan to study landscape design. When would you need me? I'm on the swim team and practice is every morning."

"Well we can usually work around student schedules. I like to have three work teams with three students on a team. That way I can get help each day and have back-ups. You could maybe have eight to sixteen hours a week. At five dollars an hour."

I thought, *enough to keep me in pool money.* "When can I start? I do have a car."

Mr. Deaver nodded. "Good. There's also good bus service from the dorms to the agriculture fields." He searched in a file for a bus schedule. "It could save you gas money." He passed the schedule on to me and started to scan my application. "Well, I like what I see here. Can you meet with all the team members this Saturday? Say two o'clock at greenhouse A. If you have time, we can walk over there now."

The job worked out well. I did four hours Tuesday and Wednesday and six hours on Saturday -- off every other weekend. Seventy dollars a week spending money eased my discomfort about Dad having to carry the full load. Although, I knew he'd be watching my grades.

The work in the greenhouse was nothing I hadn't done a hundred times: plant seeds, pot plants, tend a compost pile, water, and thin out dense foliage. The new items were the orchids; Mr. Deaver said we'd have to learn tender care before he'd let us loose on those beauties. I studied the books he offered and soon he let me work by his side.

# 5

"Hey, Jon." The voice and Jay came busting through the door at the same time. "Did you hear about the ruckus on first floor?"

"No, guess you know something I don't."

"Yeah, one of the guys asked for a new roommate. Claims his roomie's a homo. What do you think about that? Bet it's that guy who wears the ponytail and sandals. Wonder what they'll do with him? Find him another homo." Jay laughed.

"Maybe they can," I replied.

"Not in our dorm, I hope," Jay said in an ugly tone. "Can you imagine a guy fucking another guy? Perverts! Bet there's jokes about giving a helping hand or 'Look mom, I can do it with one hand'."

It was an awkward moment. "Have you ever known a homosexual?" I asked.

"No, and I ain't looking for one either." Jay shot back. "Come on, let's go shoot pool."

"Count me out. I have a test to study for." As Jay went off, my thoughts turned to Ken. How was he doing, trying to find a safe place to live? I wondered how much ugliness he had to put up with.

*How easy to become the target of jeers and ridicule . . . there are lots of Jays out there. I'd best be careful where, or if, I show myself with Rich.*

Rich was on the swim team and damn good; he out-paced me in freestyle. He also had a good-looking body -- narrow hips, tight buttocks widening out to sculptured chest and shoulders. He always managed to be in the lane next to me, and I sensed it was not rivalry or being competitive. This proved true as I listened to his banter during showers. From the stall next to mine, he'd praise my swim stroke, suggest we meet at the gym for work outs, asked who was my roommate, and finally the big question: "Do you date anyone special?" It was all done in a low-key manner, not brash or rude. But, I read his cues and found myself curious about how he'd earmarked me.


# 6

Through Jay, I got hooked up with a group of dorm students in building a Homecoming float that would represent the non-fraternity and sorority students. The committee chose a theme of music and found enough musicians in the dorms to make a swinging quartet. We planned a backdrop for the band, a large M made of yellow mums. The rest of the space on the flat bed would be for dancing. I volunteered with three others, Lori, Tim, and Becka, to make the backdrop. Lori and I worked together on the parade float, attended the game and celebrated a ten-point win over Purdue.

Lori abounded in energy and ideas. She was gutsy as she petitioned local stores for wire mesh, twine and vials. Mr. Deaver helped us get the purple and gold mums we needed for the backdrop. We were putting the last flowers on the float two hours before parade time, and Lori insisted she be one of the dancers and I her partner. How easy and fun it was to get caught up in the enthusiasm and craziness of football weekends!

Lori kept conversation going with quips, jokes, and laughter. She was cute and pert, and she knew it. Her dancing included a lot of body touching, and she was not bashful in draping an arm over my shoulder and blowing kisses close to my face. She told me, "Loosen up. It's okay to touch me, even hold me and kiss me." With the hype of music, beer, and crowds I did more necking than I'd ever done before. Lori pushed for all the way, but I said, "I'm not ready."

"What do you mean not ready?" she teased. "I've got a condom." Quite a come-on that went nowhere. I never saw Lori again after Homecoming so I never found out how serious she was. Just as well, she was more female than I could handle. Matt would've kicked my butt all the way home for missing a hot treat like that.

## 7

The first stage of a snowstorm was hitting The Cities as I left for the December holidays and the long semester break. Home sounded good. Dad said the hardware store needed extra clerks for Christmas shoppers and also asked me to help with year-end inventory at the drugstore the first week of January. Mom told me to save time to do decorations for a family get-together between Christmas and New Year's. She was planning a combined celebration of holidays and Dad's birthday on the 29th. The snow was heavy as I drove into Witherston, around the lake and to our driveway. And, there was Mom waiting for me at the living room window. She popped out of the front door.

"Oh, Jon, I'm glad you made it safely. I've been listening to the weather news since noon. Let's get your stuff out of the car. I'll bet you've got a bag of laundry."

"Mom, the walk is slick. You stay inside; I'll bring all the stuff to the porch first. When's Dad coming home?"

"It'll be late. He's staying 'til closing tonight. Grandpa's eager to see you and wanted to come over for dinner. And if he does, he'd better spend the night. Maybe you should go get him? I'll give him a call. Give me a hug, you precious boy."

She reached for the smaller and lighter items. "I'll take the heavy ones, Mom. You ought to get inside or get a coat on."

By the time Dad got home, the snow had fallen in inches and continued, making us snowbound until noon the next day. With shovel in hand, I joined the neighbors clearing sidewalks and driveways, and PaPo spread the sand. Mom suggested sculpturing a snowman for the front yard, and she found a bouquet of vinyl poinsettias in the Christmas decorations to put in its hand. It was a good start to a full, happy, and homey holiday.

**8**

"Mom, I'm going over to see Ken's mother. She was in the store yesterday and asked me to drop by. I really thought I'd see Ken over the holidays."

"They were hoping also, and were disappointed, specially his sisters. Glad you're not that far away. It would be hard for me not to see you as often as I do." Then, she added, "Have you seen Gretchen?

"No, Mom." I slipped out through the back door before she could give me her advice.

The Barrows' home was on the other side of the lake, only a twenty-minute walk. It had been zero temperatures since the snow two weeks ago, which still stood in inches on the lawns. Ken and I could have been cross-country skiing. The memories caused a sentimental twinge and a murmur, *I miss you, pal.*

Ken's mother gave me a broad smile as she opened the door. "Come in Jon. It's so good to see you, and I want to hear what is happening at school. Emily tells me you are on the swim team. Here, let me take your coat and, yes, leave your shoes on the mat by the door. You remember that from before, don't you?" She took my hand and led me to the kitchen. "I have fresh doughnuts. I'm just finishing my last batch. Here, you can help sugar them." She handed me a metal shaker filled with sugar and spices.

"Your kitchen always smells as good as Mom's and full of goodies. I remember Ken and me always beggin' you to make doughnuts. He liked the chocolate frosted ones." I held up the shaker, "Should I just sprinkle the sugar on?"

As we sat down at the table, I told her, "I thought I'd get to see Ken. This being the first Christmas away from home, I couldn't imagine him not being here."

"I guess he's too busy with jobs. Of course, California is a long drive and not good in the winter. Our offer of airfare didn't sway him either."

"What's he doing? I wanted to call him, but last time I asked, he didn't have a telephone number yet. Does he now?"

"No, and I don't know why not. He's sharing an apartment with two other boys – you'd think they couldn't live without a phone. He does call from the gallery once a month."

"A gallery? Is he showing his work?"

"No, not yet. In fact, he's working two jobs. A waiter . . . can you imagine? . . . at an upscale restaurant. Some spiffy seafood place, it sounds like. He has to wear a white shirt and black tie. During the day he works at a gallery that also does framing. Of course, this was the busy season for both places and he didn't want to lose either job. He says he makes enough money for rent, food, and art classes."

"Sounds good. Maybe he'll show at the gallery some day?"

"He hopes so. They like the pencil and charcoal drawings, so he says, and they encourage him to keep working at it. He hasn't chosen an easy profession, has he Jon?"

"I can't really say. It's good that he knows what he wants to do, and I give him credit for trying to do it."

"Here, have another doughnut. They're best when still warm."

"Yeah, they are. You must put a special spice in them. Yummy! Maybe, he'll get back next summer," I said as I munched. "Sorry for talking with my mouth full."

"I don't know Jon." She lowered her eyes and then spoke in a tone of wistful regret. "It feels like we've lost him."

"Oh, that can't be, Mrs. Barrows. It's just that California is a long way away, and you're probably lonely for him. Just like Mom."

"It's more than that, Jon. He spoke about living a different life, where he can feel comfortable with who he is. Do you know who he is, Jon?"

I was too embarrassed to answer her question and was not sure how to proceed. So I ate another doughnut.

Mrs. Barrows fidgeted with the utensils on the table, showing her embarrassment when she said, "I know Ken was teased in school and that he was called Kennie in a taunting way. He kept saying that he didn't fit in. I thought it was because he liked arts instead of the boy sports, but he did compete in swimming." She waited, fussing with the mess on the table, pushing the sugar into a small pile. "Jon, does it have something to do with not dating girls." She hesitated before asking, "Does he like boys instead?"

Wow! I felt trapped. How to answer her question? I was ill at ease and felt the flush rising up my neck. "You and Ken were very good friends, Jon. You would know if he is gay – isn't that what they call a homosexual these days? And, a lot of them live in California, so my daughters say."

"I don't know, Mrs. Barrows."

"What is it you don't know?" Her voice had a sorrowful tone to it. "If either one of you are gay?"

Now, I was embarrassed. "I know I'm not, Mrs. Barrows."

"But you can't speak for Ken, can you?" She looked at me and I shook my head back and forth. She reached her left hand across to mine and went on to say, "It's okay, Jon. I couldn't condemn Ken no matter what. I guess I'm just trying to solve my own question when only Ken can answer it. He'll have to tell me."

"Maybe he'll come home next summer." I wanted to change the subject.

"Let's hope so. I'll lose him – the longer he stays away." She stood up and started to clear the table, then stopped and looked at me. "Thank you, Jon, for talking with me. And, I assure you that our conversation stays here with the doughnuts. Can we do that?"

"Yes, Mrs. Barrows."

As I walked away from Ken's house, I pulled the stocking cap down over my ears, pushed the collar of my winter jacket up, stuffed my hands in heavy gloves and took the long way home. It was puzzling to me. What was I, really? The same old question with no answer. I liked girls and I liked boys but wasn't interested in sex. Is something wrong with me? Am I a misfit from my birth parents? Look at Matt, one of my very best friends – he liked all girls, lots of them. Ken and I had shared a lot – he wanted to be with just boys. Gretchen, my longest-running girl friend, who wanted to be hugged and kissed a lot was ready for sex. Not me! Jay was just a roomie, a guy, a pool partner. Lori, who was fake and too fast. Not for me! Now, comes Rich, with the appealing body and his invitations. What does it mean to be attracted to either one – male or female, but not interested in sex, just their friendship. I can't talk with Dad about this one. And, the question has no answer yet.

<h1 style="text-align:center">9</h1>

The second semester pretty much duplicated the first one. I studied more, pushing towards a 3.5 grade average, graduated to Team Two in swimming, swam relay to win a couple of Big Ten meets, and dated three girls – Carrie (one movie, one lecture, three cokes and two kisses), Kellie (one basketball game, two beers and a brush-off), and Becka of the Homecoming group. I met up with her one night in Dinkytown and discovered she played pool – her father began teaching her when she was ten. She became a better instructor than Jay, making me more competitive at the table, and we became regulars in the Friday night pool matches. Becka was a plain dresser and plain looking -- brown naturally curly hair encircling her head like a woolen cap and a skinny face with dark laughing eyes. She had a habit of winking her left eye just before she'd put the eight ball in the pocket. Her cheerfulness was catchy and her skill with the cue stick was envied, even if the guys didn't say so directly. After two months of dating, she told me she was going out with one of the other guys, but we'd remain friends. So the school year ended with no carry-overs. Not Jay who transferred to the university at St. Cloud, closer to home, nor Rich who lost interest in me after I showed no interest in the gay scene. He insisted I go with him one night to a club on Hennepin Street, and I worried the entire time, fearful I'd be identified by another student. I just made a simple statement to him, "Rich, this is not for me."

# CHAPTER TWO

## *Summer, 1982*

### 1

I SIGNED ON to a multitude of summer jobs -- only three provided a paycheck. I shared work hours with my cousins at the hardware store and was on call for Dad at the drugstore. I earned the most with the city parks department on a summer project to beautify Witherston. I worked long hours in the early weeks helping to replace dead trees and plant new flowerbeds along Main Street and in the parks, after that I was on the mowing brigade. My free-gratis work was coaching a swim team (ten year olds), working our lawn and flowers with Mom, and harvesting PaPo's "last" garden – or so he claimed every year.

What I remember most about the summer were three distinct conversations that altered my perspective and taught me I won't always know others fully. I would come to realize that within each person there's a private place that isn't shared – until the right moment or maybe never. It could be a place as small as an island or as large as a country. It is the home of secrets.

### 2

It was a Monday and I was free to help Mom with her long list of outside projects. We were weeding and cutting away the dead flowers, when I asked, "Mom, how come I've heard so many of your friends at church tell you that they are glad to see you."

"Well, because they're my friends and they are glad to see me."

"No, it didn't sound like idle comments, it sounded more like they were surprised to see you at church. And, I heard it being said to you the last three Sundays. And, I notice you make light of their remarks and change the subject. Even Aunt Ethel said how glad she was to see you. I remember, now, hearing the same remarks at Christmas Eve mass."

"My, you're all ears to be taking such notice. Look why don't we take out this peony bush – it hasn't done well for two summers and most of the buds didn't even flower fully this year."

"Mom, you're side stepping. Am I asking something wrong? Something I shouldn't know?"

She sat back on her heels and then moved a few feet into the shade of the garage. "I guess you have a right to know. Have you brought this up with your father?" When I responded with a shake of my head, Mom continued, "Jon, this was my individual decision . . . not made lightly . . . and one I know puzzled the whole family. You see, I'm not going to church on a regular basis. More honestly, I go only when you're home. I hoped for a long time that my feelings would change, and I'd be as ardent as I was before, but it hasn't happened."

"But you were working with the ladies, with the nursery. Have you quit that too?"

"Yes, this last year. If I wasn't going to regular services, I could hardly be involved with projects. Too awkward for everyone."

"Wow, you must get a lot of questions. Dad doesn't make you go? Are the aunts and uncles mad?"

"Yes, no, and sort of. Your father and I have had long conversations about this. You know him pretty well by now . . . and know he'd give me good reasons for not giving up my religious faith . . . but he would honor my final decision. I imagine it has been hard to explain to his family."

"What does he have to explain?"

She put her head down and soothingly rubbed the scar on her forehead – a signal that her story was serious and would be hard for her to tell.

"Jon, it goes back to when you and Matt were altar boys." *Ah, back to Father Stern,* I thought. "I've never been able to forget or forgive the priest who harmed a young boy nor the church who protected him. Your father and Father Mike tried to help me in many ways, but I cannot get rid of the picture of a priest practicing such gross conduct. Teaching young boys that sexual behavior is okay with another man and defiling the morals and teachings that stood behind the robes of the church. It soiled my belief and my faith." She stopped, looked at me and said, "I'm so sorry Jon. I must be a disappointment to you."

"Gosh, Mom, I didn't know. That was such a long time ago. Once Father Stern was gone, I thought it was all over. Matt and I did talk about it a couple of times and Matt was glad when Father left so soon." Then the truth hit me. "You went to church all that time just for me. So my school days would go smoothly. So there'd be no ugliness, no gossip. Wow! I never had a clue."

"That's good. That's the way it should have been for you . . . and Matt."

I asked, "So, when I'm home, you are going to go to church because of me?"

"Yes, if you want me to. You're older now, Jon, and should be able to cope with a mother who is a bit different than what you expected."

"I'd say more than a bit different. This has to be a big deal at St. Anne's. Did others know about Father Stern?"

"Yes, Jon, there were rumors and some believed them and some did not. After he left, I think everyone sighed with relief and most put it out of their minds. I couldn't and it wasn't just Father Stern . . . I wondered how many other priests had violated young boys. How very sordid, how ungodly." She stood up and pointed to the peony bush. "Let's start on these. How about you get the digging stuff and I'll get us some lemonade."

She walked toward the house and left me reflecting on her bitterness and distaste toward the idea that men could prefer men. That's what Ken was referring to when he said he couldn't stay here. I'd never be able to explain this one to her.

## 3

Grandpa and I ate every bit of the eggs, bacon, and pancakes that Mom put before us. She wanted to be sure we'd be well fortified. We picked up our hats and water bottles and headed out the door as Mom called after us, "Dad, don't stay in the sun too long. Jon, make him rest every hour."

"She still mothers all of us, doesn't she?" Grandpa moaned.

"Just a sure sign that she loves us a lot, PaPo. Want me to drive?" Grandpa's little grey Ford truck was twenty years old, dented and rusted. As I climbed into the driver's seat, I teased Grandpa about his jalopy, to which he replied, "Old doesn't mean unreliable. Heck, can't imagine gardening without this jalopy, as you call it. Think of all the dirt and fertilizer we've hauled in it and all the vegetables we've delivered. As long as it holds up, I will too."

"Ah PaPo, than I'd say this jalopy will become an antique."

"Yep, Bud, that's what we are, two antiques."

As I parked the truck alongside the garden, Grandpa said, "For God's sake, look at those weeds! We got some heavy work to do today – thanks to all the spring rains. Let's hoe them out of the ground. Strike the blade deep and to the side a bit, so we kill the roots. Did you put in two hoes, Jon?"

"Yes, Grandpa. But why not let me do the hoeing and you can rake the clumps into piles. Looks like the lettuce is ready for picking. Mom will like that for supper."

We worked steadily for a couple of hours, and then I insisted that we take a break. His question surprised me. "I hear you want to find your birth parents. Is that right?"

"Who told you that?"

166

"Your father mentioned it to me a while back. I've been waiting for the best time to talk with you. Bud, I don't think looking up those two is a wise idea. It's like inviting people to a party who didn't want to be on the guest list. You see what I mean? They'd be strangers and maybe they don't want to be known. Have you thought about that? You'd break your mother's heart. You know that, don't you? You have family and they live right here in Witherston. Isn't that fine enough?"

"Well Grandpa, I can see you think it's not such a good idea."

"Yep, you figured that one out correctly. Jon, it's been twenty years. You might be chasing a phantom or opening a closet full of old stuff too messy to face. You've had a fine home . . . a happy one, and parents who've made a good life for you. Why put all that in harm's way?"

"Didn't Dad tell you I don't want them to become our friends? I know how Mom feels . . . how upset and hurt she would be. I'm not that dumb. I heard and saw her reaction when I tested the subject. It's just that . . . well, it's like something that is glued to me and I can't shake it off."

I looked at Grandpa. His face was stern, eyes crinkled, and he shook his head, "No, no, no. It's curiosity, a young boy with a crazy damn dream. What's there to know? You are twenty-one, an adult . . . a responsibility to a family who've loved you as an only son. You want to twist that? You want to tamper with that love? You think it won't have consequences? If so, then you'll break a lot of hearts and trust – mine included." I saw the tears in his eyes and he lowered his head. "Don't do it, Bud. You are Jon Strutter, the son of a proud and respected family. Don't give up that honor too quickly . . . or easily. Broken items can't always be mended; they're forever cracked . . . never perfect again."

Silence hovered over us as we picked lettuce. I absorbed the words that had been spoken. Grandpa had laid a sober warning on me . . . a weight that hung heavy in my mind and on my emotions. I knew that he would not speak of this again and understood that he expected I would bring no harm to the Strutter family. All the memories of my childhood spent with this kind, generous, loyal man flooded across my mind. I made a silent promise not to disappoint him or hurt him.

## 4

We drove into our favorite woods to a small grassy clearing surrounded by large oak trees, a spot where we had visited before. I looked over towards Ken, "Well, here we are, just like old times. The woods, a fire site and a cooler full of good food. Mom couldn't resist sending chicken salad and chocolate chip cookies, and I saw your mom stacking doughnuts in that red container."

"Yeah, some things never change. Being home this week, I saw how same'o it is. California is like another world compared to here." He pushed his head back against the seat. "I would have withered in Witherston."

"Ah, come on, it ain't all that bad," I shouted as I jumped out of the car. "Let's get set up and then I want to hear about everything . . . your jobs, friends, the ocean, what's fun, your art classes. My year will be dull compared to yours."

Ken arrived last Sunday by way of Minneapolis, but it had been family time all week. We'd challenged ourselves to a few laps at the city pool, and I ate with the Burrow's one night, but we'd not had private talking time. Now it was late Friday afternoon and Ken would be heading back to California in thirty-six hours.

I sensed a change in Ken, a lightness of spirit, a freedom in his movements, a glow in his sharp blue eyes that seem to say he knew something others didn't. His body was still slender, almost thin and his thick dark brown hair came to below the tops of his ears – not quite one length but close to it. His thick hair still formed into a high mound over his forehead but now more loosely, and a few strands fell forward. He was tan all over "from sun bathing in the nude on our rooftop" he told me.

We stashed our gear inside the small pup tent, laid up chips and logs for a fire, put up our camp chairs, and left our sleeping bags for later. We played frizzbee and walked down a dirt road before settling down with a beer and our stories.

"Well Ken, have you found your place. Is it what you expected?"

"First a request, Jon. Please call me Michael."

"Oh."

"You know my middle name is Michael, and I remember asking a long time ago to be called Michael. I thought it a more beautiful sound, softer than Kenneth. But Mom said that since it was a name already used in the family – my uncle – it was best to stay with Ken. Well, one of the first things new with my move was to introduce my self as Michael." He softened the letters so that the name had a fluid tone.

"Does it make you feel different? Could you take it up that easily?"

"Yes and yes. Michael is more the real me. Like the person in me who has been waiting to come forward, be alive, live as me. Kenneth was a façade, a mask over the real person, one I didn't seem to know or even care for."

"Well, don't keep me hanging. Tell me what I might be missing. What's the golden life like? How do you live your days? Your art classes?"

"It was fortunate how I met my room mates. I stayed a couple of nights in a cheap hotel off of downtown, and it took some guts to ask the desk clerk . . . who was a young female . . . how I might go about finding a place. Like an apartment to share or a one-room in a boarding house. She asked me enough subtle questions, which I answered honestly, to know I was looking for the gay section of Frisco. She got me in touch with a renting agency in the Castro District . . . that's the gay community . . . and right off the bat, they mentioned these two guys . . . Al and Phil . . . who'd just filed an ad the day before. We had lunch, walked to their apartment, and I rented the small back bedroom.

"Rent is high in that city and you have to share or be earning a lot of dollars. Our place works out well. A big room for living and dining . . . and they had all the furniture to go in it . . . a funny kitchen that's the shape of a triangle with a tiny screened porch overlooking the roofs of other buildings. They have a bedroom off of the main room and my tiny room is in the back. And, it's tiny . . . I got a cot, a chair, a dresser I painted lavender, a lamp . . . all from the Salvation Army store. No closet, but a portable hanger for my clothes. Tough part is sharing the bathroom, which is also tiny and seems to be Al's favorite place . . . he's always in there doing something.

"I take the trolley to the restaurant, and I work every night but Monday and Tuesday. Make good money – those Californians sure know how to tip. Last week, I was given a party of eight to serve. They did five bottles of wine, thirty-five dollar dinners plus appetizers, desert and port wine . . . twelve dollars for a wee glass. Their tab was over five hundred and I got eighty-five for a tip. And that was just one table, though they did linger there most of the night.

"It's just fun to be with those people. Nothing like the ones we meet here."

"Well, I suppose not. Can you imagine our folks spending five hundred? Hell, Grandpa thinks he's being generous if he leaves a dollar tip for lunch." We laughed at the comparison. "And how about the gallery? Do they like your art pieces?"

"Well, they're not too interested in my work. I'm an amateur yet. But Jenny, who owns the store with her husband Stu, looks at my work and has aimed me towards some places that show art more in my line. I'm also going to have a little corner of their booth in the next street show.

"My art classes are the best part. I have a good teacher. He's rather funky and does some weird paintings, but he's always there and collects a good group of students. He charges by the month, so I can skip a month and still have easel space when I return. I learn as much from the other students . . . one really has an artistic touch with the pen, pencil, and charcoal."

"Your life makes you sound like a stranger to me. So different. I noticed that this week, but out here in the woods I feel the Ken I know. Oops, Michael. Guess Ken is gone, eh?"

"Yeah, Jon he is. But that boy back then had a special friend . . . you. You will always mean a lot to me . . . you must realize, Jon, that I love you. You made me feel okay about myself, you were my support. I could count on you not to put me down, not to join others in mocking me . . . and all our times on the trail, in the pool are burnt into my memory forever." With that Ken reached over to pick up both my hands and with his face close to mine, "You will always be my first love."

I squeezed his hands and blinked my eyes. "Shall we start our fire?"

The sun was below the horizon and the sky still had that soft after-glow and off to the side was a three-quarter moon ready to shine bright. We sat under that moon, letting the fire linger into warm ashes. Our beds were laid out facing the moon and ready for us, but we still had subjects to cover.

"Want another beer? Or a soda?" I asked, picking out a Pepsi for me and handed him one also. We sat still in the night silence, Ken humming softly, reminding me of Mom humming when satisfied and happy.

"Ken, oops, Michael when did you realize that boys held more attraction then girls? How does that happen to us?"

"I guess it didn't really hit me until my teens . . . maybe I was twelve. I wanted to be with guys . . . not just to play sports and kid about girls . . . I wanted to be with them . . . close like . . . listening to music, reading books, seeing movies, walking in the woods. I wanted to be alone with them, but didn't really understand what for. I had friends that were girls, but it was the boys I dreamed about, who I wanted to touch.

"Gosh, you don't know how hard I prayed that that wasn't true. What was wrong with me? I didn't hear anybody else saying what I was thinking. In fact, I didn't find another who wanted to be like me . . . until you . . . while we didn't really talk about such, you gave me a secret feeling like you and I were the same kind. But all I could do was wonder what was wrong with me. Did God make me a different way? Why? Did God even know I was different? I wanted to kill that part of me. So I did a lot of praying . . . which made me more scared . . . like I was afraid it was true . . . I wasn't normal . . . and maybe God didn't care.

"I went to talk to Father about it and mumbled enough for him to understand what I was trying to say. He said I was a boy growing up to be a man . . . to think I was different was really wrong and if I prayed real hard and asked God, it would all go away. Well, it didn't. I tried to be like the other guys . . . you know, kid around with the girls, even went to the movies with them . . . didn't mind dancing with them. But, it was just being school friends and they knew it. I was a buddy, a brother, not a date.

"One day, I snuck into the Library hoping to find a book that could explain what it meant to prefer boys. I couldn't find the right books by subject and, of course, I wasn't about to ask the librarian for help. Finally I went to the section on gender and sex and found a little book about homosexuals – otherwise, gay men. I read it behind a cover of another book for two hours. Then I knew for sure, I'd have to find my group of guys. In California, they call it the gay community . . . it's on Castro Street."

"Wow! And you were hoping that I was one of them?"

"Say it, Jon . . . say gay."

"Okay, gay! There I said it. Gay." I then wanted to share my thoughts. "I too have wondered what's up with me. I like the personalities of both, guys and girls . . . feel at ease with them . . . but any sexual desire is on the low side."

"Didn't you ever have sex with Gretchen?"

"Hell, no, and she was disappointed . . . in fact mad about that. She wanted to neck and make out just like the rest of the gang we hung out with."

"How'd you get by with it?"

"Oh, did a lot of other mushy stuff and laid back on the confession thing. You know, we'd have to tell the priest when we made confession. She'd laugh and said ' do you think the rest of these kids do that? Jon, you're nuts.' And, then one day she asked me 'are you one of them?' That's when she told me what others were saying about you and she wanted to know if I was too. That was the beginning of our end."

I squiggled in my chair. Ken was pushing his hands through his hair, and he said, "Sure took us a long time to talk about all this."

"Maybe, it was best," I replied.

"Are you still a virgin, Jon?"

"Yeah, I am. Pitiful huh. I've gone to the library also, and I guess you'd have to tag me asexual . . . attractive to the personality, whether male or female, and not the sex."

We walked in the moonlight down the dirt road, holding hands in a casual manner. We played our imagination game, sketching our dreams for the future. He would be a gifted artist; I'd be a successful landscaper. We ate chocolate chip cookies before stretching out on the sleeping bags in the clearing. It was midnight, silent, warm, but we hadn't said goodnight yet.

"Michael, what do you and your friends think about that disease that is so much in the news? I heard they call it the gay disease. Aren't you scared, at least a bit?"

"Yeah, it gets a lot of publicity. This outside world wants to ignore it, pretend it doesn't affect them, our inside world has been badly hit. Thousands of cases by now, almost fifty percent of them die. Al has a friend who has watched three of his friends suffer with AIDS. Al describes it as pretty horrible suffering."

"Hope you are careful. I bet your mother worries about you. Have you told her?"

"In a certain way, I guess I have. I've described my life style, my friends, and I think Sis has helped her realize that I'm gay . . . although she would never use that word. And, of course, my father would never even think the word. Mom came into my room the other night to tell me that she loves me and not to stay away too long. And, she said 'let's never keep secrets because that's too hard to bear'." We let the silence take hold of the night. The moon had risen above the treetops and gave a soft flow to our outside bedroom.

"Good-night Ken. Oops, good-night Michael."

"Good-night, Jon. It's been a special time."

It was more special then we thought. I saw Ken for the last time on Saturday morning as we said good-bye on his front porch. Two years later he was dead of the dreaded disease. We both would be only twenty-three, and I was the one left to live the dream. Mrs. Barrows gave me two charcoal sketches from Ken's personal belongings. One was a swimmer in Lane Four and the other the clearing in the woods, in which I found much later a self-portrait tucked in behind. It was Ken in soft brown charcoal except for the eyes – bright blue. At the bottom was his artistic signature, Michael.

# CHAPTER THREE

# *Sophomore Year, University of Minnesota*

## 1

A S I PUSHED my first boxes into the dorm room, I noticed that the left side of the room was orderly and a male standing before the closet stacking sweaters onto a shelf.

"Hi, guess we are room mates. I'm Jon Strutter from Witherston."

"Scott Nolte . . . from Bemidji," he said as he turned toward me. He matched me in size and weight but his ears were his most outstanding feature – they were long and fanned towards his face. Dumbo, I thought. Scott swept his arm across his space. "Trust you don't mind my taking this side of the room. It was a natural, as it's my side from last year."

"That's okay. I'll have the same side as last year too. And what's your preference, top or bottom bunk?"

"Either one. I did both last year. How about I do the top the first semester?" He moved his bedding from chair to bunk as I turned to my boxes. "Need help in bringing up the rest?" Scott asked.

"Yeah, I could. I got a late start out of town. I'll pay off with some of my mom's chocolate chip cookies."

"Let's go for it."

We shared the work and shared our interests. Scott was into political science and journalism. "I want to get into government work . . . hopefully on the staff of a congressman or governor. A real hit would be to hold office myself one day. It's helpful that my father has held a few city offices and been involved in state politics."

"I'm heading toward a more earthy trade. I started with an eye for architectural landscape design, but I'm switching to landscape management. I think it's more suitable with more opportunity for owning my own business, which is my mother's goal for me." I don't know why I tagged that on . . . sounds like I don't control my own life.

The change in landscape careers was right, and for the remainder of my school years, my horticulture classes would include botany, plant pathology, maintenance and design, turf grass management. Upon Dad's advice I'd be taking business related courses: economics, accounting, personnel management, and communications. And when I paid an early visit to Mr. Deaver, he was glad to hire me again for as many hours as I wanted to work. "With," he announced, "a dollar increase."

## 2

With Scott active in campus organizations – student council, opinion newsletter, and political meetings – I moved up from pool table and beer. I backed Scott for Secretary on the Council (he lost by 114 votes), and he successfully persuaded me to join with students one Friday night organizing a peace rally. Scott was pretty popular and held sway when he had the mike. For seemingly a quiet guy, he'd made a lot of connections in just one year and had a magnetic draw when in a crowd.

The rally was in conjunction with the Vietnam memorial being dedicated in D. C., for the 57, 939 names inscribed on its wall. THANK YOU AMERICA FOR FINALLY REMEMBERING

US blazed on banners. Like the homecoming parade, there'd be a float on a flat-back truck, only the music, this time, accompanied the patriotic words of *America* and the song of the day: *Let There Be Peace on Earth*. Hundreds of banners of all sizes were painted and attached to poles and routes mapped though the campus and Dinkytown. Campus police closed streets to traffic and everyone hoped for television crews en masse. I watched in awe and followed directions from anyone who made sense. Troublemakers were few.

The peace march extended from Friday night to Sunday and I was there full time. I joined the ambitious ones in cleaning up on campus and fell exhausted into bed at ten o'clock. I never heard Scott come in, and he didn't hear me when I got up for morning classes. It was a couple of nights later that we got to talk about what took place.

"Mom called yesterday and asked about the rally. She said Channel Four gave good coverage to the march. She was surprised, but pleased, when I told her I was in it. I have to hand it to you, Scott . . . I was amazed at the number of students who were there. And, not too many unruly ones. Was there any bad news with police?"

"Yeah, late Saturday night. They were beer drinkers and had had enough to taunt the police and jeer the more ardent marchers. But in the end it didn't amount too much. The police hustled them off to a side street and, I think, sat on them for thirty to forty minutes until they ambled back to a bar. Did you get to hear the speakers? Did you hear the vet named Jeb?"

"Yeah, all of them. Seeing the wheel chairs and crutches brings the war right to your face. My grandfather gave me a speech once about war never settling anything. He said war only brought the worst out in the other side . . . revenge was a natural follow-on to armed conflict and war would follow war. And that was Jeb's message also, wasn't it? He was saying, 'I went out of duty, for my country but the war solved nothing. America is hated, it's citizens are ashamed, and the leaders hide the truth.' I didn't realize that the vets were the focus for the country's anger."

"Were you glad to be with us?" Scott asked.

I nodded. "It was a big time . . . and maybe I'm wiser. I've stood up for myself but never taken on a cause. Being in the midst of it seems natural for you."

"Well, that's because I grew up in a politically active family. Both father and mother. Lot's of critique at the dinner table . . . no holds on opinions. They couldn't wait until I could register and vote a Demo ticket. Are you registered?"

"Yes, my father sees that as a privilege and a duty . . . but I'm a Republican, mostly because of family tradition. I'm not sure that I get the differences between the parties, or how politicians really exercise their power."

"Well, I'll have to see if I can win you over. It'll be good practice for me, don't you think?"

# 3

Scott always kept me informed of what was going on and welcomed me to join him. I picked and chose from his invitations, opting more to those that didn't take too much time away from greenhouse, studies, and swimming. I finally gave up swimming (it wasn't the same without Ken). I got so tied up that I was going home only on holidays, skipping weekend trips. I found Scott's friends interesting; they brought new subjects and outlooks, and stretched my worldview. I met the first of them on a Friday night outside a movie theater. Four people were standing to the side of the box office and called out their greetings -- "Hey Scott, about time." -- as we headed their way. Scott did the introductions.

"Hi, Dan and Amy. This is my roomie and new recruit, Jon." Scott looked to the two guys standing beside Amy. "This is Chuck and Robert – meet Jon. Where's Karen?"

"She's coming," replied Amy. "She chose a non-meter parking spot, so she has to walk a few extra blocks. We've got our tickets. Doesn't look like a crowd. Hope we can all sit together. Maybe we should do two rows, and then we can talk over our shoulders."

A tall girl in a bright red sweater came hurrying cross the street. "Here I am. Had to nose out another car for a space. Made her mad and she gave me the finger. I politely looked the other way. Hi everyone . . . guess I haven't met you."

Jon took the hand held out to him. "I'm Jon . . . I'm tagging along with Scott."

"As a friend, date, or . . ." to which I answered, "roommate and new recruit."

"He's such a consummate campaigner. Guess, you'd like to know I'm Karen Hoth."

The plan for the night was to see the movie *Gandhi*, and afterwards go to a coffee house to follow up with discussion on non-violent revolution. Chuck and Scott were preparing for a debate on the subject in their communications class, and Scott thought the movie, discussion, and debate tied in nicely with the Peace rally two weeks ago. Movie previews were ending as Scott, Karen, and I took the three seats behind Dan, Amy, Chuck, and Robert. Karen playfully squeezed both of our hands, "It probably won't be hard to see why this movie won all the Oscars. I've heard Kingsley is awesome."

I stole a sidewise glance to get a better look at this spirited person. Fresh looking, no make-up, lips that raised on each side, as if molded from a constant smile. Cute wasn't the right description; pretty, just a bit shy of beautiful.

The movie was long and by intermission we were pretty intense. To watch the brilliant determination of the Indian who stood down the English rulers seemed more movie drama than real life. Scott made notes of what we'd get into when we'd do our coffee discussion later - Gandhi's intellectual background; spiritual activism, leadership qualities, courage or destiny, and the arrogance of imperialism.

I'd stepped into a new arena meeting thoughts, concepts, and an outside world that was not everyday thinking for me. I realized how tightly wrapped up I'd been in my home and family and our town. I sensed my education expanding beyond classrooms and professors. I wanted to glue myself to Scott and his friends and would play the novice before I became an equal. *I don't know how this helps a landscaping career but, who cares? Boy! it's time I came out of the boonies.*

By the end of the evening I began to see how everyone fit together. Amy, a senior in home economics, lived with Karen in a two-bedroom apartment on Mott Street south of campus. They'd been friends since they met on their jobs at the university hospital three years ago. Dan was studying civil engineering, planning to join the Peace Corps when he graduated in December. He and Amy were steady dates in a casual relationship. They both stated they had too many personal plans and goals to get too serious. Chuck and Robert did not disguise their partnership; although, even if they had not spoken of it, one would have suspected that they were a gay couple. Later I would learn that they'd gone to the same high school and were glad to now be able to live a more open, but still somewhat cautious relationship. They were into Literature, Communication, and Arts. Karen was twenty-four, one year younger than Amy and Dan and a junior in education, majoring in history and civics. Her goal was teaching junior high students.

Our discussion centered on how one follows in the footsteps of Gandhi through civil disobedience. Scott referred to the peace rally. He pointed out how it raised the energy levels and attention of the crowds but unless it touches an individual who can walk out in front and hold the energies together until the higher goals are attained, it is just background noise. Karen rebutted with, "the energies are important . . . whoever will know how many people in the crowd are touched to move to a higher level? . . . they may lead in invisible ways." And Dan added, "I agree. It was the 'peace not war' marches I walked in my earlier years that headed me towards the Peace Corps. I want to make a difference, I want to change a village."

Karen picked up Dan's thought with, "Hitler changed a whole

continent with energies, leadership qualities that reached into the pride of the German soul and their desire to be victors, to wipe out being losers in the first World War. He knew how to use all the elements that excite emotions – music, uniforms, decorations, a cause, and mass meetings. He moved a whole nation and led them into unthinkable deeds. Was he a leader? He sure was, just as much as Gandhi . . . only he had different dreams."

Karen leaned towards me. "What about you Jon? You're being quiet."

"You gotta remember that I'm new here. I mean to rallies, world politics. I know of Hitler and the war from history through my grandfather who fought in Italy and Germany. I'm sure we must have touched on India in high school but how one man did so much was lost somewhere. I am intrigued . . . strong people catch my interest . . . my father is a man of principle, loyal to honesty and integrity. Would he lead a movement? I'm not sure. Of course, if it was centered in Witherston, he couldn't help but get involved.

"I'd like to be invited back to your group. Let me listen and add my two cents when I can. And, I'd march again for a good cause."

"All we have are good causes. Right Scott?" Chuck threw out.

## 4

It was a bitter, cold, January afternoon when I drove into the parking lot of Catholic Charities. I lingered until I could calm my jitters – my emotions were riding high. I knew there was slight chance of finding family history, but I was excited to have this chance to seek it. I took a deep breath as I trudged up the snow-packed walk. Inside a receptionist announced me with a telephone call.

"Mr. Strutter," a woman of mid-age dressed in a blue suit held her hand toward me, "Hello, I'm Mrs. Conlay." She pointed down the hallway. "This way to my office."

As I took the chair in front of her desk, I asked her to call me Jon. She picked up a sheet of paper from her desk, read it quickly and then raised her eyes to mine. "I have here your request about adoption information. Your phone call was passed on to me." She relaxed back into her chair as she asked, "Please give me some background and what you're hoping to find. I do have the record that the adoption did indeed take place through Catholic Charities back in 1962, but there is little information to share with you. In fact, really none at all. Our files are confidential, laws regarding adoption were, some still are, quite stringent, and I find no contact being made from either party after the formal adoption. So how can I help you?"

"Simply stated, I'd like to see my birth parents. See is the key word. I'd like to know what they look like, what they do, how they live. It's like wanting to complete a picture puzzle. I want to fill an empty space, an unknown. I just want to know."

"Curiosity, you mean. Nothing more than that?"

"My parents ask the same question. Naming it curiosity relegates it to non-important . . . sort of like just a passing fancy. I want to see them, not become a part of their lives. It wouldn't fit for my mother and would be too awkward . . . it's too late."

"Are you saying, Jon, that you could just see them as an observer and be able to let it go at that?"

"Yes."

"Then you have no idea the emotions that would surface at that moment when you stood across from them . . . knowing who they were and they not knowing who you are. I know you're young . . . let's see twenty-two, twenty-three . . . what you are suggesting is quite naïve." She rubbed her hand across her chin and shook her head. "In any case, Jon, we can't help you in any way. There is not one piece of information that is open to you, and, in fact, we have no information about the birth parents at all. Just as I said before, the file was closed on April 1, 1962 . . . . no inquiries since that time. Which is a strong indication that the birth parents have no interest. As hard as that seems, that is what it means.

"Jon, let this go. It is one of the hard parts of adoption . . . the unknown. Focus on your life forward. I presume you've had a good family experience . . . you are in college preparing for your adult life . . . have faith that the young people did what they thought best at the time." She paused and leaned forward in her chair, "Believe me, it is not a casual event to come face to face with birth parents, even under the best of circumstances. When you say that you just want to see them, I don't think you understand that it will involve more emotions than you realize." She waited a long moment, letting her words hang there before me.

"There is nothing that I can offer you, other than the advice I've already spoken. Do your parents know that you made this inquiry?"

"No. They know of my interest. They don't know about this visit, but I will tell my father."

"Why not your mother?"

I hesitated before answering. I thought of how fiercely Mother pushed back. How adamant she was that our family should stay intact. Her fear of any outside intrusion. "Mom loves me very much . . . I am her perfect boy . . . we are the happy family . . . and she makes it so. She is such a good mother . . . both Dad and I know she should have had a slew of children. But since I am the only one, I do get the intensity of her love. She would not be happy if she knew I was here."

"Jon, it sounds as if your adoption had the best of outcomes. What you are looking for may not, would not, add very much. May I suggest that you talk with a counselor in this area? We have a good one on our staff, Dr. Edwin Mabry. Would you like to talk with him? We could set an appointment."

I stood up. "I'll think about it. Thanks for seeing me. I didn't think that I could find much here, but it was my first place to look."

Mrs. Conlay came around the desk and put her hand on my

arm. "Jon, find your way to give up this pursuit . . . it is a dead end." As she opened the door she said, "When adoptions work as well as yours, we celebrate. Do the same, Jon. What are your studies? Your career?"

"Landscape management, thanks to my mother. She loves the dirt, the flowers, and the beauty of growing things. At age three I had my plot of ground, my shovels, my flowers."

"Those are the blessings of a whole family. Treasure it, Jon. Good luck to you."

# 5

Karen and Amy's apartment was the gathering place of friends on weekend nights. Sometimes it was standing room only, usually when a political event had taken place during the week – an outcome from Scott's involvement. Those were nights of different opinions and viewpoints – a platform for airing student rhetoric. By the end of the evening, at around midnight, the gathering usually wound down to Karen, Amy, Dan, Scott and myself. Chuck and Robert preferred to stay when it was just the five of us. We'd make pizza: Karen did the crust, Amy the sauce, and I chopped the veggies. If we were lucky, there'd be a few beers and a bottle of wine left for our late snack.

Our discussions could go on for hours. It was a somber group the night that Chuck and Robert spoke about the gay illness that was plaguing San Francisco, the only city open to reporting the cases. Hundreds were dying of an unusual disease, a rare type of pneumonia. All homosexuals. Robert said Los Angeles reported that five men died in that city in the last four months.

"How is the medical community following this?" Dan asked. "Who's trying to identify the cause? Where's the research?"

"Well, I bet they don't want to be associated with it." Karen spoke with an edge to her voice. "After all it sounds as if they have tagged it to a segment of our society that deserves to be punished. Isn't that the way the thinking is on gays?"

"They have ignored it through the seventies but the deaths are now in the hundreds and no medicine, pills, or help is there for them." Chuck continued, "I read that clinics have been set up in Frisco, spearheaded by the gay community itself, but New York is basically ignoring the fact that they have people dying of the same disease. Rumor has it that cases are showing up in Europe also. And it seems that our government is ignoring it all."

I couldn't help but think of Ken and our last time together in the woods. How excited he was to be in California, being a part of that community. Could he get the disease? . . . would he tell his parents? . . . would he tell me? It was scary thinking about it.

"Tell us, Scott, if you were elected how would you handle this potential crisis?" Amy asked the question and we waited for Scott's answer, which came slowly.

"First off, it has to be a hot political issue, one which most politicians would prefer not to address."

"Well, that's a given," said Karen. "That's exactly what's taking place now."

"I guess, I'd want the facts, get the Department of Health involved . . ." Scott tried to form a logical reply.

"Well, I bet nothing happens, Scott, until other segments of society, or some celebrity, gets hit by the same disease," Robert growled in an angry voice. "You politicians will sit on your hands bound with your prejudices, and let us all die."

*Not Ken. Please, not Ken.*

# 6

One Friday night, Karen was not there; she'd taken the evening shift for a co-worker at the hospital. I was disappointed, yet it was then that I realized I looked forward to seeing Karen as much as the discussions. It was her voice that energized the evenings; it was her intensity and seriousness about her ideas that captured my attention; it was her emotional responses – head thrown back and the fullness of her laugh – tears for a touching human story

– her excitement and hand-clapping, her enthusiasm – always encouraging, urging others on. She was bright and sensible with a strong personality. I was attracted to her – and I trusted her opinions.

During the week, I kept thinking about Karen and found my eyes scanning campus surroundings for her. She'd be easy enough to spot. She was about my height; five feet ten, maybe five eight. Her body was full but not heavy or fat, and she walked straight and tall, proud of her stature.

I flushed out Scott. "How well do you know Karen?"

"What do you mean, how well do I know her? You sound as if you wonder if I have any interest in her. Have I dated her? No. Do I want to date her? I could, she'd be a fun date. But I have my eye on two other girls, neither one giving me much of a break."

"Does she go with someone? There's no sign of a special male around in the group."

"Jon, why don't you just ask her out? It's the easiest way to find your answer. You haven't taken many girls out have you?"

"Not in college. Only one really and she went for the guy who played better pool than I did. What an excuse huh?"

I dragged my heels. I found excuses. *I am not as worldly as she. She'd been to Germany and has lived in other cities. I am younger than she. Three years make a difference when you're in your twenties. She loves history and government. Maybe landscaping would not be of interest. Listen to myself. I sound like I'm going to marry the girl. Jeez, it's only a date. Gosh, Mom will be happy to hear that.*

By the time that I got around to asking, it was spring, April, with only five weeks of school remaining. I made my move on a Friday night in her kitchen while she was fixing a tray of snacks and I was opening a bottle of wine. I had to wait for Amy to leave, then another person came in and I waited again. I quickly said, before anyone else came through the kitchen door, "I'm going biking tomorrow would you like to join me?"

Without hesitation she replied, "If it's in the afternoon after two . . . though where would I get a bike. Do you know anyone or can I rent one?"

"Scott has one."

And my secret became public as she yelled into the living room, "Can I borrow your bike tomorrow, Scott? Jon just asked me for a date." I blushed as I heard the sound of applause from the living room.

Our next time together wasn't a true date, except I'd planned to make it so by stopping at a small family diner on the way home from the university arboretum, twenty-five miles outside the city. I'd volunteered for a spring clean-up headed by Mr. Deaver, and asked Karen if she liked to work as a gardener for a day. She teased me, "Cheap labor, eh?"

"Sort of, I guess. They're serving us breakfast and lunch, and I'll buy you dinner. Have you ever been to the arboretum? It's really quite beautiful, in the summer that is."

"I'll say yes under one condition, Jon. Only if I work side by side with you."

Saturday was one of those clear, cool, upper-Midwest spring days. Mr. Deaver had recruited 25 people who split off into work groups of five. Our team first took on the rose garden, removing the winter coverings. After that we raked the stretch of iris beds along an oval pond, before joining others in a wide grove of oak trees clearing the dead branches.

"Ouch, these thorns are wicked. I see why Deaver gave us heavy gloves." Karen remarked while we helped the professionals prune rose bushes. "And you want to do so this all your life?"

"It's where I am the happiest. Outside. Physical exercise. You get to see immediate improvement, and it's a swing back to childhood memories."

"Will you go back home? I've heard you say that there is a family business."

"Yes, and yes. Although the family businesses are a drug store and a hardware store. Mom envisions a landscaping business; wants to see me add to the family tradition of hometown. It all started with my great-grandfather. From the family stories, he

187

was quite the stern German and good businessman. He was the best contractor in the county – built most of the barns in the countryside that still stand."

"I wish I had those same family ties to our family town in Germany. Hitler's war wiped that out. The Russians destroyed everything as they came through, and my grandparents fled to Berlin where survival wasn't easy." I could hear the sad regret in Karen's voice. "My parents came to America in the late fifties, and Grandpapa and Grandmama stayed in Berlin."

"Have you visited the old town? I've heard you mention trips to Germany."

"Yes, we've visited Warzburg several times and wanted them to move back. There were a few old neighbors but Grandpapa stood pat, 'What has been, has been' is his mantra." Karen jerked her hand back, "Ouch. How do they know where to cut the bushes?"

"For me, it was trial and error. I use to be timid and with time I became more aggressive. Of course, I didn't start with rose bushes. My early pruning trials would have killed them."

At the end of the afternoon, we all gathered in the hosta garden – large and spread our near the Japanese pagoda. We took our rest with sodas in hand on the steps leading up to the rose terrace. Karen eyes searched the landscape of the gardens; my eyes searched out the person beside me. A sculptured nose, not small, rather long set above a wide mouth with thin lips, defined her profile. The eyelashes were long, extending out before curling up, almost touching the eyelid. Her thick brown hair was cut long to mid-neck and pushed back softly behind her ears, all tucked under a billed cap for today. With her sturdy body in overalls, one could mistake her for a guy, except when she'd face you, the feminine eyes and beautiful white teeth would deny your guess. *Mom would like Karen.*

"Have you and Scott talked about the apartment downstairs?"

"Yeah, Scott is dealing with the renting agency. I guess a single guy is taking the small room in the back. Who will take Amy's bedroom?"

"I think Mudge – cute nickname, isn't it? Remember, she came several times, once with the tall basketball player who gave us the speech about civil rights. Remember, he was taken back because no one disagreed with him."

Karen leaned forward, took off the cap and swished her hands through her hair. "How about I take a rain check for dinner. This is hard sweaty work. My body will need a tub soaking, and we'd looked pretty scruffy going into the diner. How about tomorrow night or later in the week?"

"I'm on the hook for whenever you say."

When we drove up in front of her place, she opened the door and in an instant leaned over and kissed me on the cheek before sliding out. "Jon, you're a keeper. How about Wednesday dinner?" she said looking back across the car seat.

"Thanks, Karen. I'm glad you came along; it made the day go faster." She bounded up the steps and turned to wave good-bye. Already, I was looking forward to the next time. I liked being with her and felt the first pull to wanting her as my girl.

## 7

The Wednesday night date was followed with a Saturday night supper. Karen wanted to cook a German dinner – pork, kraut, and dumplings with a Riesling wine from the Ruhr vineyards. Amy was across the river in Minneapolis with friends for the weekend, something to do with General Mills and Betty Crocker and maybe a future job. Scott was in Des Moines, tied up with political sessions at Drake University. Chuck and Robert's schedule was always a question. Without the posse, the weekend gatherings waited for another time. I was a bit nervous that it would be an evening of two instead of many.

It was my Saturday at the greenhouse, and I worked longer than usual. Mr. Deaver had a full task list since the year was coming to a close and his student help would vanish in a few weeks. We lingered over his orchids. He'd been unusually talkative today, wanting to share his plans for entering the smaller hybrids in the State Fair. It was six o'clock when I knocked on Karen's door and heard her bright voice, "If it's Jon, come in."

"If it's not, what do I do?" I kidded. "I smelled your cooking as I came up the steps. I haven't had kraut since Christmas. Mom always includes it with the turkey, a Strutter family tradition."

"I was thinking about family today and wondered if we shouldn't share some of our histories - traditions, as you say. I pulled out a couple of albums. There are pictures of relatives who still live in Germany and then those of me growing up in New York. Ought to go well with wine. Or do you want a beer? I found some German beer at the liquor mart."

"I'll take a beer, save the wine for after dinner and your family pictures."

Karen played down cosmetics and I liked her plain look. Her skin had a natural beige blush, her lips well defined and not needing lipstick, her eyelids and lashes tinted in a soft hue, her thick brown hair curled behind her ears. She didn't lack self-confidence, enthusiasm or interest in the events and people around her. Her eyes had a constant sparkle.

"What did Mr. D have you doing today?"

"We spent quite a bit of time on his hybrid plants. He is growing some unusual specimens, especially the orchids and iris, working towards smaller blooms and new color varieties. He's entering some in the State Fair. I've learned a lot from him. He asked today if I wanted to work next year. I told him to count on me, and I mentioned that I wanted to work a summer with a large landscaping firm. I'm hoping he can help place me with one."

"Here in Minnesota?"

"Or Iowa, Illinois."

"But Witherston is your final destination, isn't it?"

"Well that's what my mother wants. Most of the home owners are their own landscapers, but she sees how I could service the entire county and play a role in city planning."

"Tell me about your parents, Jon. Not what they do, but who they are. You have German ancestors also . . . right? With the name Strutter."

*Do I blurt out that I am adopted and I don't know the nationality of my parents?*

"My father's great-great grandfather came from Germany, no record of where, though. His grandfather is remembered as stern and stoic; he was a great influence in my father's upbringing . . . Dad was only five when his mother died, and a strong bond was created with his grandfather."

"Does that mean your father is also stern and stoic? I find it amusing that most people tag those attributes, along with stubborn and hardheaded, on German people. I don't find you to be that way." Karen gave a quick wink and smile.

"No, I've never seen myself as rigid or inflexible. Are you? Being a hundred percent German is surely a test."

"What do you think? Are those my notable strengths? We haven't butted heads yet."

"No. You are more like my father. You have determination but you're not rigid. I suspect you have a sense of right and wrong and are not afraid to stand firm on what you believe. My father is very loyal to his principles, family and town. He has the patience to see the whole picture but stands pretty firm on what is right to do and say. People trust him. So do I. He's helped me talk out a lot of stuff. He's a great father."

"My father is a quiet man. The days of Hitler and war crushed his spirit, and I think he regrets leaving his parents behind. But, when he sets his mind, it's not changeable. He doesn't re-visit decisions, passes on with 'what's done is done'. In other words, 'let it be'. I see those same characteristics in Grandpapa."

"You say they live in Berlin. That is the one place that my father speaks of visiting. He wants to make that trip but doesn't plan for it. I wish he would while he's still in his fifties." As I cleaned my plate of second helpings, I admitted, "Good supper.

Good cook." I softened my eyes hoping they'd show a glint of affection.

Karen asked as we cleared the table, "Do you have a picture of your father?"

"Yes, and Mom too."

"Here, Jon, you open the wine." Karen carried two glasses and we headed for the davenport, side by side. She snuggled close as she picked up a brown album, two inches thick, ragged on the corners, with a photo of a church encased on the front cover. "Get your pictures out first before I start this tome."

In my wallet I had a picture of Dad and Mom from several summer ago. It'd been a family picnic day in the back yard and cameras were in busy hands. There were probably better ones, but both Grandpa Frank and Carl were in this one.

"This is Dad and his father, Frank, on his right." My finger moved to the right, "Mom and Grandpa Carl next. He was almost eighty when he died. He's the one who fought in the war. His unit drove on into Germany from Italy and he told me about the concentration camps."

Karen studied the photo. "No grandmothers?"

"No. Both died young, well before I came along."

"Where did your blue eyes come from?"

"Mom thinks from her side."

"And who has the cowlick like yours. It intrigues me how it curls into a circle."

*I could tell her that both come from people I don't know and how I wonder about what else I don't know. This is not the time to talk about adoption; it'll detract from the album.* "That remains a mystery to all of us."

"Let me touch it. I've wanted to rub my finger around it." She turned my head so the back of my neck faced her. "Smooth. What a distinctive mark." As we turned toward each other, I couldn't keep my hands from reaching for her face and bringing my lips to her mouth, softly, slowly. Her lips took my kiss, held it, and then pushed into my mine, lingering in slow motion. This was no ordinary kiss such as with Gretchen or Becka. I felt the sensations in my mouth and down to all the right places. Our first kiss went from second to third before I mentioned, "Album, pictures, should we?"

"Jon, you are terribly sweet."

We clinked our wine glasses, I kissed the tip of her nose and, with a sigh, Karen opened the album.

"This is my grandparents' town . . . Warzburg, Martin Luther's city. Their parents were born here and Grandpapa and Grandmama have known each other their whole lives. This building here was Grandpapa's home. You know, in the old country, the family lives upstairs and the animals downstairs . . . all in one building."

"A bit smelly, eh?"

"Yes, but one tends to keep the stalls clean. The animal heat warms the floor above them. And, it's convenient for animal care in cold winters." Karen rubbed her hand over the picture before turning the page. "Here is my father, as a young boy, with his sister. A brother was born later. He died during the war. From measles. He was seven years old."

"And the sister?"

"She stayed behind when Grandpapa and Grandmama left for Berlin ahead of the German soldiers. They had to walk twenty miles to finally get a train. Adele is no longer alive and that is one reason my Grandpapa doesn't go back. The Russians ravished the town, like barbarians . . . pent-up emotions, frustrations, and hatred led them to do terrible deeds. Adele was gang raped, left in a cold barn where she hanged herself. His parents died from the hardships of the winter and Grandpapa has no family. Well, some cousins, who they don't see too often anymore. 'What's over is done with' are his words."

"Is this one of your grandparents?" I pointed to an old couple.

"Yes, we took this in front of their building on our last trip to Berlin four years ago. I'm glad that we are going back next summer after graduation. I want to stay with them for at least two months.

Their time is getting short. They don't speak of their age, but I know they are nearing ninety." Karen spoke directly to my eyes. "I want to capture the old stories - their history - and write their story. If I can, maybe I'll visit the cousins to include their stories. It's important to me and for my children and grandchildren."

"You'll make a great history teacher. Where will you go to teach?"

"Like what town or state? I don't know. I'm not inclined to head back to New York, but then wouldn't mind being close to my parents. It's a decision I should make this summer. I'd like to teach and study for a graduate degree, so I'll need a college town or one close by."

In another hour, her photos took me through her childhood in New York City: baby pictures, parents, school days, playgrounds, pets, days at the seashore, and graduation ceremonies. Photos introduced her brother, Ernst, older than Karen, who lives outside of the City, a High-School principal in New Rochelle. "Well, that's the Noth family." Karen said as she laid the album aside. "When do I get to hear about your family history?"

"The best way would be to come for a visit to Witherston." *Boy won't Mom love that. A real girlfriend for Jon would be perfect. And Dad could ask about Berlin. But maybe my suggestion is too soon. How serious do I want to be? More than before, I think.*

"Well, Jon, I wouldn't be disappointed if that worked out." She stood up and held out her hands. "It's a lovely night, let's go for a walk. Okay?"


# 8

The final weeks of the school term were too filled with tests, graduation, parties, and final moving day to have the time alone with Karen I would have liked. We looked forward to next year; we'd see more of each other with Scott and me living in the downstairs apartment. And, we made tentative plans to see each other during the summer. After all, it was only a two-hour drive between Witherston and the city. We both admitted to an interest in a relationship beyond being just friends.

"Karen, I've never had a serious relationship." The closest had been Ken, but that was for me to know, not others.

"Not even in high-school? What is a serious relationship for you?"

"One in which we share ourselves. Thoughts and dreams. Be together. Care about our feelings. Learn to be close with each other." I brought out each word hesitantly.

"And where is the intimate part? You know, sex?" Karen gave a quizzical look with raised eyebrows. "You do know sex, don't you Jon?"

I felt my cheeks turning hot, and I heard my embarrassed chuckle.

"Jon, you're a virgin, aren't you? Now that explains your timidness with affection. Well, you are sweeter than I expected. Now, now, Jon take that as a compliment."

"Does it matter to you that I might be? Does that make me an oddball?" I heard the edge come into my voice as I stood up. "We can drop it here, teacher."

"Jon, no, no, no. Please. Sex will happen when it should. The right time shall be the right time. To be truthful, I am cautious myself. I was in a very serious relationship three years ago, one that I thought had long-term dreams. It ended quickly and unexpectedly with a lot of hurt, pain and bitterness. I vowed, the next time I gave myself so fully, I'd be sure that the guy was committed to our relationship. You might be that guy." Karen stood in front of me and waited in silence. "Are we okay? Let's let it happen, whatever happens is meant to be. Jon?"

I wrapped my arms around her and held her tight, whispering, "Yes, let's. I like you very much Karen. These are my first serious feelings for a girl. I feel awkward, like a grown-up novice who's behind the times."

We stayed encircled, our heads tucked together cheek to cheek until we heard Amy at the front door. A squeeze of our hands gave

*Ann Wade*

a message of promise.

## 9

Exam week was all that was left of the school year. I'd had my head in books and class notes, particularly those for plant pathology and botany. My concentration was interrupted too often by Karen, not in person but in my thoughts. I kept thinking forward, wondering where our relationship was going. I held thoughts of love, but I was leery of me. I'd never done sex, but I wanted Karen. I had secrets not ready to share. I guess I was studying the pathology of Jon.

Dad would be in the cities tomorrow, and I looked forward to having time with him over dinner. I planned to bring up finding my biological parents once again. I wondered why I thought he could be of help anymore than the agency – what else could he know that they didn't? Somehow, it seemed like he was my last chance; if Dad didn't have an answer, I'd give it up.

## 10

Dad was sitting at a patio table when I walked into Simon's. The night was warm and inviting for outdoor eating. He stood up as I came through the doorway trellis and toward our table by the green wall of shrubbery.

"I thought this would be a good setting for our landscape professional," was his first comment as we clasped in an embrace. "How's the prep for exams going?"

"Oh, you know the late hours, trying to find your notes, guessing what will be asked on the exam. I've boned up on the tougher subjects. I'm aiming for nothing below a B." As the waiter stood ready to take our order, I asked, "Do you have the beer from New Ulm? Good, I'll have a draft. No? Okay, then, a bottle."

Over our beers, I asked about family. Mother? Busy with spring planting and planning a summer get-away with Clare.

196

Papo? Still at the store every day keeping the inventory in balance and saddened by the illness of one of the coffee fellows - his group of old farts.

"I wish Grandpa Carl was still here. Some of my best times with him were in the workshop. He was so patient, never tired explaining the right way to put things together. I had to redo a birdhouse three times so there were no spaces where the joints come together. I miss him."

As we enjoyed a salmon dinner, Dad asked about classes for my junior year. I told him that even though I'd switched from landscaper architecture to landscape management, I planned to take a design class anyway. I thought it a 'sort of a good to know' skill. I'd be into landscape management, botany and turf grass management, and starting economics classes. I planned more business classes in my last two years. "I need to be as good a businessman as you and Papo."

I insisted on dessert of chocolate turtle cheesecake and then broached Mom's forbidden subject.

"Dad, I went to Catholic Charities and met with Mrs. Conlay . . . nice lady but no help, no information, no encouragement. Not surprising, is it? You knew that."

"But you had to hear it for yourself, Jon." He waited a few seconds before saying, "Now what? Can you let it go?"

"No, Dad, but I'll have to. There are no avenues open, no clues, and no possibilities. All I wanted was to know who they are, what they look like, what they do. Even pictures would be something. Do all adopted children want this?"

"I suppose they do, son. At least those adopted at birth and who never lived with their biological mother or father. There is a natural curiosity to know about oneself, the whole self. I do understand your need to know."

"Mom's not like that, she doesn't understand that need to know."

"Well, maybe about some things, but she's more for life going smoothly. It's the ugliness she wants to keep out. I think of her as wanting to be an angel, making 'perfect' happenings. It's not bad having people who strive to make life good, enjoyable, pleasant. Her frustration and pain come from the necessity to control, because perfect is not an absolute.

"Well, son let's play 'what if'. Let's say you knew where your biological parents lived. What would you do?"

"Gosh, what would I do?" *Just like Dad to make me think this through. To make it specific.* "I'd want to go to that town, that city, and hang around, maybe get a job. I might have to stay a while. Surely, one of them might have a business or work in a store or in a public job. I'd have to know their hang-outs, be there when they'd be there." With a laugh, I said, "For sure, I couldn't just hang out in my car on their street. I'd be picked up for stalking."

"How are you so sure that you could just see them and not reveal yourself?"

"Because I wouldn't know what to say to them. I guess it's hard for you to believe that I don't want to reveal myself. I'm not looking for their recognition. They aren't looking for me either, that's for sure. Why would I make it awkward for them?"

"How would you tell your mother about this?"

"I wouldn't, Dad. After I saw her reaction when we talked before, I've thought a lot about her ways of thinking. And, I don't want to hurt her or give her any concern. She loves me too much, I know that . . . and I do have to protect that. This would have to be my secret, but one that doesn't appear that I'll need to keep."

As we waited for the waiter to bring the bill, Dad told me, "Mrs. Barrows was in the store the other day and we had time for a brief chat. She asked about you, what you were doing this summer. I could see that she was very disappointed that Ken was not coming home for a visit. They haven't seen him for a while and she sounded a bit concerned. Have you heard from him? Is everything okay with him?"

"Just a brief conversation a month ago. I called him and caught him just as he was going out the door . . . to some party with his roommates. He said he was doing okay, still working both jobs, had sold a couple of his pieces at an art fair. There wasn't time to talk about this summer."

"You two were pretty close."

"Yeah, we were. I found it wasn't the same being on a swim team without Ken. My interest wasn't as strong when I joined the team here. Just as well I quit."

Dad left a ten-dollar tip, not stingy. "We kept his table for over two hours," he explained. As we said goodnight in the parking lot, Dad suggested another meal together. "My last session tomorrow ends at eleven. How about we meet for lunch before I head out. Could you do that?"

"Well, yeah, if it was after one o'clock and we eat in Dinkytown."

"Name the time and place."

"How about one thirty at the Chinese restaurant? That one on the corner that Mom likes. You'll find parking in the lot across the street. Easy in and easy out." I added a last minute request. "Would you have time to stop by the dorm and take some of my stuff? It would ease the load for my car. You know Scott and I are renting an apartment next year, on ground floor. I'll be glad to be out of dorm living." We hugged and waved as we both drove off.

*Dad's a neat guy, always there for me. He'd be the best advisor if I do start a landscaping business. But do I want to be in Witherston the rest of my life?*

## 11

No greater surprise could have been dropped on me the next day. I was stunned and cried when I read what Dad gave me in an envelope; a piece of paper I read three times before I could speak.

During our meal, for me my favorite shrimp and pea pod platter and for Dad chicken chow mien, we talked about my morning test and his meeting. His next words were mysterious, words carefully chosen it seemed, and they caught my attention immediately.

"Son, I am about to take an action about which I have ambiguous feelings. Once it is done, I won't be able to put it back in the box, so to speak. Being a cautious type of guy, I hesitate. Being the father of wonderful young man, I feel obligated. This envelope and its content must never enter our house or family. You'll know I've kept a secret and you must realize the trust I'm placing in you." He handed a white envelope to me, light-weight and sealed. I was glad we were at a table tucked into a back corner.

"Dad, does this have to do with my birth parents?"

"Yes, Jon."

I lost my appetite immediately. My stomach churned and tears brimmed around my eyelids. "Wow. I never expected this. How come you have information?"

He shook his head. "That's my secret."

"Dad, I'd rather open this in private. Let's check out and go to the car." The cashier handed us fortune cookies and I put mine in my shirt pocket.

My hands were shaky as I slid my finger under the flap of the envelope. A single sheet was inside. I gave a big sigh before unfolding it in my hands. My eyes went over the lines, again and again.

Nora (Paulsen) Allen 37 years of age
    Owner of Print/Frame Shop
    Married to Ben Allen 38 years of age
    Owner of Insurance Agency
Home and businesses in Brandeis, Illinois
Bio father: Tim Parsons  died in Vietnam War

In my hands rested two photos, an arrow pointing to a man on one with Ben written on top and to a woman on the other with the name Nora. Her photo had been taken at a distance, and she was a shadowy figure in the middle of several people.

I felt like a silly little child as I broke into short gasping sobs. Dad stretched his right arm across my shoulders, "Jon, this has more weight than I'd presumed. Are you okay?" He circled his hand between my shoulder blades, attempting to soothe the little crying boy.

"I don't know how you did this, but thank you. This is her . . . a bit fuzzy, but maybe a magnifying glass will help," I said as I sniffled the moisture up my nose. "And, thank you for trusting me so much."

"Well, son, that is a key issue. It is a leap of faith to let you see these, and I must have them back . . . I keep them in a private and secure place. And, of course, your mother has never seen this or even knows about it, and it must stay that way. I do have your word on that, don't I?" I nodded. "Do you understand why Jon?"

"I think it would destroy our family, as we know it now. Mother would never forgive you . . . and maybe hate you for telling me."

"Hate is a strong word, but we could say, she'd be crushed . . . her trust in me shattered . . ."

"Yeah, just like what happened to her Catholic faith."

Dad let me hold the pictures for several more minutes, then held his hand out. The names were burned into my brain, and with one last look at Nora, I put the paper and photos in the envelope and handed it to my father. "Thank you Dad." I paused before I said firmly, "I'm going to see her in person one day."

"Jon, promise me that you will tell me beforehand. It's important to me, just as seeing her is important to you. I was hoping that a picture would fill the void you speak about, but I see it won't. There must be more you have to have."

"Yes, there is Dad. But, it may have been the guy, Tim. Now I'll never know about him."

I got out of the car, walked around to the driver's side for an embrace that held more than just a casual farewell. I admired this man who'd been a true father since my birth. He'd always made me feel worthwhile, never damaging my self esteem, and I realized that I had just witnessed an ultimate sacrifice – sharing with me a secret kept from his wife. I gave one last wave as I watched him drive away.

I forced myself to stay alert as I biked through the heavy traffic back to the dorm. I had one hour to calm my racing mind before a late afternoon class.

*Thank God, it wasn't a test. I wanted to yell out the good news. I'd seen her! Who could I tell? Karen? No, she'd need to know more than I was ready to share. Who else but Ken . . . Michael. I'll call him. I want to know his summer plans, anyway. I miss him.*

I found a cryptic message when I opened the fortune cookie: Good intentions pave a straight path. Set your sights to the horizon. Your lucky numbers are 4, 5, 21. *What Chinese god rigged this cookie? Four, my birthday month, twenty-one my age, 5 one of my lucky numbers.* I slid the little piece of paper into my wallet behind my license.

In the emotional last minutes, we'd forgotten about sending boxes home.

## 12

"Hey, Michael, this is Jon. Glad you were by the phone. Got time to talk?"

"Yeah, you sound excited. What's up? Are you going to tell me you're coming to California this summer? I hopa, hopa!"

"No, it's better than that."

"You've had sex! With who? Male or female?"

"Boy, you aren't shy anymore. The answer is 'no' to both."

"Well, that's even more disappointing. Man, it's getting a little late for you, isn't it?"

"It's not too far off. I've met a girl that's caught my interest and juices, as they would say." I shook my head in disbelief of my words. "Michael, I saw a picture of my birth mother today and her name is Nora." I heard a 'no kidding' on the other end of the line. "Yeah, she's in her mid-thirties and so is her husband. My birth father died in the Nam war."

"How did you find this out?"

"From the most unlikeliest of people, my father. I didn't inquire how and why he had the information, and he probably wouldn't have told me. The less I know, the better, is where he's at. You know Mother can't ever know that we know. And, that means you. Promise to keep this between us."

"Of course, you think I'm stupid. What are you going to do, now that you know who she is? Do you know where she lives?"

"Yes. In Brandeis, Illinois. Looks like a small town on the map. It's close to the Mississippi River outside of Moline, Davenport, Rock Island . . . called the Quad Cities . . . spreading along the Iowa and Illinois border lines. I'd just have to drive cross Iowa."

"Are you going to do that?"

"I don't know yet. First I need to get my emotions in check. I want to see her in person, but did hope to see him also. My plans have to go through Dad first . . . fair enough."

"Jon, did you want to find out if one of them was gay? You know – heredity? - a gene from your birth father. An answer to your sexuality."

"You sure put it bluntly, don't you?"

"Well, I didn't come to California to hide anymore. I know who I am and I don't have to hate myself or be ashamed. Say, I have good news also. I've found a partner and guess what his name is."

"Not another Michael, is it?"

"No, his name is Ken. Can you believe that? Seems like the perfect match, or what?"

"Well, I glad for you. Is he an artist too?"

"No, but he owns a gallery in a refurbished warehouse and lives in one of the lofts upstairs. He's ten years older than I am and has been here a long time. Gives me a lot of confidence and a venue to show my works. I'm happier than I've ever been Jon."

He wanted me to come out to visit this summer; he was not coming back. "It's getting more awkward to be around my father, he still ignores the issue and me."

I admitted to myself that I was curious as to what it meant to live the gay style; but my preference was as an observer, not a participant; Karen had settled that question.

I told Ken (Michael) about our Friday night group and our discussions on the gay disease. "Be careful. I don't want any bad news from you."

"Neither does my mother."

## 13

"Mr. Deaver, do you know of any alumni who own landscaping businesses? I'm particularly thinking of Brandeis, Illinois."

"Well, I do have a computer file of some who've stayed in touch. I'd have to check to see by that city. Why? What's your interest?"

"I thought it would be a good summer job and experience to work in another city. I did Witherston last summer, and off and on before that. You know, get to see how others might run a landscaping business."

"If you have time after you finish here, stop by my office and we'll call up the file and have a look. I'd be glad to make a contact in your behalf with whatever city you choose." He started down the row and then turned back to me. "Why Brandeis? Something special there?"

"Sort of."

"A girl, no doubt?"

# CHAPTER FOUR

## *Summer, 1983*

### 1

T HE CAR REEKED with emotions as I headed south into Iowa on Highway 35. I felt queasy; the kind of nausea that tags along with fear. My mind told me the wise thing to do was to go home; my heart told me differently; *so which one is the smart one?* I kept my attention on driving and an eye on the speedometer; *don't go over the speed limit.*

Mom's image arose again and again before me. I'd never felt her anger before: "Then go, Jon," were her words last night. "Off on some foolish lark. You're not telling the whole story, I can sense it, and I don't like that of you. Keeping secrets is not of our family, and secrets come out of their hiding places in due course. Go, have it your way for now, but let me tell you how much this hurts. I feel I'm being punished." With that, she sliced the peach pie, one piece for Dad and one for me, and then pushed herself from the table and slammed the door on her way to the back porch.

Dad looked at me, shaking his head, his left fist jammed into his upper lip. "Jon, I've misplayed this one. I hope you can hold it together and not let it get any worse. What a role for me; the dad does the sin and asks the son to hold back the harm. I'd better go to her. Why not clear the table?"

I heard their snatches of words. "John, did you encourage .

. . ?"

"Em, he's twenty-one"

"Freedom, what do you mean freedom? Am I some kind of an ogre?"

"Em, for God's sake don't blow this out of . . ."

"Don't you tell me what not to do. You're siding with him."

"Don't let him go with your anger. You'll regret that."

Then her voice went low, "Why do I do this?"

I hadn't realized until now what it really meant to be an only child; the sole focus of an over-attentive mother. My life had been planned without me while I was basking in the limelight. *Wow! If I'd gone to California! Poor Mrs. Barrows.*

I drove into the next Rest Stop, needing to pee. I followed the walking path around the back of the grounds to settle myself – I'd been driving down a busy highway without conscious thought. I remember her final words beside my bed early this morning. I woke to feel her stroking my forehead, wanting me to awaken softly. "Maybe if there'd been others, I wouldn't need you so terribly much. Maybe I expected too much of one child to fill an immense void." Her eyes were moist. "Let's not part unhappy." Then she beamed one of her mother's smiles on me, "Be easy with me, Jon, and don't stay away too long. We should have some summer time together." She kissed my forehead and I squeezed her hands.

"Mom, I'll be back in July for sure, ready for whatever you wish to do. I may ask a friend from university to visit us. If you'd like that."

"Oh, your roommate, Scott?"

"No, a friend of ours, Karen. Scott and I are moving into the downstairs apartment of the house she lives in. She rents the second floor with another gal. I'd like you and Dad to meet her."

"Well, dear heart, what a nice thing to look forward to . . . a girl friend. Yes, that would be nice. Now get a few more hours of sleep. I love you, Jon . . . sometimes I think even more than your

Dad." She stopped at the door to tell me she'd make my favorite breakfast, sausage and pancakes. "So no skipping out early."

*Be cautious. Be careful. Look, see and come home. And, don't blow it by saying something stupid.*

I drove along the green, emerging cornfields and passed Ames at eleven o'clock. Soon the skyline of Des Moines was ahead of me and Highway 80, which was a straight line across eastern Iowa into the Quad Cities. I'd estimated eight or nine hours on the road and wanted to be in Brandeis by six. I'd pick up lunch at some quick stop along the way.

Other than the guilt of keeping a whopper of a secret from Mom, I begin to feel okay with myself again. I remembered my fortune cookie promised good luck. Then Mr. Deaver's files rolled up a landscaping business between Brandeis and Moline. He even called the owner, Ted Anderson, who said he had a lot of summer work and extra hands would be welcomed. After I heard Mr. Deaver praise my experience and work ethic, I felt sure I'd find work. Then Dad handed me five hundred dollars to tide me over until payday.

*Dad. What a risk he's taken. Bet he regrets doing so. He has to trust me that I can handle this without mistakes. That's a lot of trust to place in a twenty-year old. I'd be nervous if it were me. God, I'm nervous because it is me. If I just stay true to my goal – to see her, not to reveal myself. And bring nothing back into our family.*

My anxieties had lessened as I drove by Iowa City and I turned my thoughts to Karen. Between bites of a ham sandwich and swigs of soda, I fiddled with the radio knob looking for music. My ear caught the distinctive voice of Willie Nelson, one of Mom's favorites. She'd wiggle up to Dad and say, "Hey handsome, how about a dance?" I'd seen them dance in the kitchen, back porch, living room. She loved it. I envisioned dancing with Karen. *Does she dance? Am I good enough? We'll dance at the Owl's Inn when she comes in August. I want to go camping, walk in the woods, get to know her better. Will Mom take to her? Dad'll like the Berlin part.*

The mileage sign for Davenport came quickly, only thirty miles. I squinted at the map to check if I should stay on Highway 80 past Moline to Brandeis. I'd be there in an hour or so, looking at my watch it would be close to six-thirty. Brandeis was a suburb of Moline, just twenty miles from its outskirts. Half-way between, I read a road sign:

Allen Insurance Agency
Serving the Quad cities since 1938
Full Service Insurance by Certified Agents
1 309 795 7500
Ben Allen, Owner

I had arrived on Saturday, and on Sunday I explored my surroundings. Brandeis had a typical Midwest town square with a village green at the center. Stores and shops, extending four blocks each way, indicated an upscale community. Large pots of flowers adorned the street corners. Hanging flower baskets brightened the sidewalks, and sculptures made the park a work of art. I could see that Ted Anderson was in the right business.

After traveling around the downtown area block by block, I turned back to the main street looking for a place to stay. I turned left in the direction of a black, red and white sign directing me to Molly's Home and Lodgings. I noticed its homey, inviting appearance as I drove into the front parking space. A small park across the street was lively with young children playing tag, hiding behind trees, and squealing with glee. I stood by the car to watch their play. Mom would like this scene.

## 2

Molly's Home and Lodgings was a two-story colonial and the walkway from the car led to a large screened-in porch at the rear of the house. An office sign hung on the door. To my left was a building, one long porch with six doors, apparently leading into separate units. Flowerbeds were scattered around the porch steps, and rich green grass extended to the street. Six large old-fashioned pine rocking chairs, one by each door, gave a hint of southern charm.

It looked like the right place for me, and I hoped that there was a room. As I started forward, a spry gray-haired lady walked toward me, her hand reaching for mine. "Hello, young man. I'm Molly Gibbons. It's a grand summer day, isn't it? Suppose you'll be wanting a room."

I took her slim hand and was surprised by the strength of her handshake. "Yes, I do. The park, your lovely gardens . . . I'll be disappointed if you're full."

"Well, these outside units here are taken, but I have two rooms in the house. You'd have to share the bath if someone takes the other room. Is it just for the night?"

"No, I plan to be here for a couple of weeks. Is there a special weekly rate? But, would I be disturbing you to be in your home that long?"

"Only if you are the carousing type. And, of course, no girls in the room. Any trouble like that and I'd have to ask you to leave." Her eyes held mine, as if she was sizing me up. "I'd enjoy the company. Young people bring the outside world to me. How about thirty dollars a night and I'll make breakfast for you."

"Oh, I can eat in town."

"Oh, I know you can, but I'm an early riser and breakfast is my best meal. Morning talk with coffee is a good way to start a day. Or maybe you sleep in late? Guess you'll think me nosey, but what are your plans? I suppose if you had relatives or friends here, you'd be staying with them."

"I'll be working for Ted Anderson . . . landscaping work . . . really just a pair of extra hands for him. I'm a horticulture student and wanted to see what different landscapers do. I may start a similar business in Minnesota where my family lives."

"Well, we are going to have some good chats. I love flowers and working the soil." She took my hand, running her hand over the calloused spots. "Feels like you do too." Keeping my hand in hers, she said, "Let's go look at your room."

Along the way she added, "There's old Ted and young Ted, and they own a large chunk of property out on County twenty-one. You'll be busy. They do work in all the surrounding cities, some big commercial jobs and a lot of the homes here."

"How long have you lived in Brandeis?"

"Forever. I grew up in Moline, married Warren who grew up here and became the mayor of Brandeis. Not much I don't know about the town and the people."

*Yep, I'd come to the right place. All the history and background. . . . Anderson's on road twenty-one, one of the lucky numbers of the fortune cookie. Gotta be right.*

After Molly was sure I liked the spacious room and we made arrangements on how I'd pay for telephone calls, I paid her for a week, and she invited me to share her diner with her. I smiled and said, "Thank you Mrs. Gibbons."

"Call me Molly." She clenched her hands around my arm, "I think we are going to have a good time together. Now, go get your stuff and I'll set the table."

*Think I've just found a grandmother for me!*


# 3

As a signal of my presence, I hummed as I walked across the hallway from the stairs to the kitchen door. Molly was at the stove tending to a large soup pot, she looked over her shoulder and said with a smile, "Almost ready. Chicken noodle." She looked small in her large kitchen. There was a long row of cupboards along two sides of the room and her cooking area on a third side. Gazing at her frame, I noticed her legs lightly bowed at the knees and a slight curvature between her shoulders. Her pure white hair curled around her hairline and a small, thinning spot showed on the crown. I guessed her to be in her eighty's, although her face with few wrinkles could deny this guess.

The table was set for two: heavy white soup bowls and plates for the large slices of bread in a basket (*bet it's home-made*). There were shining soup spoons (old silver with an ornate design), and yellow cloth napkins. A small bouquet of yellow daisies sat to the side in a cut-glass vase.

"Ice tea, Jon? Otherwise it's water. I'm out of soda and liquor left this house when my husband died."

"Ice tea is fine. Can I help?"

"Ice is in the freezer and the tea is in that pitcher." She nodded towards the end of the counter. "Hope you like chicken soup. Noodles are one of my specialties."

Molly kept the dinner conversation focused on Brandeis. First she told me the background of the Anderson family. Ted being a hometown boy, drafted during the final years of the world war and returned to Brandeis with a French bride. "Surprising to a lot of people. Ted started with borrowed money and has grown a successful business and two boys who work with him. People got to know his wife Edith when she started their flower shop. Business got to be so heavy, she moved it into town – right down on the square. They are one of our success stories and are well liked. Edith's cousins came from France one year, and the town gave them a real nice party – right on the square."

"Looks like I've come to the right place."

"Give Ted an honest day of work and he'll help you with what you want to know."

"I noticed other billboards along the road into town. Mae's Diner?"

"Use to be our best food in town, but since Mae died, you'll get better food in my kitchen. Her daughter sold out to a couple from Indiana who don't know a hoot about cooking."

"Guess I won't invite you there for dinner, huh? And then there was one for Ott's Antiques?"

"Oh yes. That family has scoured the countryside for every last piece of old furniture. Old Will Ott was a master at re-furnishing wood. His grandson, Bill, is walking in his footsteps.

Worth visiting their barn just to see their work. They have people coming even from Chicago to buy." Molly motioned to his bowl, "There's more soup."

"Two bowls, and these are big bowls, have filled me up. Your bread is good." I helped her clear the table and, as we did the dishes, I asked about another sign. "Allen Insurance, is that a home-town business?"

"Ah, yes the Allen family. Bernie with the backing of his father built that business from scratch. My husband didn't think Bernie could do it with the little bit of knowledge he had of insurance and finance. But what he had was a way with people; they trusted him and they never had to pay for any of his mistakes. His son became his partner and then they both sold to a cousin. That Ben is a real go-getter, they say."

"Do you know them? I assume they have a family."

"Just cousins, nieces and nephews. Not many childless families in our town, but Ben and Nora grew businesses versus a family."

"What does the wife, Nora, do? Do you know her?"

"I've been in her framing shop a couple of times, and she's fairly active and visible in the town. In fact, they both are. Country club people, and they get involved in our town celebrations. He's at the head of our parades every other year."

"Their reputation? Is it respectable?"

"Rumors were, at one time, that he liked to gamble. If he still does, he must be a winner. I understand they are debt-free. Of course when you not raising a family . . ."

I didn't push for any more information, but I could see that Molly knew the families of Brandeis pretty well. Getting to Nora's frame shop was number one on my list.

# NORA AND BEN

# CHAPTER ONE

## *Attraction and Adventure*

### 1

"**H**URRY JEN. MRS. Groton will be here in ten minutes." Nora yelled up the stairs. "Your suitcases aren't down here yet. Are you still in the bathroom, fussing with your hair?" Nora shook her head and mumbled, "Teenagers."

"I'm hurrying," was the return from upstairs. "I'm there in a minute, Aunt Nora."

"It doesn't seem like that. What about breakfast?"

"I'll just grab a breakfast bar. Put a blueberry and a raspberry on the hall table."

"That's hardly enough. It's five hours before the bus will stop for lunch." Nora added, "I know, I know. You're watching your figure." Nora repeated her mumblings, "Teenagers wanting to be slim . . . all about looks. I probably should have another discussion about good eating, anorexia – just to let her know I'm watching." Nora wasn't sure who had the most influence, she or Jen's mother. Jen stayed often at her aunt and uncle's house because her closest friends lived in the neighborhood. She had grown up on the next street over and left her best friends behind when her parents moved to a newer suburb outside of town. It was like having two homes and two sets of parents.

Jen flew into the kitchen with brush in hand. "Look Nora, it won't stay down. It makes me look weird." Nora saw the swatch of hair on the left side of Jen's bangs sticking out to the side. The hair was wet from Jen's failed attempt to make it lay flat.

"You must've of slept on it wrong, honey. Don't worry about it. Wear your strawberry cap, by lunchtime it'll be in place."

Nora started for the staircase, "I'll get your luggage. Mrs. Groton will be honking the horn and you're not ready." *Not a good start for the day. I've got ten different things stacked up for the day . . . think about those later . . . gotta get Jen out the door. What a blessing for summer camps.* Nora saw the clothes on the bed and started to pack them in the suitcase. "Is this the last of it, Jen? Where are your hiking boots?"

"There in the duffel bag," Jen snapped as she came into the bedroom holding a toilet case. "Nora, where's my slicker? I think I left it here last time."

"How would I know? Why have you waited to the last moment? Is it still down in the hall closet?" Nora heard the doorbell ring. "Here they are Jen. I'll look in the closet while you say goodbye to Uncle Ben."

Nora saw Ben sitting up in the king side bed as she passed their bedroom door. He was holding his arms out to Jen. "Why are you crying, honey? You miss me already, and you haven't even left."

"No, it's my hair. Just look how it sticks up. It ruins everything."

"Honey, you always look pretty to me. Maybe you ought to push all your hair to that side . . . forget the bangs. Hell, you'll have a cap on most of the time at camp. Forget about style, have fun, that's what camp is all about. Come on, time for our bear hug."

"Come on Jen," Nora yelled from downstairs. Jen jumped off the bed, "Bye Uncle Ben, see you in a month. I'll be ready for our golf lessons. How many cousins are playing this summer?"

"Five of you," Ben yelled as Jen hurried out the door, "and

we're going to take the trophy."

Nora waved from the front porch steps, as the mini-van backed out of the driveway. She threw a kiss to Jen and waved a 'thank you' to the driver. She was glad Betty Groton had offered to drive Jen and her friends to the bus that would take twenty-five girls to a Girl Scout camp in northern Wisconsin. Jen had been going to a scout camp since she was eleven years old, but this was the first year of four weeks in another state.

"Like a whirlwind, isn't she Bash?" Nora asked as she ambled into the bedroom. "I'm taking Jen to Richard's when she returns and splurge on a hair cut for her. He ought to be able to style those bangs to hide the patch that sticks out. May cost seventy dollars, but it will be worth it."

"Be careful. Elaine may not want you taking that on. I think she's jealous when we do too much."

"Yes, I'll okay it with her mother first." Nora started for her closet to make her selection for the day. "God, I've got a busy day. How about you? Is it golf or office?"

"I was thinking more of coffee and juice, served by the most beautiful gal in my bedroom."

"Do I have to start your day also?"

"Yeah, with a morning quickie between the sheets."

"Oh, you're making a joke. We've never been quick in our lives."

"Come on, you've certainly got thirty minutes for some lovin'."

"No, I've got to get ready to fly out of the door. It's a busy day." Nora replied over her shoulder while she pulled underwear out of a dresser drawer.

"Aw, don't leave me now. I could be the best part of your day, and every day for the next thirty."

Nora turned around and, with an impish grin, made a flying leap for the bed. Ben caught her and nuzzled into her neck. "You always smell so good."

"Ouch, don't give me a morning whisker rash." Nora moved

on top of his body and with a satisfying smile, "My God, you feel good . . . my ever ready lover."

Sixty minutes later, they were off in separate cars; Nora in her white Blazer and Ben in his silver Mercedes.

## 2

"What a guy." Nora said to herself as she steered her car through the morning traffic into town. They'd been the best of playmates, right from the beginning when she'd met Ben on the ski slopes of Colorado. He skied recklessly, like the risk taker he was, tackling the moguls with speed and style. He was quick, bold, and self-assured. Nora remembered their first meeting, on the ski lift headed for the top run. He'd jumped out of nowhere, it seemed, and took the empty spot next to her on the lift chair. His most striking feature was his thick dark brown hair – too much for an ordinary ski cap, so he wore earmuffs.

"You're a good skier," he smiled at her.

"You've seen me on the slopes?" Nora quizzed. Sunglasses hid their eyes.

"Who could miss you in that golden outfit. Going to the top? We could ski down together."

"Ho, ho, I'm not up to that challenge. I take the more gentle slopes . . . I'm getting off on the third stop."

"Hey, my name is Ben, also answer to Bash. What's yours? You here alone?"

"You're moving too fast Ben."

"And so? What's the answer?"

"I'm with a girl and her boy friend, and I answer to Nora."

As Nora pulled her hat tight over her ears and placed her poles in her hands preparing for the next stop, he said, "I'll buy you a drink at the Staghorn . . . your friends too." Nora didn't answer him, but he yelled to her as she skied away from the seat. "See you on the lodge deck in forty minutes." She held up her hand as the lift passed over her.

They were both happy-go-lucky, free, fun-loving singles in their early twenties. She was a medical assistant for a prominent clinic of doctors in Boulder; Ben, who considered himself one of the lucky ones (a Vietnam vet back home with all his limbs) was a salesman in a stylish up-scale men's shoe store in Denver while working on his business degree. The ski slopes were an integral part of their romance -- every other weekend for two months. After that, a weekend in Boulder and two in Denver and they were committed to a long-term relationship. Nora moved to Denver and eventually into Ben's condo.

## 3

They were approaching thirty and had been married three years when Ben received the proposition from his cousin in Brandeis.

"Nora, guess who called today?" Ben asked as he came into the bedroom where Nora was changing from work dress into comfy jeans and lavender top.

"How would I know? You sound so excited . . . an old girl friend?"

"Well, it is an offer I can't refuse," Ben answered with a wicked chuckle.

"When are you leaving me?" Nora played the role of the injured wife, throwing herself on the bed, pretending to cry.

"As soon as you pack."

"Your bags? What an evil man you are." She cried out, "Boo, hoo, hoo."

"Enough kidding around." Ben stretched out beside her. "My cousin, Judd, called today to ask about my interest in the insurance business."

"Your cousin, Judd. Isn't that the family from Illinois?" Ben nodded, as Nora continued, "His wife is Elaine and they have a couple of daughters. A handsome man, in fact a good looking couple, as I remember." Ben nodded again. "What's his proposition? Not to sell us insurance? We're already insured." She stared intently at Ben, attempting to understand what he was implying, before she shouted out in disbelief, "No! Not to move to Illinois. There aren't any ski slopes there. Where in God's creation is Brandeis? Some rinky-dink town in the Midwest?"

"A suburb of the Quad cities by the 'ole man river'. We could have a yacht on the Mississippi, a big colonial house like you've always wanted. A business for me and a business for you."

Nora raised herself on her elbows, "Okay, let's have the details before you start the sales pitch."

"Listen to this, he wants me to buy in as a partner with him. His dad, my Uncle Bernie, built the business and now wants to move to Florida. Judd said he didn't think it would take long until I learned the business and became certified." He couldn't resist giving himself a pat on the back, "I'm not sure that he doesn't have an eye on my outstanding selling skills." Ben turned playfully serious, as he said, "And, we would become the new citizens in Brandeis and on our way up, I might add."

"Whoa, Ben. Why are you so excited about this?"

Ben rolled on to his back, stretched his hands high into the air and answered Nora's question. "A host of reasons. One - I'll have ownership of my own business . . . Judd hints he might want to sell out someday. Two - I'll continue selling . . . you know, I'll do well with the clients . . . those now and those I'll bring in. Three - I'll be able to put my business skills into management. I'm only thirty and Judd is going on fifty . . . he'll retire before I do, I hope, and I'll have a business to leave my son."

"Whoa, you're moving too fast. I'm not even pregnant."

"You promised by thirty. We could start right now." As Ben reached for Nora, she backed off the bed.

"Might be a girl you know," to which Ben replied, "we can always try for a second."

Nora winced inside. She'd pushed herself, and regretted it, to commit to one child just for Ben who wanted to be a father. But two was not in her plans and, if she could get out of the one, she'd do it. Nora knew herself to be too self-centered to find the patience for raising children although, without a doubt, Ben would be no absent parent. She wished that she had a natural maternal instinct as most women did, but she'd lost that inclination a long time ago, if it had ever been there.

"Come here, you sexy doll . . . all this excitement has a good thing going." Nora laid still as Ben reached out his arms to encircle her. He kissed her mouth, eyelids, mouth, ears and when his hands slid down her back to her butt, "You have got the sweetest ass, bar none. It captured my attention from the git-go."

"Oh, Ben, you are a charmer. If there were awards for sex, just as for sales, the walls of this house would be covered with plaques." Nora knew they were ideal mates and a perfect match in their sexual desires. She doubted they'd mismatch as a business duo.

"I vote for a time out," Ben whispered in Nora's ear.

"I'll second that." Nora pulled her sweater over her head, tossed it to the floor and fell back onto the bed. Ben held the cuffs of the jeans and slowly pulled them down the slender hips and thin legs and tossed them on top of the sweater. He cupped her feet and kissed her toes, then his hands moved up her body, stroking her legs and thighs. He sunk his face into the smooth firm flesh of her belly and whispered softly, "nice and easy, all the way." Slowly, his tongue slid up her body, from the navel up through the narrow valley, across the flat upper chest, "nice and easy, all the way." As his tongue found hers, her legs parted. "Let's go slow babe. So warm. So soft. Nice and easy."

### 4

Much later in the kitchen, Ben motioned to the table, which held a pad of paper, pens, and two beers. "Let's list the pro's and con's."

"How long will Judd wait for an answer?" Nora asked.

"He'd liked to know within the next two months; of course, the sooner, the better. He says there's no specific time business is more demanding than any other time, but there's always work in romancing new customers. He says they have a lot of commercial accounts and that area could grow a lot more. That's where Ben the salesman shines." Ben held his beer up as a toast and waited until Nora reluctantly tapped his bottle with hers.

"Okay, let's make a plus and minus column," Ben said as he drew a line down the middle of the paper, "and see what we have to resolve."

"God Ben, you make it sound like it's a given. What if I don't like Brandeis? What about our other great sport? You know, besides sex, there's skiing."

"Okay, 'no ski slopes' in the minus column. We aren't all that far from Colorado, just a drive across Iowa and Nebraska or a flight from Chicago to Denver. Come on now name an opportunity. The obvious one is the chance for us to have our own business and not having to work for others. It's a business that is mature with lots of good customers and plenty more to capture. You'd have to help me with office management, maybe for a year, but that gives you time to find your business opportunity."

"Colorado's been my home for so long, Ben. I've grown accustomed to its charms. There are a lot of memories here for us." Nora's face tightened. "I know you're going to say that we'll build memories wherever we are. Right?"

"Yeah. Just think, Chicago is only a couple of hours away. It's a great town for fun, has all the things a big city offers. Indy is just across the state, another big city with the races. We'd have fun there. In fact, those two cities go in the plus column.

"We're young, Nora, and can use our thirty's to build our future. We'll be well established in ten years when we turn forty. We'll travel wherever you want." Ben's enthusiasm was building.

"You're starting a sales pitch with me, Bash. Why don't we look for a business for sale in Denver?"

"Nora, this one is with people we know, people I can trust, a family whose integrity and ethics are without question. That's like having the best of all worlds. The move is perfect timing - we have few possessions to bother with. Our schooling is complete, just the two of us, no children to uproot. We have little debt and good savings. I need a new car and the company will buy that.

"And, we'd be among family. Besides Judd and his father, there are Uncle Bernie's two sisters. Aunt Ethel and her husband Jim living outside Chicago and Aunt Charlotte in downtown Chicago. I'm not sure where her two sons live, but that's another couple of cousins. I hear they have great family parties. Look at it like we'd be going from one hometown to another." Ben caught Nora's hands. "How about it sweet-stuff? Let's do it! You were ready to change jobs anyway and always wanted to run your own show."

"I don't know, Bash, it's so sudden . . . I need to assimilate it all. I'll sleep on it for a week. That's the best I can do for now. How much is cousin Judd asking for your buy-in? I'd like to keep my inheritance money to myself. It's my security blanket."

"I want to be your security blanket. We're a team, aren't we?" Ben put the pen to paper saying, "I have forty thousand in the condo equity, we have twenty thousand in savings and only a thou on credit cards. We should be able to swing a loan easily . . . Bernie and Judd have to have influential contacts with banks. We won't touch your inheritance. It was from your grandmother and should be for you to use, maybe for your business when you find it."

"Why don't we drive over and see Judd and your uncle. Walk through the town. Look at houses. See if the poor relations fit." Nora suggested, thinking she might find enough reasons not to move.

"Great idea. Can I tell Judd a week from Friday?"

"You trickster, waiting for me to make the suggestion. I fell for your famous line, 'you can always rope them in better when it's the clients idea'. What a smooth-tongued charmer you are, Bash." She grinned at him hopelessly.

"You know I love you, Nora. You are my one and only forever, even if you do renege on children by age thirty." Ben thought *how dumb to say that now.* "Look, I want you to be happy along with me. This will be great fun for both of us - a new adventure."

"Like skiing the extreme slopes?"

"Sort of. And why not? We are expert skiers about to become the up and coming entrepreneurs of Brandeis, Illinois."

"Oh, Ben, life is such an adventure for you. You are contagious."

"How about we celebrate? Dinner at the Olympia and music at the Jazz Club."

"Shouldn't we be saving our money?" Nora teased.

"Get your bod into that sexy black dress; this is a big date."

"Should I ring Bill and Jocelyn?" Nora laid out a second tease.

"Absolutely not. I want you to myself all night long." Ben patted her backside. "Still the cutest one around and it's mine."

# 5

"What a gal." Ben said out loud as he followed Nora's car into town. His senses hadn't left their morning romp in bed. *Jeez, I'm getting a hard on just thinking about it. You're a sex addict, Basher.* He laughed at Nora's caution when they first met. His tried-and-true technique of romancing a gal into bed, by at least the second outing, did not work with Nora. She was a savvy date, and she read his behavior for what it was and held back, making the challenge all the more enticing. The instant, deep attraction that seared through him when he watched Nora, without her hat and sunglasses, walk across the Staghorn to his table was likened to a lighting blot. His eyes admired her confident stride, body held high but not rigid, shoulder length, sexy hair – light brown with golden highlights. As she came to the table, where he stood waiting, he was captured by her vivid, crystal blue eyes; the intensity of the wide iris, the brightness of color, it was like sinking into an island lagoon. *"What a babe."* It was on their third trip to the ski slopes that she let him into her room and bed. She was an equal partner in sex, as eager to enjoy and please as he was.

Her first words of that first morning were, "Where did you

get the name Bash?"

"A hand-me-down for three generations."

"A family name?"

"More or less. A great-great grandfather reported to be illegitimate was called a bastard, finally shortened to Bash."

"Not a good tag for either of you. What does it mean now in this generation?"

"Well, believe or not, there is some honor to it. His real father . . . back to that old grandfather . . . was a merchant -- a banker for shiploads from Europe. He hired Caleb, my great-great grandfather, and taught him the business."

"Did Caleb know he was his son?"

"The family story says not for sure. He only guessed. The mother died when the boy was young, with sealed lips. She'd worked in the merchant's household, and Caleb was conceived of the master and a servant. The mother never told him of his ancestry. His real father had four daughters, no sons and, when he died, he boldly left control of the business in Caleb's hands. Anyway that's the way the family tells the story."

"How come the name is tagged onto you and not some one else in the family? Are you the only male?"

"It happened at a little league game. I was six and had just hit my second home run for a win. I heard my father yell from the stands, "Way to go Ben . . . what a basher. I'm meaning I could really swat a ball over the fence. The moniker hung in there as I bashed my way through championship games in baseball and golf.

"My team mates were envious of my homers, long drives, low handicap and, over time, they quit referring to me as Ben. I was Bash all during high school."

As he approached the turn to the agency office, Ben watched for the wave from Nora, their morning ritual. She then made a mime of holding a phone to her ear. Ben was quick to know what she meant, 'don't forget to call Ted Anderson about meeting us at the acreage'. *Gotta get a call into Skeely by ten. Sunrise in the third and Fortana in the fifth. I need a couple of wins to break even for the month.*

A wave of satisfaction and pride swept over Ben for their status in Brandeis. Much had been attained in the last seven years: He was sole owner of Allen Agency and its building; Nora was sole proprietor of The Frame Shop; they lived in their dream house -- colonial style on the golf course, and had just purchased a 160 acre parcel of pristine land five miles outside of town. It had not been an easy sell to displace Nora from Colorado and the consolation was allowing her to renege on promise of a pregnancy by thirty. *Gotta be glad for Jen and her cousins . . . there're neat kids to let me play dad. Man, I'll bet money on my golf team this year.*

# CHAPTER TWO

# *Nora's New Customer*

## 1

NORA PULLED INTO the parking spot behind the store. Neither Peg nor Don's car was in the other reserved spot. Don, who sold her the store, was the original owner. He'd done only framing and was skilled at the task. Peg, equally as skilled, had been his part time worker. Both of them were meticulous in choosing the right frame for a piece of art and equally precise in judging the edges and width of matting. Nora enjoyed their friendship and knew they were instrumental in tripling the customer base due to the good words they spread about her. She'd met many of the people who came to her store while helping Ben at the insurance office the first year. Half of his client list had eventually become her customers.

Nora was in the store half of each day, at least, to keep a personal touch with customers. The rest of her time she functioned as an interior decorator; not a role she'd planned on. Her customers had bestowed it upon her. At first they asked her to help hang pictures. When the requests included choosing color themes and redoing offices, she began to charge for her services.

At the time she bought the store from Don, the income mainly came from framing and the sale of a few prints. In six years she had fashioned a different store; framing was still the main activity, but she had upgraded the artistic quality of prints, featuring more local artists (she was amazed at the talent she had discovered in the Quad Cities) and had added her own photography (a hobby she had taken up shortly after moving to the Midwest). Two years ago she'd dedicated space for an artist from Eugene, Oregon who she'd met on the Colorado ski slopes. The room displayed hand blown glass by Rene: high-priced sculptures, bowls, vases, and figurines.

She had to finally admit that she was happy in Brandeis. Ben loved his work, which made every day with him a time of excitement and enjoyment. His nieces and nephews became his family of children, and left her off the hook for bearing children. Although it was not the perfect solution for Ben, it proved to be his sacrifice for their move from Colorado.

They socialized in a wide circle of friends, and Ben was in his element – people who needed insurance, people who put him in the forefront of community, people who voted him to board of the country club, people who spoke of him in the most favorable of words, and family who adored him.

Nora was inside at the panel of light switches when she heard the back door open and a voice alerting her, "Hi, just me. Running a bit late this morning. Good morning Nora," Peg said as she came into full view, adding, "Wow! What a cute outfit. What's up for the day?"

"I'm meeting with Crystal Development at their new offices east of Moline. I'll have to leave around ten. They want us to do the wall decorations and there are no competing bids. All three of us will work on this one. I'll size out the wall space and color scheme today. They'd like me to put a store in their new strip mall, but one store is enough for me." Nora went to unlock the front door, asking, "What's your schedule today?"

"Don's coming in before noon. We have six major pieces to do." Peg looked up as the door opened, "Good morning Sally. Are you back to look at the Harris print again?" She moved from behind the counter, "I have several frames to show you that will compliment it."

Nora was rearranging the glass pieces when she noticed a young man stop outside and look at the items on display in the window boxes. He squinted as if to see inside the store. He was of slight stature, nice looking and sported the new style of sunglasses that flowed away from his face to his hairline. *Doesn't look familiar.* He stayed in the same spot for quite a while before she heard the tinkling of the door chime. Nora watched as the young man gazed around the shop, a look of curiosity more than that of a buyer. She busied herself moving a vase from one position to another, slyly watching.

Peg was still tied up with Sally, prints and frames laid out on the counter, so Nora approached the visitor with, "Looking for anything special?"

She sensed some awkwardness as he responded, "Just looking. I thought I might find a birthday present for a girl friend."

"What might be her fancy? We have some lovely prints by local artists, also photo prints. Or maybe a beautiful piece of glass." Nora looked at her watch. "I apologize, but I do have an outside appointment that I need to leave for. Peg, the other lady will help you when she's finished with her customer."

"That's okay. I have several weeks to decide." He took off his glasses as Nora stepped away, but in that brief moment, she was startled by the bluest of blue eyes. Her reaction puzzled her, and she glanced back as she hurried to pick up her briefcase and purse. The bothersome spell distracted her and she came close to running a red light. *What's going on? It's some sort of déjà vu? One quick glance into a pair of blue eyes.* She took her sunglasses off and looked at herself in the rear view mirror. *Crazy.*

Nora had recovered her high spirits when she returned to the store. She had found Crystal's office space to be large and the owners had given her free rein. She was excitedly telling Don and Peg, "Lots of wall space, a large foyer bathed in light, muted colors, and room for us to be ever so creative. The office manager, Ann Moyer, would like some extra large pieces in the reception area. I thought of Priscilla and those paintings of irises she showed last month at the gallery."

Without interrupting his work, Don asked, "Can we have access in off hours? We could take a few pictures and measurements."

"Yes, any night after five, except for Friday. They do a TGIF over at George's Den . . . the bar for the professionals. It's Ben's favorite Friday night stop also." In a casual manner, Nora asked, "Peg, did that young man buy anything?"

"No, but he did look at all the photos and inquired about the photographer. He was quite interested that it was you and remarked how much he liked the ones with fall colors." Peg's hands and eyes were at work measuring and marking a buff-colored mat, and it was a few seconds before she realized Nora had halted as if waiting for the rest of the story. "So, he said he'd drop by again. He asked about Nora, the photographer. I told him he'd just spoken with her."

## 2

Two days later around noontime, the young man returned. This time he was dressed in work clothes – jeans, T-shirt, well-worn ankle-high work boots, and a billed cap, which he quickly took off after entering, smoothing his hair with both hands.

Nora busied herself behind the counter, watching his movement, trying to see where his eyes focused. He glanced around the store and, when he saw Nora, he moved to the wall of prints. His interest seemed cursory to Nora. *Was he casing the store? But what would be of value to steal?. . . the glass art . . . a print or two. It's not a familiar face.*

Walking from behind the counter, Nora asked, "May I help you with something?"

As he turned around, he squeezed the cap in his hand. "Yes, I'm still looking for a present."

"Your girl friend, wasn't it?" Nora moved closer and avoided looking directly into the blue eyes.

"Yes, but I can't decide on a print or a photo. The other lady told me you are the photographer. Are these all from around here?"

"Mostly, yes. Some of the snow scenes are in the Colorado mountains."

"Do you ski? I cross country, but I've never done downhill."

"Yes, my husband and I are avid ski buffs. He's the expert. Does the challenging slopes."

"Are you from Colorado? Or have you always lived here?"

*Why am I feeling like I'm being interrogated? Let's see how far he'll take this.*

"Yes, I lived in Colorado for a long time before moving here seven years ago. Where are you from? You seem new to the town."

"You guessed that right. I'm not here for long – just a short work assignment. Would you tell me about this photo? I like fall and the colors. Are these woods around here?"

"Yes, there's a wooded area just outside of town that has these old trees. See how big they are with large strong trunks and tall branches. They've stood there for ages, like they own the ground on which they stand. They are strong, independent, and mature like tall sentries guarding our land. It's one of my favorite places. Here's the same scene during winter. I want to get a good spring and summer shot and then frame the four in one frame. Can you see that effect?" Nora wondered why she was sharing so much, but noted that the young man was listening to every word. "What's your name? You're new in town, aren't you?"

"My name is Jon . . . J o n. Jon Strutter. I'm from Witherston, Minnesota. We have lots of wooded areas, great for camping. I do a lot of that. And cross-country skiing." He turned his attention to the prints and Nora sensed an awkwardness again. She noticed the swirl of hair at the nape of his neck, which stirred an old sliver of memory tucked away in her mind. She took a couple of steps back and involuntarily shook her head.

"Well, I'd better get back to work. I'm trying to decide between the print of the woods or that print over there of the Mississippi River." He really intended to buy both of them, but held off so he could come to the store again. "Do you have any other photos?"

"Yes, in an album. Why not look at them before deciding." Nora wanted to bring the young man into the store again though she was not sure why. "I'll be here all day on Monday. What time do you get off of work?"

"I could be here by four." Jon knew that if he asked, Ted would let him quit early, particularly since he would be working all weekend. "I'll see you then." He pulled his cap down on his forehead. "Thanks a lot."

### 3

"Hey, I'm late but here I am. Had a late caller. You know that big farm over by Devon? I think he's my next new account." Ben couldn't reveal that the late caller was really Skeely. He'd won big on Fortana and so-so on Sunrise. He had promised Nora he'd quit gambling when they made the move. That was her final prize for leaving Colorado. And he had kept that vow for the first year while Nora was working in the office. Ben's addiction for betting on horses and sports hadn't died; he just did it secretly now, by telephone.

"Hey, I'm home." He called again, as he walked into the empty kitchen, looked out the porch door to an empty yard. He saw no lights in the basement when he checked the stairwell. "Hummm, is it one of those times?" he muttered to himself.

Nora was subject to dark moods that came suddenly, without spoken cause, and would silence her quick laughter, bright spirit, and eagerness for fun. Ben would see that buoyancy die; his playful mate gone quiet, private, retreating into mundane tasks like cleaning closets or basement, re-stacking bookshelves or taking long, lonely walks. He used to try to cajole her out of these moods, to come back from the dark quietness, but she would sting like a scorpion – quick, sharp, deep and unexplained.

Ben had learned to find other solitary things to do when Nora masked his fun-loving companion. He had tried several times earlier in the marriage to act as normal or to tease her out of the mood, but a flying object or retreat behind a closed door had been his payoff. The moods didn't come often and lasted no more than two to three days; one day the happy, exciting Nora would disappear and return just as suddenly on a later morning. It was like a twin had moved in, a twin that Ben did not know or understand.

*I guess we've been lucky. She's not had one of these for a long time - several years, maybe. Tread lightly, Ben.* He talked to himself as he climbed the stairs to the bedroom. The door was closed but fortunately not locked. His gentle tap was the only sound as he opened the door. He saw Nora sitting in one of the wingback chair on the sun-porch. "Hi, hon. Beautiful day outside, isn't it? How about we go out to Walden's on the lake for a fish dinner? Would you like that?"

"No, Ben, you go. I need to be alone. A little silence will help." She sounded aloof and didn't look his way. "Not to worry, nothing's wrong – just one of those moods. I ate a snack and no I don't want a drink. I'll be okay." Her voice was taking on a sharp edge giving Ben a clue that it was time he left the room.

"Ted said he'd meet us late Friday afternoon out at the acreage. I'll put it on the kitchen calendar." He paused before closing the door, "I'll find something in the frig to eat and watch some TV." Then, he stuck his head back in to say, "I'll be right here if you want anything." No response.

# 4

Ben and Nora were strolling hand in hand across the lower meadow when they saw a cloud of dust rising out on the dirt road leading up to the entrance into their acreage. "Have you any new ideas on a name for our place," asked Ben. "I want to get a sign designed for the gate." He let a soft chuckle grow into a loud laugh. "Since we've blessed the ground with our love making, how about 'The Love Nest'?"

"Or 'Bash's Grazing Ground'," Nora replied. "Oh, Ben, it is so beautiful out here. It feels as if no one has ever walked this ground except the animals and us. Names such as Heaven's Land . . . Bountiful Meadow . . . Peaceful Acres . . . Nirvana . . . Shangri-La . . . Paradise Meadow seem well suited. We'll need to make the 'No Trespassing' signs more visible."

"I like the meadow theme." Ben slipped his arm around Nora's waist. He was delighted she had re-appeared yesterday morning from the silent mood. He missed her presence even if only for a day. Nora's attraction, besides her anatomy and her sharp personality, was her boldness in both action and words. It kept him alert, on his toes, pushed to the edge to where he could say, 'Come on, let's play,' whether it be skiing, exploring new territory, or romping in a love-fest.

A green truck was winding down the narrow road lane toward the flat land. "Here's Ted." Ben said, waving his hand. "Looks like he's brought a helper along with him." Nora squinted at the passenger in the truck and mumbled, "Oh, no."

She felt unsettled inside. That young man's presence was starting to make her feel ill at ease, lifting a nagging memory she wished not to visit. She had locked away an experience that had been her private secret for over two decades, and this blue-eyed young man, twenty-one years old, sporting a cowlick, was a threat to her safety. She hung back as Ben walked toward the truck.

Ted Anderson unfolded his legs from the driver's seat and stood to his full six foot four stature. He had a tall, lanky body, and his skin was weathered and tanned, making him look much older than his fifty years. He stood five inches taller than Ben. "I always think of Mutt and Jeff when we stand side by side," Ben said as he stretched his hand to Ted's for a hearty shake.

Ted let his eyes roam across the land, "You've got a right nice place here. Never thought old lady Hamilton would ever sell this. It's proof positive that you are the ultimate salesman." Ted turned to the young man standing by the passenger side of the truck and motioned him forward. "This is Jon Strutter from my alma mater. He's here working for me and learning the ways of landscaping. Wants to start his own business one day. Jon this is Ben and Nora Allen."

Ben took Jon's hand, "Well you certainly came to one of the best. Ted Anderson is tops in managing a thriving business. If there was an Anderson tag on every tree he's planted in the county, it would equal a national forest." Ben gestured toward Nora. "And this is my wife. She owns The Frame Shop in town."

"Yes, he knows that." Nora stepped forward. "Hello Jon. Still thinking which prints to buy?"

"I think I'll stay with the ones you put aside for me. I'll be by tomorrow to pay for them." He turned to Ben, "Your wife is a good photographer."

"Which reminds me," Ted butted in, " I have a client who gave me permission to do before and after pictures of a big project I'm doing for them. Are you interested in taking it on Nora? I want pictures for my professional portfolio, and I presume you'd get permission to take photos for your shop wall, maybe year after year. Their flower gardens will remind you of those in England."

"I wish this young man was staying for the whole summer. He knows his stuff enough to work independently . . . sure would be helpful. I've got Tom Strabala's big place, and you're about to tell me how big this job is going to be. Shall we begin?"

Ted handed a pad of graph paper to Jon. "You can sketch the designs this time. Do it in sections, much like we did at Strabala's. Okay? On the margin estimate the number of plantings. Then we'll work on drawing a full layout and proposal. Where do you want to start, folks?" Ted moved alongside Ben, "How many acres are here?"

"A hundred and sixty." Ben pointed up, "Let's walk the higher land this time. It's been a cornfield, but this is its last year."

When they reached the top of the hill, Ben continued. "Over there is where we are thinking of adding most of the trees, making the open space in the upper meadow smaller. We were wondering if prairie grasses could be a good replacement." Nora followed the three men, Ted on one side of Ben and Jon on the other, but she quickly moved in front to be privy to their conversation. She had her camera out of its case, planning to build her own picture album of the land before and after.

Nora was impressed by how much Jon knew about trees and how Ted allowed him to offer suggestions, following up with, "Why would you choose that species?" Ted looked over Jon's paper work, making a few corrections and additions before the three turned back to the rim of the hill overlooking the lower meadow. An hour had passed and it was now five o'clock, and the June sun still cast its full light across the green land.

"This is magical," Nora exclaimed. "I feel like we are looking down on holy land. I've always pretty much poohed-poohed those who practice meditation but, from here, I think I can see how one could sit quietly and let the mind drift to wherever it wishes to go."

They stood in silence for several seconds, then Jon said, "Mr. Allen, would you consider putting a pond down there, off to the right? If it had water flowing in and out, it would be great for stocking trout."

"Wow! That's a hell of an idea, Jon. Could we do it, Ted? What do you think, Nora?"

Ted answered first. "We'd have to work the drainage issue. It could cost an arm and a leg - big bucks. I'd have to get an engineer involved. How do you plan to use this lower meadow?"

Nora was quick to chime in, "For gatherings, family picnics, maybe small community events, though I'm not eager to have a lot of strangers trampling over the grounds. We thought, at first, we'd build a cabin, but we've decided not to burden the land with structures." She looked at Ben, "Isn't that right?"

"Yeah," he answered. "We'll camp in tents and I may get a small camper that I can pull in and out. I can see some good times here with nieces and nephews and cousins. There's plenty of room for net games, horseshoes, lawn bowling. We want to keep the area green and grassy, but a few leafy trees could be nicely placed to shade a picnic area. And we'll need to consider how to feed the animals and birds. I'd like to attract them to the land without letting them take over this lower portion.

"Well now that you've seen our dream, I think we'll have to walk these areas several times after you have a layout. Feel free to come out on your own as you need to. I think I'm safe in saying . . . (right Nora?) . . . that we want to beautify without overdoing, and we are willing to entertain your ideas such as Jon's trout pond. We'll handle the money issue at the end. Now, let's head down to the picnic table. I brought a cooler of beer for an end-of-the-week drink. And let's talk about trees."

"I put a bottle of wine in for me and anyone else," Nora added. "How about you Jon? What would you like?"

"Either one, Mrs. Allen. Students usually take to beer, cheaper you know. But a glass of wine sounds good for now."

"Jon, how about calling us Ben and Nora? It makes us feel younger." Ben said as he headed down the slope.

## 5

Jon stood while Ben got two beers and a bottle of wine out of the cooler. He was alert to where everyone sat, as Jon wanted to sit across from Nora. This would be his best opportunity to observe her and learn more of her ways.

Nora poured wine into two plastic wine glasses and brought one to Jon. "I hope you like this. This is one of my favorite Chardonnay's. We have a wonderful wine shop a block over from the store, and they feature wines from other countries. I bought a different country each time, until I decided I liked the white wines from New Zealand and Chile the best. Portugal and Australia for the reds."

"Thank you, Nora." Jon held his glass up in a toast before taking a sip. "Maybe I'll visit the wine shop. My mother favors red wine, but a bottle of this would work for a date."

"When you give your girl friend the print? Very romantic, Jon."

Ted took the conversation back to the landscaping layout. He spread out the rough layout Jon had drawn. "We ought to settle on the type of trees. Did you want any fir trees on the upper meadow? Or in either meadow? Look, there are several ways we could use them. I always suggest pines and cedars. They provide cover for game and birds when the other trees have shed their leaves."

In the murmur of their voices, Jon's eyes shifted from Nora to Ben but mostly centered on Nora. He let his senses etch Nora into his mind. She was slim from head to toe, a tiny waist accentuating her curves. Her oval face, softly browned with a summer tan, framed a slightly pointed chin and a straight slender nose rising up to brilliant blue eyes. He listened to her conversation, which was quick, sharp, and animated as were her hands – all part of a body language that kept people's attention. She laughed easily with big smiles pushing her cheeks up and crinkling the skin around her eyes. Even then, her blue eyes shone through the slits of eyelids. She was very feminine and it was obvious that Ben adored her.

*I was born of her. Carried in her body. Her genes are my genes. I saw her write left-handed the other day, something we have in common. I wonder what she thinks of our eyes. She's not mentioned the color, and I'd better not. I might stumble into a stupid remark. She's tiny. I suppose he was too. My body is short and slim. No cowlick tufts on her head . . . so must of have been him. Mother would be devastated if she saw this.*

"Ted do you have time for another beer?" Ben asked. Ted gave a nod.

Nora got her legs from under the table. "You stay, Ben, I'll get them." After the beers, she filled the wine glasses. "Jon you're being quiet."

"Well, I won't be part of the planting. Ted knows his stuff, and I'm just along as a gofer and a student. I wish I could see the place when you're done."

"Well, you're welcome back anytime," Ben said with a broad grin. "Why aren't you staying the entire summer? Ted says you're a damn good worker and pretty smart yourself."

"I'm going to work at other landscape companies this summer. Trying to see what differences there might be," Jon lied. He was going nowhere but back to his old summer boss in Witherston.

Ben asked Ted to talk about a pond. "Was it feasible? What was involved?"

Jon returned to his mental reflection. *I thought I'd feel more emotions in her presence. Like maybe a sadness, cause I can't tell her who I am, or anger that she doesn't care about that baby twenty-one years ago. But I feel glad, satisfied that I've met her, seen her, heard her. I like her as a person. She loves the woods and that gives me a connection. The hardest part is this may be the only time I'll be with her. But I got my wish – thanks to you, Dad.*

"Well," Ted said as he stood up and drained the last of his bottle of beer, "better be on my way. I'll have something back to you in several weeks. It'll be a first proposal, one that we can refine, as we take second and third walks of the land. How about you taking this on this week, Jon? Make a layout, research the trees . . . are they appropriate, and price the trees and planting. I'll do a separate estimate for the pond."

"We've got plenty of time, if you say we have until September." Ben said and turned to Jon, "Would you consider coming back for the planting?"

"Yes, I might. Semester ends towards the end of May. I could come after that."

As they walked toward the truck, Nora asked, "Then you'll be in for the prints this week?"

"Yeah, around mid-day. Would you like to have lunch? Maybe you could introduce me to the wine store and some selections." Jon looked at Ted, "Which day would be best? Monday or Tuesday when I'm in the office doing the proposal."

"Either one. After that I need you at the Strabala's rest of the week. Sure you can't stay another week?" pleaded Ted.

"I'd have to call back home to work that out. I'll let you know."

Ted and Jon waved their hands as they drove away, leaving Nora cuddled into Ben's right arm. "Nice couple," Jon said.

"Yes, they are. They've been here for over ten years now and people in Brandies like them. Ben has been high profile in the community and is one hell of a golfer. They call him Bash because he can drive that ball straight down the fairway with a roll on it to get one hell of a distance. I've teamed up with him several times in tournaments and we never lose. He's a great competitor without being obnoxious about it. Great sense of humor."

"Do they have children?"

"No, just lots of nieces, nephews and cousins. They hang with Ben a lot. He makes a family golf team every summer and coaches them. He'd made a great father."

"And Nora, she must have a nice business also. I've been in there looking at her stuff. The photo prints are good. I'm going to buy a couple of them. Is it okay if I take a longer lunch on Monday?"

"Yeah, if you promise to stay another week," Ted bargained. "I could really use you here if you can work it out. And, come back next year for the big planting."

*Maybe I will make it back here again. Better be cautious though. Familiarity could loosen the tongue.*

"I appreciate coming with you today and letting me put the initial proposal together. I'll be checking reference books about trees. With so much ground, we have a lot of choices." Enthusiasm entered Jon's voice. "Maples for color, oaks for size, and the hickory tree is sturdy. Walnuts are beautiful but messy. Should we put in some large bushes in the lower meadow? Ben's idea of prairie grasses in the upper is not a bad idea either."

Ted smiled as he nodded yes. "Nice project for you."

## 6

Ben and Nora walked the land back up the hill to a stand of old tall oak trees overlooking the corn. A breeze slanted the tassels to the east and bent them around like dancers dressed in gossamer. "Our farmer is not happy about out decision of no more crops," Ben told Nora. "He called again yesterday asking what he could do to persuade us. I said I was sorry but it was a done deal. No buildings; no crops. We're taking the land back to what you call pristine."

"The grasses will be so beautiful, waving in the breezes that seem to blow across this meadow all the time. Letting the ground renew from tilling might bring new spirits," mused Nora. "I'm getting excited by the picture of what this place could be. It's going to take some money. Good that we are free of business debt right now."

"No problem with the bank. Improvements will enhance the land and make our loan on the property more attractive." Ben pulled her towards him, "Do you know that this is the first time, except for getting married, we have been in sync with a money decision?"

"Ah, come on, Bash, we didn't hassle over the choice or price of our house." Nora halted their steps and turned around, "Let's go back and watch the sun set. I think there's enough wine for another glass, and you have plenty of beer."

"Interesting young fella, that Jon. I noticed his eyes. Other than yours, I've never seen such striking color . . . a piercing blue, rather hypnotic. When we first sat across from each other in the ski lodge, I could hardly concentrate on anything but your eyes."

"You mean my eyes took precedence over my butt?"

"Well, no, I honed in on your cute figure first." Ben leaned towards her and whispered, "Say maybe we should bless the land with a little of our love. I got a blanket in the car."

"Sorry, not a good time of the month."

They strolled along the fields, into a thicket of trees, down to the edge of a small stream, really not much more than a fat trickle. They both pointed to a flat green patch of grass and sat down with their backs to the tree. Nora reached for Ben's hand, "This would be a nice spot for a bench. Such a lovely spot. I could lose myself . . . disappear into nature . . . be the wind, the fields, the leaves, the water."

"Whoa, I prefer for you not to disappear on me," Ben said as he stroked the inside of her palm with his thumb. "We'll probably find several spots for benches. I'll start looking for some one to build them. Ed at the construction company ought to know a name or two. We could go really sappy and put brass plates on them with sayings, quotes by poets . . . who write the nature stuff."

"I don't think that's so sappy, Ben," Nora remarked casually. "I'll look for the quotes. Thoreau, Emerson, Frost." Another silent moment, Nora bowed her head, "Jon's a really neat young man."

"Have you taken to him that much?" Ben teased.

"He touches my heart. You know how that can happen . . . you meet a stranger but he doesn't seem like a stranger. You know deja vu . . . you've been here before."

Ben kept up with his teasing. "So you're telling me you're about to have a fling with a guy twenty years your junior."

Nora looked into Ben's smiling face and shook her head. "Ben, sex is forever on your mind, I swear." With a twitch of her mouth and eyes wide open, Nora said, "Ben, he could be my son."

Ben's face went from smile to frown, and his words came in slow motion, "What are you trying to tell me, Nora?"

"A secret."

"Of what kind?"

"A solitary one. An old one buried deep. One I've shared with no one else."

Ben grew even more serious. "I thought I knew all there was to know," and after a long moment and with a skeptical glance said, "go on Nora."

"Ben, I wonder if Jon came here to find me."

"Why? For what reason?"

"He's, . . . well, I think, looking for his birth mother."

"That's you?"

"It could be possible. I know, it sounds like a run-away imagination . . . like I'm sounding loony."

"Okay, Nora, I'm ready to hear your secret, though I thought we had none between us anymore." Ben had to wince inside at his words, for his gambling was his secret, his private habit and strong enough to override the promise he'd made to her to quit.

"I know. I know. Everyone keeps a few private items to just themselves. But this one has been so deep for so long, like it hasn't seemed a secret because it's been forgotten. Or, more accurately, denied."

"Until now?" Ben quizzed. "And Jon has triggered it, brought it out of the deep dark hole, has made you remember something that you wished never to surface. Okay Nora, from the start." But he quickly said before Nora had a chance to begin, "Will I be able to handle this, Nora?"

"Oh Ben I think so. You were once young, brash, taking risks, dating girls, having sex." Nora paused before she went on and looked out over the stream as she began her story.

"I was fifteen years old, a rebellious daughter, angry, hated my mother, and longed for my father. He'd be easy on me, wasn't likely to set boundaries." Silence and a deep sigh. "I was a fallen teenager, a dismal student, desperately looking for someone to care for me."

"And, he did?" asked Ben

"Maybe. The first boyfriend didn't. He just wanted to operate his penis. I'd let him sneak into my bedroom at night."

"He's the father?"

"No, it was the next one . . . funny I can't even remember his last name. I used him because he wanted to make me feel like I was loved."

"Did he do that? Did you feel loved?"

"No, not really. It was impossible. In my anger, I'd turned

away from a normal world." Nora looked down at her hands, "A teenage boy was not going to be able to save me."

"You've never spoken of your teen years in this way. The angry girl who felt unloved. I know your parents divorced before your teens. Is that why you were angry?"

"I suppose it made me rebellious. I wanted it my way. I wanted to do things that mother objected to -- big time. It was a constant struggle, constant conflict, and I didn't care. I believed she didn't love me, and I guess I wanted to prove to her that I didn't like her either.

"I don't go back there to think about those ugly times. When I was eighteen, Mother and I began to mend our ways and promised to start anew. We finally could let the past be past, buried. We now have a relationship that works for us and respect for each other's personality."

"What happened to the baby? That's part of the secret, isn't it?"

"Yes, it was a boy." Nora said hesitantly, "Funny, we only had sex twice, and I denied the pregnancy even though I'd missed three periods. He talked about us being together and didn't run away from the problem like a lot of boys would do."

"I'm not seeing the picture yet. What did you do?"

"When we finally told Mother, she left the ball in our court, so to speak. Said we had three options: abortion, adoption, or parenting. Her words were like, 'it was your choice then and it's your choice now'. She came across cold and unemotional. She suggested we go for professional counseling to help us make a decision. She was emphatic, said she'd not provide a home for the baby. I sensed my teen years had come to an end – squandered in dumb foolishness."

"And your father?"

"He was not one to face conflict; he'd turn away from it, deny it. He'd feel sorry for me but let Mother solve the problem, and she didn't want this happening any more than I did. She couldn't comfort me, make it okay. We'd been through a lot of conflict, arguing, and meanness. Our love bank was depleted. I think we hated each other for what we didn't like in ourselves."

"A lost little girl looking for love. How sad for you. I've never suspected any of that early turmoil in your make-up, even when you withdraw at times. I see a sharp, bright, witty, happy, sexy gal. Guess you must know that I've always felt I won the best prize in life when I found you." Ben kissed the tip of her nose. "You want to tell me the rest of the story now? I can handle it and - isn't it time to empty the coffin inside."

Nora straightened her spine and moved her buttocks to the base of the tree. Like telling a story with the book in her hand, she recounted the visit to Catholic Charities, moving into a house for unwed girls, and the birthing day. It became disjointed; she didn't try to fill in all the blanks. They were unclear in her remembrance. This time, the talkative Ben listened in silence, absorbed in the unfolding tale.

"I decided on adoption. His family argued with us, urging us to live with them. He sided with his family and made pleas many times over. But, I was adamant. How could two teenagers, who hardly knew each other, become parents and provide adequate care for a baby? My defiance of authority and control was in my every thought and action.

"Mother made arrangements with her aunt and uncle in Minneapolis. Working with Catholic Charities they provided me a home, school classes, hospital delivery, and a husband and wife who wanted a baby."

"Did you get to see the baby?" Ben looked into Nora's eyes searching for tears.

Nora turned her face away to stare into the stream. "Yes. I had to hold him . . . twice . . . for an hour each time. It made me more scared of playing a parent role and my decision for adoption more firm. My stubbornness, my refusal to change my mind, my unkind remarks to the boy finally swung him over to accept my decision. We signed the papers, and I walked away without a regret. We never saw each other again, although he called several times wanting to see me. I wanted the episode gone, forgotten. No reminders, please."

Ben held out his arms, "Oh babe, come here." He wrapped his arms around her, held her to his chest and let her cry away her secret. There were no more questions he needed to ask; he just wanted to protect her, let her come back to the present, help her let go and forgive herself. His thoughts about the land were confirmed – this is our paradise, our haven, our safe ground. It was a sanctuary and this had been a sacred moment.

As Nora relaxed against him and the flow of tears lessened, Ben remained quiet, letting himself look back to two sex encounters with a sixteen year old when he was seventeen He'd forgotten her name. One never forgets his first love, but she wasn't it. Her parents were away from home each time. She cried, repeating, 'what if . . . what if'. He assured her, without proof, that withdrawal was safe. He could easily have been the boy in Nora's scenario. He now presumed he understood the resistance to having children. Distasteful memories, painful experiences. No maternal instinct is what she told him. *Always admired her for the honest answer.*

Nora pushed her elbows out to disengage Ben's arms. She sat up, closed her eyes and let her head drop back. She breathed deeply several times, making a loud sigh as she exhaled. Her voice quivered with emotions as she clasped Ben's hands in hers. "Thank you for today and all the days we've had together. You are my best friend, my adoring husband, my audacious business partner, and my tender lover. I wish I could have given everything you wanted as a family."

"I have all I need with you. Extras are nice, but you come top and foremost. I love you, Nora."

"I know you do . . . I knew that from the git-go. Someone finally loved this person, Nora. You've never asked me to be anyone other than who I am. Thank you, Ben." She laid a light kiss on each eye, the tip of his nose, each cheek, and then his mouth.

"You're welcome sweetheart." Ben gave a nervous cough before adding, "It's hard on the psyche to keep secrets and hard to let them out. It takes a lot of courage and a lot of trust to let go of a secret. Thank you for telling me." He shook his head, "We can silently thank Jon's presence, I guess, for the role he's played here without his knowing."

After several silent moments, Ben asked, "Any regrets, Nora?"

"Never. It was the right decision then and if Jon might be a product of that kind of decision, I believe even more so now.

"Ben, I was too selfish to raise a child at sixteen, seventeen, eighteen. I didn't believe I could give or do the right stuff. In fact, I didn't want to. When I held that baby boy, I knew at the deepest level I could not do him right. I knew a loving set of parents was the kindest act I could do . . . his chance for a good life was with them not with me.

"For years I dreamed of a child who was faceless. It was always a boy; he might sit at the foot of my bed . . . in a long nightshirt . . . another time he was on the other end of a teeter-totter dressed as a clown. One time, he jumped out of a bush as I walked a path and was dressed as a knight. In the final dream, the child walked ahead of me on a stark, barren road that stretched towards a far-flung horizon blessed by a double rainbow. He wore a long coat and never looked back, just kept walking until he was a tiny, tiny speck."

"And, what happened after that?" Ben asked.

"I had a sense everything was okay. Might have been wishful thinking, but I felt we had separate directions to our lives and respect for each other's motivation. For me I knew the decision remained the right one for both of us.

"I've not been hung-up with those days until Jon walked in my store and I saw the blue eyes and cowlick." Nora laid her head back on the tree as if recalling that moment.

"I don't think I'll be in the store when he comes by this week. I'll leave a note for Peg to give him."

The sun was setting as they drove down the dirt road to the highway heading home. A peaceful silence embraced them as they headed back to town. When Nora turned on the radio, Roy Oberson, their favorite country/western musician was singing: 'Moving on down the line . . . gonna do right . . . do right all the time'.

"Keep you hands on the wheel, Bash."

# Going Home

## 1

I DROVE AROUND the block several times checking the parking lot for Ben's silver Mercedes. His agency was in an old, historic brick house, two stories for offices and the third floor dormer windows scrolled with gingerbread lattice designs. I backed my car into a street parking space, flicked through the folder holding my proposal, gave a sigh and thought of questions to take our conversation beyond trees and shrubs. Maybe, I'd ask advice for starting a business and advertising for new customers. I wanted to know Ben Allen more than the brief encounter we'd had that day on his land. Through him I hoped to know Nora in other ways and leave with a better sense of her world.

A large porch wrapped around the first floor and the entrance was a designer double door – looked hand crafted – thick glass framed within dark wood, maybe walnut. I stopped to read the lawn sign telling the history of the house; designed and built in 1865 by Jeremiah Stout . . . family home until 1925. *I'll ask Molly to tell me more about the Stout family tonight.*

The plaque at the door listed Allen Insurance, Bett's Bookkeeping Service, and Eric Steffan, CPA. I walked into a large circular foyer, decorated with antique furniture around the sidewalls. A middle-aged woman was behind the oval receptionist desk in the center of the room. "Hello, I'm Jan. You must be the landscaper here to see Mr. Allen." I nodded my head, and she pointed down the hallway to an open door, "He's been waiting for you."

I tapped on the doorframe, "Mr. Allen?"

"Hey, Jon, come on in. How about a cool drink? Soda? Tea?" He called out to Jan, "Jon will take a glass of water. You can bring me iced tea." He motioned to a round table to the right of his desk. "Let's sit here, more room to spread out your plans." As I put the folder on the table, he asked, "Did Ted work on this or is it all yours?"

"I did most of the research but ended up with too many varieties, so said Mr. Anderson. He was very helpful at placing the trees." I pointed at the upper level on the layout, "We suggest adding oaks, here and here, tall bur oaks and red oaks . . . they'll get to eighty feet." I went on to describe the other trees and shrubs. "Place hickory and basswood in this grove and add another walnut opposite the one that's there. We thought you'd like the Canadian cherry, it's a hardy native tree and pretty . . . white flowers in May, red fruit in July (Ben muttered, "the birds will like that.") and a purple color in the sun. No elms because of the disease prevalent in the Midwest right now." I paused and let my finger circled two other spots, "Ted thought a couple more large evergreens provides cover for game in the winter. Of course, it would be a number of years before they were full grown." I joked, "But you're still young."

"Yeah, I don't consider myself full grown yet." Ben tapped his finger on the layout. "Does this say aspen?"

"Yes. The quaking aspens do fairly well in this area and are good cover and food source for wild life. They also attract butterflies." I looked at Ben for verification and he was nodding his head. "And, Ted wants you to consider turning the cornfields into meadow grasses rather than prairie grass; it's not as high. I brought these pictures along so you can see the difference." Ben nodded his head as he scanned the three photos.

Ben knew this must be my first go at a presentation to a customer and patiently gave his attention to the rest of my talk. "On the lower level, there'd be an ash and maples of several varieties . . . the colors in the fall would be awesome. Even a black walnut would be nice if you want the mess of nuts on the ground." I paused and looked at Ben's face scrunched in a 'maybe or maybe not' look. "And then we are suggesting a string of lilac bushes along this side of the pond and serviceberry on the opposite side. They have white flowers in the spring and small dark fruit that birds really love. Here, I've attached pictures for all of these."

Ben took at quick look and said, "Good, Nora will like this."

He posed no questions, so I moved along. "I understand you are going ahead with the pond."

"Yep, Jon, that was a great idea." He'd given the proposal no more than ten minutes, saying he trusted Ted's wisdom and complimented me again on the work I'd done. He motioned me to a chair and changed the conversation asking, "Well, Jon tell me about your ambitions."

After I spoke about my plans to build a career in horticulture and botany, Ben asked how my love for nature came about. "My mother and grandfathers." And, I told him how I began gardening as a child with Mom.

"Later, Mom's father took me camping and we'd study his guide books for identifying the trees, wild flowers, and birds. And my other grandfather, Papo, made me a partner in his big vegetable garden. Guess, you could say I was programmed into this profession."

"That's very impressive Jon." Ben eyes hadn't left my face as I told my stories. His genuine interest kept me talking more than I'd planned. "And your father. What did he teach you?"

"My father is the pride of Witherston, as is the Strutter family. People still talk about my great-grandfather. He was one of the best carpenters in the county; he and his sons built most of the barns around Witherston, and most of them still stand. He started two other businesses and his sons became good businessmen because of it. They all are involved in either the hardware store or the drugstore. My father is a pharmacist and has the drug store, just like his father. Papo still goes in every day, but really, Dad manages the business." I stopped abruptly. "Gee, I didn't mean to give my history."

"No, no, I'm very interested. I'd even like to hear why you think your father is so respected."

"He's honest, fair, listens to people and gives good advice. He and Mom both do a lot for the town, and the church. They can always be counted on. People trust my Dad." I paused. "I do too. He's never short changed me in his time and love." I leaned back and rubbed my hand through my hair (a motion I do when emotions arise), "Neither has my mother."

"Seems you've had good family around you . . . that's means a lot." Ben stared at me, not a hard look, rather a soft hint of affection. "Will you have your business in Witherston?"

"I'm thinking that through. It would be my mother's desire, and she can be a strong force."

"How's that, Jon?"

"Dad tends to let things flow in a natural order and handle them as they come into being . . . that might seem perfect to him. Mother has her own definition of 'perfect', and perfect would be a landscaping business for me in Witherston." A sobering thought as I realized how true this was.

"Is that your plan . . . your goal?"

"I'm thinking that through. It's hard to deny parents their desires."

"I'm sure you'll make the right decision. You seem quite bright and thoughtful for your age." Ben stood up, looked at the plans again, "Well, you let Ted know we can begin according to his schedule and what's best for planting. Will we see you back here then?"

"Probably not." I wanted to ask him why he was a success but could see that he was ready for me to leave. "I'd hoped to get a few pointers from you on how to be successful."

"Jon, I think your father can teach you those." He patted my back, "Just be enthusiastic about what you choose to do."

As we shook hands, "Good luck, Jon. Life just might be more perfect than you realize."

**2**

For the first time, I really missed Karen tonight. I wished I was in Minneapolis with her but had to settle for getting no closer than a phone call. So much she didn't know about me yet, but a telephone was not the manner in which I wanted to share my history. Maybe I could get back to Witherston through Minneapolis without Mom knowing of the detour. Molly and a renter had gone to a concert in the park, which gave me the privacy to make my calls. Karen first. She was breathing heavily as she said hello.

"Did you just run up the stairs? This is Jon."

Panting, she said, between gulps, "Yes. Give me a second."

"Want me to call back?" I could hear her 'no, no'. "Listen, I wanted to check an idea out with you. I'm thinking of driving to the Cities on my way home. I'd like to see you. Maybe for a couple of days. Ted, Mr. Anderson, wants me to work another week, and I've opted not to do it. That puts me here until Friday. I'd have to leave late Sunday or early Monday; I can't get out of Mother's plans for me on the Fourth."

"It would be great to see you, Jon. I haven't been doing anything but work, work. I've taken extra hours, which means overtime, as I can use the money. My new roommate doesn't move in until the end of July."

"How about next weekend? I could be your roommate. Is that okay?"

"Hah, is this a test? We each have a bedroom? Wait and see who crosses the hallway first." Karen laughed. "Shall we place a bet?" When I didn't laugh, she quickly said, "Okay, okay, I'm kidding . . . for now at least.

253

"I'll get serious. Next weekend would work. I won't be home until around eight on Friday night and we could walk up to the Grill for eats. I assume you'd stay until Monday morning. I'm up early on weekdays. I need to report in by seven."

"Sounds like a deal. I have to let my parents know of the change, and I may be pressured into leaving late Sunday. It would help to tell Mom that you'd be visiting us in August. Is the first week still on?"

"Maybe not a whole week, but three days at least. I'll ask for more but can't count on it. They are really short-handed this summer, and since I want part-time work during the school year, I feel I can't demand too much now."

"How about I call you the night before, on Thursday? I'll have some idea when I'd be leaving. I may not get there until nine or ten."

Karen added quickly, "In which case we'll have beer and sandwiches here. It'll be good to see you. I'm eager to hear about you're experience. It's a bit of a mystery to me why you'd go to Brandeis for a three-week job."

"I'll explain the mystery. Two days by ourselves and you'll know the real Jon."

"Well, this one isn't too bad. You really have me puzzled now. I suppose you're going to let my imagination fill in the blanks until you do."

"It'll be okay. I want to talk some things out before our friendship goes further." I paused before saying, "I like you Karen and I don't know how it will go, but I want a clean slate with you."

"This is intriguing. I suppose we'll have a fair idea if this is going to work for us, by the time you reveal your secrets and after my visit with your family? At least I see us as friends, if not lovers." She added and when there was no response from me, "I can't wait to see you!"

"Thanks Karen, me too."

*Pretty bold, Jon-boy. Adoption will be easier to talk about than*

*Ken. Should I? So some guys are attractive. But for now it's Karen. Guess I'm going to know soon.*

►┼◄►─◯─◄►┼◄

"Hi, Mom"

"I've been thinking about you all day, wanting to talk with you. We must be telepathic." She rushed on to tell me, "We've decided to do a family float for the 4th of July parade. And, I promised that you'd help with the decorations. I suggested we make a flag out of flowers, which you could do . . . you made something of flowers for a homecoming parade, didn't you." I tried to interject a word, but it was dismissed by her excitement. "A loud speaker for music. Your cousins are working on that. We want to get the parade watchers singing patriotic songs as the parade goes by. At the end of the parade, by the lake, we're going to serve root beer floats . . . your dad and uncles are working on how to set that up. Doesn't it sound great?"

"Well, yeah. How big is the float? Who's in the driver seat? I mean what's pulling the float?"

"Well, when you get home this week, you can help work that out, if the family hasn't. When will you be home? Sunday?" When no answer from me, she asked, "Monday?" When I didn't respond, her voice went from soft to hard. "Jon, are you about to disappoint us?"

"No, Mom. I'll be there for the Fourth. I just won't arrive in town until Monday -by noon. Wouldn't that work? A day and half to get the float ready. We can't put the flowers on until Tuesday anyway."

"Jon, I can't believe that you are reneging on a commitment. What could take precedent over your promise to me?" She waited for my answer, one I was trying to form. "I knew that this job in Brandeis was a fake . . . a cover-up . . . I'm not sure that you are even there. What's happening Jon?" Her voice had turned cool, and I detected a sob being held back. "This is a real disappointment. I trusted you and your promise to be home after two weeks. Does

255

your father know what's going on?" She allowed my silence for
only a few seconds and asked, "Tell me Jon, how can you shatter
a happy family, with impunity?"

*Impunity? Free from guilt? No, I feel guilty. Gonna have to tell
a fib or two.*

"Look, Mom, I had a chance to spec out a big project, a layout
for a large tract of land . . . the trees, a pond, lilac bushes . . . the
works. If I stay another week, I get to finish the proposal. Don't
you think that's important for me to experience?" *Ted really wants
me to do labor on the Strabala job, but I can't say that . . . it won't
hold merit enough.*

"He's asking you to work both weekends . . . Saturday and
Sunday? Why don't I believe this Jon?"

"Because you want me home so badly," I replied. Her silence
was heavy and I broke it with, "Say something, Mom."

"Like what, Jon? I'm happy you won't be here until the last
minute? You should know better than that." *I sure did.*

"How would this be? I'll come home on Sunday next, late but
I'd be up early Monday morning. Mr. Anderson can get me the
tubes for the flowers and I'll bring them with me." Silence. "Can't
one of the cousins make the frame for the flag? Rick and Steve are
good with tools." Silence. "Ah, Mom don't make this so hard."
Silence. "You'll have me for the rest of the summer."

"It's already half gone. Doesn't the semester start in mid-
August?" Her flat response told me I wasn't winning.

"Well, I do move in the week before school starts. Maybe
you could go up with me and we could have a week in the cities.
Would you like that? And, Karen is coming to visit us the first of
August, so you'll know her."

She finally yielded, "Guess I'll have to resign myself to you
having your way. I don't hold on to being contrary, it's just that
I love you, Jon, and I see so little of you. You're still my precious
boy."

*And I guess I will always be.* "Yes, I know, Mom. But I'm
grown up now. Well almost. And I have to make adult decisions.

We can work 'em out, can't we? Isn't that what love is suppose to do? Give and take?"

"I trust one of those decisions is to settle in Witherston."

*She can't resist.* "We'll work that out, you, Dad, and me."

"Give me a call next week and please work on Mr. Anderson to let you go on Friday . . . at least Saturday."

*Another fib.* "He's short handed next week but I'll be home on Sunday night for sure." *That cuts an evening with Karen.* "Say hi to Dad. Look forward to the Fourth. Love ya, Mom."

"I want to believe that, Jon. Still, I don't understand why you had to go to Illinois in the first place." *Just let that go and get off the phone.* "Bye, Mom, gotta go."

"Oh, wait Jon. Have you talked with Ken or his mother?"

"Why, what's up? Ken coming home for a visit?"

"No, it seems Ken is having health problems and the doctors can't define what they are. Jan told your father she's trying to talk Ken into coming back here but he's saying no. She may go out there with one of the girls. She seems quite worried."

"Thanks Mom. I'll give Ken a call." I almost said Michael.

*Please, not that gay disease . . . he hasn't been there that long . . . he said he was being careful . . . it can't happen to him . . . he's just beginning his real life. Please, not Ken.*

### 3

Molly would be coming home soon, and I decided to wait for her on the side porch. The evening air was heavy with summer humidity, but air flowed through the breezeway cooling my damp body. Leaving Witherston was becoming less and less of an option. I ask myself, 'Will that satisfy me?' I think so. I'll have Dad's management experience on hand, and the Strutter name over another business is a sure winner. I'd be up and running with enough cousins who might work for me. Dad suggested a buyout of the other nursery; after all, Guy Ferguson was up in years and no family to follow him. *I'd feel a deserter leaving Mom and Dad.*

*They've done so much. It would have been different with a teenage
mom. Nora probably would not be who she is now if she'd kept me.
One decision by one person set the course of two lives. She has a good
life, a business, and a good partner. And, I can have the same. My
partner can only be female, if I haven't tried the other. Can one be
called gay if he doesn't know he's gay? Surely I can love a woman.*

"Good evening, Molly. How was the music?"

"Oh, Jon, you should have gone with me. The little Winslow
girl, Mia is her name, only nine years old, and she plays the violin.
So talented. She did a classical piece. One I didn't know, but
no difference. She's quite amazing. Then a teenage boy played a
guitar. I always forget his real name. People call him Butch. He's
a nephew of Ben Allen. Anyway we sang along with his tune and
just filled the town square with happy voices."

"Were Ben and Nora, Mr. and Mrs. Allen, there?"

"Yes, right on the front bench. That man should have had
a parcel of children. He dotes on his nieces and nephews, even
has made a golf team out of four of them. I always wonder why
a woman doesn't have children. I trust in this case, it just wasn't
possible because that Ben is father material. Oh well, isn't any
of my business, is it?" She said with a grin, "I try to keep myself
from being too nosey.

"What did you decide for next week? Did you give Ted a 'yes'?
Which means I also have you for another week."

"You've got me, Molly. If you're tired of cooking for me, I can
always go to the diner."

"Not on your life." She reached across and patted my arm,
"Whew, it's hot out here. Let's go in and have another dish of
peach cobbler. With vanilla ice cream or plain?"

As we went through the kitchen door, I told her, "I'll have
time to do some yard work for you, maybe weed your flower beds
and cut back those bushes overhanging your front walk."

"I'd like that Jon. Wouldn't it be a good time to move some
of those tulip bulbs? I'd like to put some back by the last unit."
Setting out the dishes, she added, "If it cools down, I'll weed with

you."

"Better you sit and keep me company. I love your stories about the town. I want to hear about Jeremiah Stout."

## 4

Nora and I never got out to lunch or the wine shop. I missed the first week; Ted had us working away from town. Now it was my last week. I called the store on Monday and left a message: 'I'd be in on Wednesday, around eleven thirty'.

I wanted a photo of her but couldn't devise a scheme for taking her picture without her knowing it. I wished I'd had my camera when we'd been out at the acreage.

I had two emotions welling inside as I parked the car and walked the three blocks to the frame shop. One, the excitement of seeing her; second, that I'd found her and would always have a mental picture, knowing I was a part of her – I'd see those blue eyes every time I looked in a mirror. My emptiness inside now had evaporated. The other emotion pulled in an opposite direction; I'd leave bearing the secret, no parental words spoken between us, and no invitation to see her again. Contentment and satisfaction coupled with regret and sadness. I stopped in front of a bookstore, two doors from Nora's, pretending to window shop as I swiped at the tears. *I can't give myself away, I promised Dad. What a tremendous gift he'd given me. What a sacrifice of his integrity to do so.*

Peg, Nora's clerk, was talking with a customer by the door when I entered and nodded at me. My eyes scanned the store, expecting to see Nora but the only other person was a man behind the counter. He looked up and waited for me to approach. "Can I help you?"

"Yes, I have several photos being framed, but I also expected to see Mrs. Allen."

"Hum, we don't expect her back today. In fact, Peg said Mrs. Allen would be out all week. Was there something special?"

I stuttered as I tried to keep my emotions in check, "Well, I . . . she and I . . . I thought . . . but it wasn't for sure . . . we'd have lunch today."

"Hum, I didn't see anything on the calendar. She's pretty strict about keeping her appointments on the calendar. Helps us to plan the day. I haven't talked with her this week, but Peg probably has." My face must have looked crestfallen for he seemed sensitive to my disappointment. "Peg will be through in a few minutes, maybe she has better information for you. Mrs. Allen may be in next week and you can leave a message for her . . . a new day to meet her."

"Not possible. I'm leaving Brandeis this Friday. My work is done here." I moved back and forth in front of the counter. I pulled out my wallet and said, "Guess you can get me my photos . . . there were four of them."

"Yes, I did the framing. The white glossy frame around the flowers is nice, real nice." He went into the back room. I heard Peg say 'good-bye' to the customer and then her greetings to me. "Hi, Jon." She avoided mentioning Nora's absence, and my instincts held me from pushing for anything further other than what the man had told me. She had not wanted to see me, for whatever reason. After all I was just a passing-through laborer. I hadn't given anything else away or said anything that hinted I had other motives.

"Is Don helping you? You're probably here for the photos. I'll go help him find them." Only the man came back to the counter and spread the four photos on the felt section. There was no cause not to admire them.

"These are gifts for two different people. Do you have a brochure or write-up on the photographer? I'd like to include them with the packages."

Don brought a box up from under the counter. "We used to have a postcard of her with her camera. Taken several years ago, but it does have her write-up on the back." He rummaged through the bundles in the box, while I silently prayed he'd find what I wanted. "Ah, yes, here they are. Her hairstyle is different, but no mistake that it's Nora. Gosh, I don't know why we've tucked them away. You want two?"

"Thanks. Could I have three? I'll just put them in my shirt pocket for now."

Upon request, Don wrapped my gifts in two tissues; the flowers for Mom and the fall scenery for Karen. I'd show a picture to Karen - maybe Dad, send one to Ken and that would leave me two. I'd need to find a secret hiding place, certainly not at home.

"Good-bye. I'll tell Mrs. Allen you were in and asked about her. Do you want to be on our mailing list?"

"No, it's best not." And I added quickly, "I'm away at school and don't always have a constant address." My emotions were back in place. After all, I had gotten more than I had bargained for.

Just as I stuffed my wallet in my back pocket, Peg came out of the back room, "Here is an envelope for you."

I waited until evening before I slit the seal and read the inner message: "Sorry I had to renege on today, other considerations took precedent. Thank you for your purchases and the suggestions for our land. Any white wine from New Zealand is good, and for the red wine, I suggest Jardot Beaujolais. Please take my best wishes with you for your success in your landscaping business." Nora Allen

*A note in her handwriting. More than dreamed of.*

# 5

Molly cooked pancakes, bacon, and eggs for my last meal in her homey kitchen. I'd talked her out of dinner as I planned to return to the house just to shower and move out of the room, hoping that Ted would let me leave at mid-day. She insisted on having sandwiches, chicken salad no less, and iced tea ready to send along with me. I knew she'd bake cookies also. Molly would be engraved in my memory as deeply as Nora; I now had experienced the sweetness of a grandmother. I'd come back to Brandeis to see either one of them.

"Jon, I'm going to miss your company. It was just like having family here. I wish you were staying the summer."

"It would have been easy, but my Mother would be down here to get me if I didn't make it home for the rest of the summer." I gave her a wide-eyed grin and a chuckle.

"Your parents must be very proud of you. They surely did a wonderful job of raising a fine young man. Not every twenty-year old would hang out with an old woman every night."

"And I didn't have to pretend to enjoy it. You're the only grandmother I've ever known, if I can call you that. If I'd stayed longer, we'd put your stories in writing."

"Oh, Jon, you are a precious boy." She put her arms around my chest and gave a mighty squeeze. I kissed the top of her head and she said, "Thank you, Jon. I'll take another hug this afternoon. Now on your way, it's six o'clock."

⤞⬦⬦⬤⬦⬦⬟⤝

The last flowers were in the beds and the new sod laid in the back of the yard, when Ted came around the corner of the Strabala house. He had hired two high school boys to help me for the week, which gave me my first experience at supervision. I did more telling of what to do and how to do it rather than explaining why; I was hell bent on being done today.

"God damn, you made good progress." It was a gruff welcomed compliment from Ted. "It looks like there nothing but clean-up work left. You must have worked their butts off. Hey turn around and let me see." We all laughed.

"It's noon, Jon. Think you can get finished by one? What's left to do?" He walked back and forth, taking careful note. I came to realize, in the first few days of working with Ted, that he had a memory and recall that didn't need check lists or the layout in front of him to know the work was going according to plan. "Looks like just cleanup left. I'll go talk with Mrs. Strabala and see if we can do the rest of it tomorrow. We'll take the tools now and haul the junk later."

"It'll work for me if it works for you."

"Well, damn it, wish you were going to work for me all summer. I could make good profits on you." He yelled to the other two, "Come on, let's load the tools." Then he walked up to the house, a man of few words but they said it all. He was no slouch when it came to promises, both to customers and employees. These weeks had been like attending a class in management one-o-one.

# 6

Molly set a paper bag, my lunch, on the front seat as I closed the trunk door. As I went to receive her last hug, her eyes were filling with tears, "Jon, I'll miss you." She held out a piece of paper. "I wrote my address for you, thinking maybe you'd drop me a line . . . doesn't have to be a long letter . . . just how school is going. Of course, I'd love to hear that you were coming back to Brandeis. If so, you have a room here." She opened her arms and I moved in for a tender farewell. I didn't try to hide the tears in my eyes. Molly smiled and pulled my head down for a kiss on my check. "Now, you get on your way."

It was three o'clock as I gave my last wave to Molly. She kept waving until I turned the corner. *I'd come to town to find one woman and was leaving with two.*

A six-hour drive stretched before me; a lot of time for thinking, for reflecting, for sorting it all out. Something had transpired these last few weeks. I now felt different, like a new person had emerged, or maybe it was the real person, the one I had to find. Maybe the void, the mystery, the unknown was being filled in ways other than knowing my birth mother; or, maybe the quest for her was the journey for finding me.

Who was I? Not Nora's son. I was her baby, but I am the son of John and Emily Strutter. My blue eyes, writing left handed, a stupid twist of hair from genes from a line of people who possibly have marked me also in other ways. Was there, in that line of trait makers, someone who preferred men to women? Had there been a Ken? Am I gay? Hell, I don't know. I had feelings for Ken more than just a buddy, a pal, an ordinary friend. What kept me from living out those feelings? Religion? Mother? Yes and yes, but more so, it was the lifestyle that would follow. To be snubbed, ignored; to be the brunt of jokes, laughed at; not to have a family, children or to be a part of the hometown community. Ken needed to live that lifestyle; I did not.

What did I need? First to finish school, then start a business, build a life. With whom? If not a male then it has to be a female. Karen was in the spotlight at the moment. Sex. My test . . . would I pass or fail? My first time. The first time to even want to go all the way. Time to find out.

I let my mind play forward to what I was going to share with Karen. Tell her about Molly who was a talking history of Brandeis; her kitchen and our meals together, a grandmother found unexpectedly. Ted. Not so much him but the projects; supervising the Strabala landscaping and preparing the layout and proposal for Ben and Nora. Good lead into why I went to Brandeis. I'd be using Karen, using her as the ears of what I need to say out loud.

*"I'm adopted. My folks picked me up at the hospital and I became a Strutter. They told me when I was five or six about adoption. It was no big deal to a kid who was living a happy life, surrounded by a loving family. I had no reason to question, to feel short-changed or that life could be better only if I'd been with birth parents. As I grew through the teen years, I began to wonder about that boy and girl. Where were they? What did they do? Were they still together? What did they look like? I wanted see them to replace the faceless persons in my mind."*

It's Karen's nature to delve into details; she'll want the emotions along with the facts. She'll ask a lot of questions. What was my folk's reaction to go looking for my birth parents? (*Mom was hurt, angry, became the obstacle to pursuing it any further*) . . . How did you find them? (*That has to remain a secret from everyone*). I can hear her next question, "You're saying adoption is an off-the-table discussion in your house?" (*Yes, Mom doesn't know why I went to Brandeis*). She'll ask the next logical question, "And your father?" (*He'd be supportive if he could.*) Dumb answer. (*He's the one who gave me the lead, told me about them and where my mother lived.*) Wrong answer. Only dad and I can know this. It's our secret to keep. *Guess that narrows my story. I can dare to reveal only the adoption part, and leave out the searching part. I must admit - and believe - I'm a happy, satisfied, precious son of Emily and John.*

The sun smarts my eyes, as I head directly west on Iowa Highway 80. My ears pick up the top-of-the-hour news story, "The latest count of AIDS cases now number over 2,500, forty percent resulting in death. All the cases have been confined to the gay community with San Francisco and New York having reported the most cases. AIDS first appeared in 1978 and has now been diagnosed in thirty-three countries. Today, a case was reported in an older woman and the possible link is to blood transfusions she received for another illness. Her name. city, and details are not being identified at this time. Authorities urge people not to forgo transfusions, if needed."

*Wow, a high price to pay for a different lifestyle. Ken, I hope you're okay. You could be in the wrong place at the wrong time. He never said how many partners he's had . . . maybe it's just one. I hope he protected himself. AIDS is enough of a persuasion to keep sex to the female side.*

I thought of tonight with Karen. *I want to hold her close, stroke her bare skin, kiss her face, her neck, and I want the same in return. I want to be held, feel sexual stirrings . . . its time my penis went to work. I need to know if I can satisfy her. Not just once but how often in a night, a weekend. If not with a female, then am I gay? Or, am I just not passionate? Who passed on that gene? If, I can't perform over time, how do I explain that to Karen? How do I explain it to me?*

## 7

Without realizing it, I'd started a journey with no road signs except the one I just passed; 185 miles to Minneapolis. Behind was a love lost twenty years ago and ahead is a love to find. Nora never knew the full love of raising her child, and I must find the extent of my love for a life partner. My blessing is that I have been a recipient of love. Mom, who never held back, never skimped, nor was ever false in her deep affection and devotion. And Dad, a model of everything I want to be. How could my loyalties lie outside of family? I thought of PaPo and his words, that day in the garden, came back to me. He'd reminded me that I was the son of a proud and respected family. He urged me to not give up that honor too quickly, or too easily. The most vivid was his final warning: 'Broken items can't always be mended, they're forever cracked – never perfect again'.

I'd gone to Brandeis, putting family in jeopardy, to find someone and that someone, it seems, turns out to be me. My name is Jon Strutter, son of John and Emily, and I know that I want to grow old with my family in Witherston, build a happy home with a wife and two, four, five children. They'll have grandparents who will enhance their lives beyond measure. Mom would say the world was perfect!

*I sound like an adult and if I've crossed that threshold, then I must think and act as one.*

I was humming to the music coming from the radio . . . *day by day . . . my love seems to grow . . . no end to my devotion . . . deeper than any ocean . . .*

My mind began to form what I wanted to say to Karen; if not tonight, then tomorrow. Tell her she's the first girl I've wanted naked next to me. Stress that it's the intimacy with someone I care a lot about, not just the sex. We can laugh at my inexperience. Whisper: "I could fall in love with you. Please give me a chance."

# Acknowledgments

SINCERE APPRECIATION FOR my family and friends who read the manuscript in varied stages of completion: Kristin Espinoza, Rose Meer, Patsy Vessey, Deanna Wagner, Jo Wagner, and Robert Zoller. Their feedback and encouragement was just what I needed. Special thanks to my friend, Milli Gilbaugh, for editing my manuscript. Milli is a gifted writer herself with a distinctive style. Her suggestions for words, sequence, and dialogue were invaluable. She helped me make the story richer in so many ways. And, kudos to Lori Popp for her creative talents in designing the book jacket. In working with her, I found a new friend.